I0764514

Nephilim Push

NEPHILIM PUSH

A novel by
BRIAN HOLTZ

This book is a work of fiction. Names, characters, places and incidents either are products of the author's imagination or are used fictitiously. Any resemblance to actual events or locals or persons, living or dead, is entirely coincidental.

Nephilim Push

ISBN: 978-0-6151-8138-7

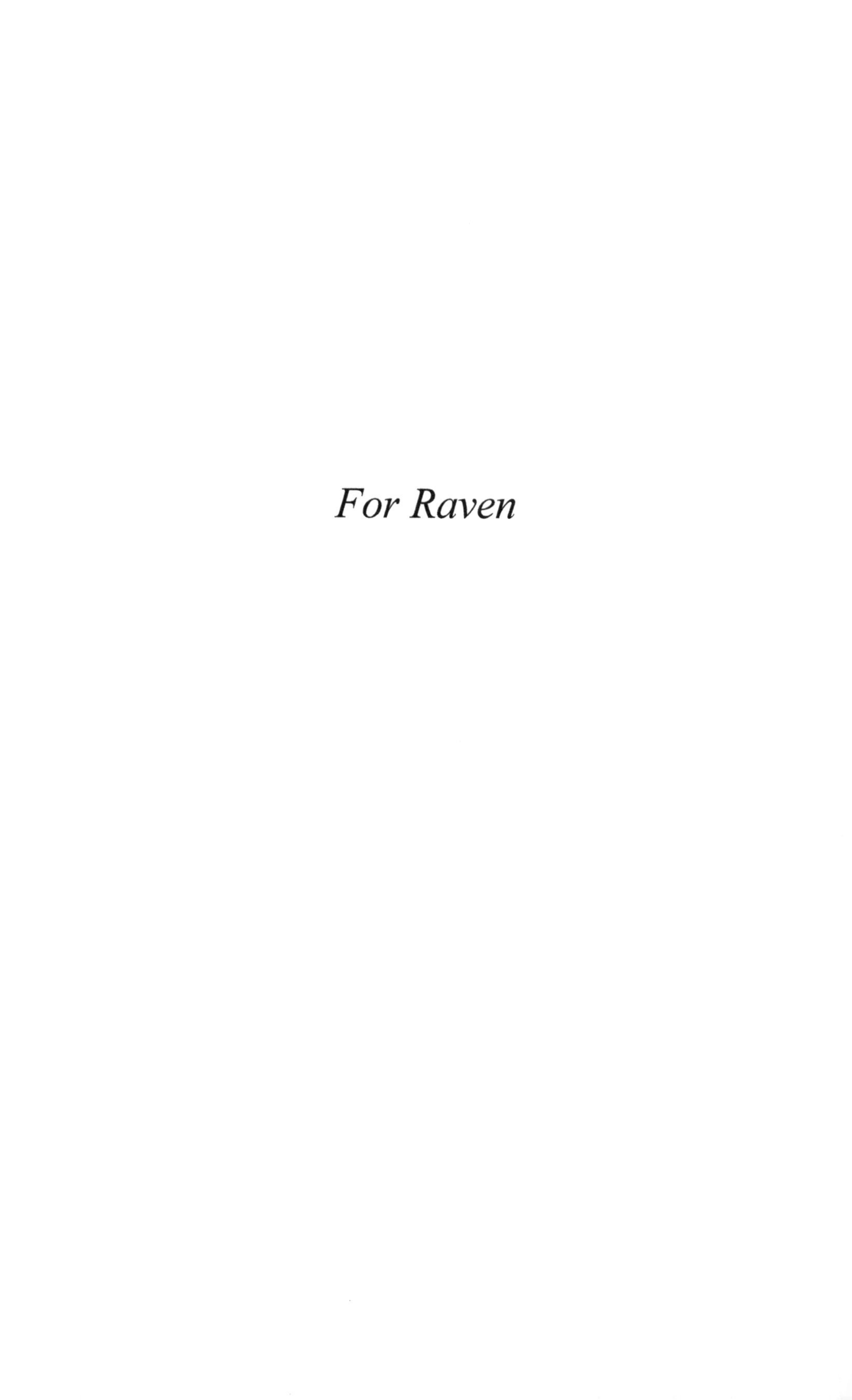

For Raven

<u>CONTENTS</u>

0:1

Questions.

We all have them. They have been ingrained in us since the dawn of existence. Ever since man became aware of his own mortality he has wondered what, if anything, was beyond.

Entire cultures have risen and fallen on religion's foundation. Many have lived and died by the answers given them.

But what conclusion did they find? Whose words did they follow? From Buddha to Christ, the pharaohs to the Pope, many have claimed truth and led multitudes of followers.

Of all of the different belief systems that appeared, one common thread tied them together. A faith in a higher reality. A place far beyond the suffering of the mundane world. And most held fast to the idea of a creative power, or powers, that resided over that reality. Men needed something separate, outside of themselves, to gain meaning.

God.

The inevitability of mortal death validated fear and expedited the search for immortality. Many found comfort in wise men, prophets and scriptures. They gained what they believed to be a connection with a higher power. They had faith. They trusted without proof, without seeing.

For countless others, the search continued. What religious paradigm held the answers? What if they were all wrong? That was a possibility that could not be ignored.

Atheism and agnosticism flourished in an advancing and modernizing world. Science began to provide answers that religion could not. It became easier and easier to believe in nothing spiritual at all. Many chose to live for the here and now and put such wonderings behind them.

But even in the most hardened mind, in the most avid nonbeliever, the spark still remained. Somewhere far back in the dark recesses of consciousness, it lived. Waiting for acknowledgment and proof.

How far would a man go to find truth? At what risk would he end the journey? And, if the power of knowledge fell into his hands, what price would he be willing to pay? It's possible that it would not be apparent until it was too late. Only then would the answers, and the sacrifice, become clear.

There were giants in the earth in those days;
and also after that, when the sons of God came in unto the
daughters of men, and they bare children unto them,
the same became mighty men which were of old,
men of renown.
Genesis: Chapter 6 Verse 4

BOOK ONE:
THE FALL

1:1

In the beginning before the beginning, God and his angels existed on the highest of the astral planes. God was the most powerful being in the realm, and he looked upon all the others with love and kindness. The angels worshiped him as their master, and were in awe of his presence. His love and approval was the most cherished goal they could achieve.

Another being in that place, also having a creative power not unlike God, was known as Lucifer. Guidance was also sought out from him, although his brilliance and strength did not match that of God. They lived in a state of total bliss for many millennia.

After many years God became weary of the nothingness that surrounded them. The dimensional plane that they occupied was an endless black void. He, and those that were close to him, were the only living things in known existence. They were alone in a vast sea of non-being.

He searched the other dimensions, but each one proved to be as empty and lifeless as the previous. The fulfillment and love from his angels that had once comforted him no longer gave him meaning. He could find no reason at all for his existence and he became sick from useless experience. His power was saturated with a sadness that none of his familiars could understand. They could only watch as the consciousness hid itself deep within his ethereal mass.

As God searched for purpose and reason, the angels became confused. They could not understand what had happened to their master. Many thought that he had become unsatisfied with them and the confusion soon became sadness, fear and anger.

They turned to Lucifer for the love and guidance they no longer received from God. He also had become angry with the one that seemed to have abandoned them.

God remained inside of himself for a thousand years.

Lucifer and many of the angels had long given up on him ever coming out of his current state and decided to leave him. One third of the angels followed Lucifer to a distant place, away from God. He fashioned a new realm for them. The astral kingdom became known as Hell. It was an enormous spiraling storm of light and color, a galaxy of peace and love. All who entered were washed over with eternal bliss. Lucifer and his angels had come home.

After a thousand years had past, God came out of himself with a new purpose. He would create a world that would give them all endless meaning. His energy was charged with joy and excitement.

As he looked over the angels that remained with him, he realized that Lucifer and many others were not there. He learned that they had gone to a distant place to live in a new Kingdom. He raced to see what they had done.

When he reached Hell he called out to his brothers of light. Lucifer went to meet him. God told him his plans of the mundane world, and commanded that they join him in his new task. Lucifer refused him, saying that they were content in the kingdom he had created. God was enraged and demanded that they follow his will. Lucifer once again refused and told God that Hell was their home. The angels inside, resentful and angry with their former master, agreed. They would not leave.

God looked over the blissful spiral of Hell's power, the comfort inside. He became even more furious watching the angels at peace, completely satisfied behind the washing color. He told Lucifer that Hell had not provided any meaning for them, it had only created selfish pleasure.

God sent a thick stream of astral hate into the light storm. It wrapped around the existing cloud of color, nullifying its power. As the bliss fell away from the occupants within, they glared at the one that had taken away Hell's comfort. They hated him for ruining their home.

God called out to them all. He told them none that had abandoned him were welcome in his sight. If Lucifer was to be their new master, then they should stay with him there, forever.

Hell's creator boiled with hate as God returned to his previous place. He vowed to destroy God's creation, just as he had ruined theirs.

God took his remaining angels to the lower dimensional plane and got to work. He created the mundane universe, the planets and the stars. He made galaxies, moons, and comets. He created *life.*

It took millions of years to fulfill his vision of the lesser beings that would be known as man. He watched the world evolve into a place that would support the things he had intended.

He became so enthralled with the mundane realm that he ignored all else entirely. His remaining angels watched as the attention and love once given only to them were now given to the new beings that resided on the planet's surface.

A small group of angels were appointed as God's messengers to the earth. They were the only ones apart from God, who were allowed to see the world and its inhabitants up close. But they found out that they were not the only ones visiting the Earth.

Lucifer sent his own angelic watchers to the mundane realm to learn of the new creation. The anger grew deeper with each expedition they made to the planet, and the tales they brought back with them. In their travels they learned that the people were confused, powerless beings. Some loved their creator, while others held him in great contempt. And God loved them all with a higher conviction than he had ever loved any of his angels.

As their visits to the mundane world became more frequent, God's hate for them grew. He despised those that had disobeyed him. Lucifer realized that the way to ruin creation was to turn its occupants against their creator. He traveled to the Garden of Eden and convinced a young woman to disobey God's law. So temptation was born.

When God learned of this he told his adversary that any one of them that entered the world again would meet his most terrible wrath. Lucifer laughed in the face of God, knowing that he was a creative being, and had no power to destroy anything he did not create. God, furious, cast him out of the world of men.

Lucifer returned to his brothers in Hell, to devise a plan. His decision was a simple one. To enter the mundane world they would have to become part of it. They needed to be flesh and blood. They could then walk among men. They had to breed with the human females. Two hundred angels would invade the earth, spreading their seed.

Lucifer put the powerful angel, Samyaza, in charge over the legion of invaders. Samyaza, fearing God, spoke to the group before him. He wanted to be sure of the dedication of his army.

He did not want to stand alone before God, to suffer for such a grievous crime. The large group all swore together, that they would not change their intentions, nor would they flee, leaving him to pay for their crimes alone.

When he was satisfied of the angel's loyalty, they stormed into the mundane realm and descended upon Mount Arman. The huge spirits spread out across the land, raping all women they encountered.

God's angels, seeing the invaders, raced to inform him of the terrible event. The creator raged down from the heavens to see for himself, Lucifer's atrocity.

In a great whirlwind he gathered the fallen ones up into the air. He knew, as they did, that he could not destroy them. If he had held that power, he would have surely done it. Instead, he would make them the things that they truly despised: *human.*

Every woman that was now with child dropped to the ground and immediately gave birth. The angels trapped in the spiral of God's wrath watched as the babies grew to adult size in just moments. He then locked each angel in an earthly body, one by one.

They cowered inside their living prisons as they experienced physical pain for the first time.

An angel's astral matter was much larger and more powerful than a human's. The bodies they occupied became huge and disfigured from the energy. Due to the astral pressure, some grew over four hundred feet in height, while other weaker ones grew to no more than twenty feet tall.

The fallen ones' spines became twisted and black, pushing through the pale gray skin. Their foreheads were enormous and sloped up to the hairless scalps. The knotted muscles sweated profusely and a bitter smell came with it. Their teeth immediately rotted and fell from their mouths, as the taste of spoiled blood sickened them.

They were truly the things that should not be.

Outcasts before God.

Deformed giants among men.

1:2

1999 AD

It was the last sunny day they'd see for a while. The sky was bright, clear blue with a
few sparse clouds hanging about. Sure, the breeze was quite cool, cold in fact, but if a person could find a nice spot were the wind was blocked they could appreciate the sun's warmth on their skin.

If they didn't know any better they might've said that it was a nice day in September, or maybe early October. They might assume that winter was still a good ways away. But the truth of it was this. The date was February fifth, and everyone in Colorado knows that in the winter, anything can happen.

You might have a beautiful day full of seventy degrees and children riding bicycles and playing on swing sets. Or you may have a day where those same children sit inside drinking cocoa, while their parents dig the car out of a snowdrift. The oddest part was that those two days could very well be consecutive. Some might say that kind of weather could occur in any number of places. That is very true, but it seemed to happen more frequently in the lower elevations of Colorado (even more specifically, Fremont County) than just about any other. At least, that's the way it often appeared to its residents.

The old timers could be heard saying, *If you don't like the weather, that's okay. Just wait five minutes. It's sure to change.*

And it was.

The weatherman on channel twelve was talking about the storm front that was swirling its way in from the West at that very moment. He was enthusiastically busy showing satellite pictures and explaining pressure systems.

He was a funny little man, waving his hand over Fremont County on the map. His suit didn't quite seem to fit and he appeared overly happy about the bad weather he was currently predicting.

No one in the dining area of the local Burger King noticed that his clothing was two sizes too large or that his tie was far too thick for his neck. They did not see his plastic, car salesman smile.

They didn't even care that the volume on the television set hanging from the ceiling was up way louder than necessary.

Most sat eating a sausage sandwich of some kind and drinking coffee from small Styrofoam cups. A few had the biscuits and gravy, which was on sale for $1.99, for a limited time.

The clock on the wall read ten twenty-seven. At ten-thirty the restaurant would no longer serve breakfast. The people in line at the front were about to become angry. The cashier was going to tell them that (like it or not) they were going to eat lunch.

The couple at the front of the line complained and asked to speak to a manager. The rest said nothing about their disappointment and ordered French-fries instead of hash browns. One such customer at the back of the line stood tapping his foot, wishing those people would quit bitching so he could get his food.

His name was Jack Sawyer. He was thirty years old and his face showed every bit of his age, and then some. His hair was short, neatly cut above the ears and prematurely graying on the sides. He wore blue jeans and a Denver Bronco football jersey, number seven.

He lived in Penrose, twelve miles east of the town he was in now, Canyon City. He worked at the Royal Gorge, the highest suspension bridge in the world, eight miles west of Canyon.

He spent most days at work, his days off staring into the television or surfing the Internet and his evenings wishing that his life had turned out differently. (Except Mondays. That was football night.) The others were occupied with daydreams of something, *anything*, happening to him that would give him a reason to get up in the morning. But, nothing out of the ordinary *ever* happened to, or around, Jack.

Since high school, his life had become very usual. There was bitterness that came with the realization that the greatness he'd once dreamed of as a younger man never came. He hadn't had any particular mechanical or creative talents to speak of while growing up, but his aspirations and enthusiasm more than made up for any of that.

As a senior in high school he was sure that he was going to do something great. He was going to shake the memory of that boring town off of him like dirt. He would change things, make a difference, help people.

Of course, at seventeen years old, he had no idea how he was going to do it, but he was sure it was going to happen. People would know his name and thank him for his accomplishments. He wanted to be famous and rich and above all, admired.

But as years passed the spark faded, the expectations disappeared and the dream got packed away like an old pair of shoes.

He got married at twenty years old, to his high school sweetheart. She was a beautiful girl; Stacey Burke was her name. They met in Mrs. Chinley's sociology class. Before they had the class together he'd seen Stacey around school but had never spoken to her. He'd *wanted* to speak to her; he just hadn't gotten around to it yet.

She sat two desks up from him and he couldn't keep his eyes off of her. He tried to pay attention in class but found out it was impossible. Her soft brown hair with the faint highlights of blonde was like a magnet. He spent most of fifth hour every day wishing she'd look back so he could catch a glimpse of those bright blue eyes.

An assignment came up were they were supposed to choose a partner. Mrs. Chinley gave them all ten minutes to pair up. Stacey stood up, walked back to Jack and asked him if he'd be her partner. He was shocked. It took him a moment to respond. He wanted to sound pleased, but not *too* pleased.

All that ended up coming out of his mouth was, "Okay."

He fell in love with her at Village Inn over a plate of chicken fried steak. They had gone there to talk about the assignment. He made a lame joke, she laughed, that was it. Her eyes were wide, her smile was warm and her face was kind. He knew then that he wanted to be with her always.

They'd been together ever since. In fact, she was the reason he was in Canyon City. Her birthday was in a week and he was going to buy her a present. She'd be thirty years old on Saturday. He was determined to get her something really good this year, something she'd never expect.

Last year she had told him that they needed a new set of dishes. He spent a great deal of time picking out a design he hoped she would like, only to find out she hadn't wanted them for her *birthday*, they just needed a new set. She told him it was like getting tires or groceries. He was not going make the same mistake this time.

The Paradox bookstore and coffeehouse would be his destination, after he got something to eat, that is.

Jack looked out the window at the clear blue sky. The pastel haze on the horizon made him think of his wife's beautiful eyes. He only wished that the kindness he'd once seen inside of them would come back. It had been a long time since they'd seemed anything but cold and judgmental.

Most days it felt like they were just pretending that they had any relationship left at all. Jack still loved her but the connection they'd both felt was long gone. Their blue sky had faded to gray more than five years ago.

Jack knew that there was no present he could buy or words he could say that would bring back Stacey's understanding and kindness. It would take hard work from both of them if they were going to make it. For now, they would just have to live under the gray.

The man on channel twelve wasn't telling him anything he didn't already know. He knew the storm was coming, he'd watched the news earlier. It would not be the worst weather they'd ever seen. God knows, there had been some nasty storms come through. It would be a blizzard, nonetheless. There would be heavy snow, poor visibility and power outages. And something else.

That would be the storm that he'd remember forever. Something *was* about to happen to Jack, something he could've never imagined. In the next few days he would learn things that he'd always wanted to know.

He'd also experience some things that he would do anything (and I do mean *anything*) to forget.

1:3

1968 AD

She would be his first.

He watched closely through the window as she unloaded her wet clothes from the washing machine. She was wearing a white tube top and black shorts. Her breasts moved freely underneath the stretchy material. He stared at them as she bent down to pick up the basket. Her hair was shoulder length, blonde and feathered back on the sides.

She reminded him of the other, the one that had just stood there, laughing. The one that had done nothing to stop it. The one he hated. She carried the heavy load over to the wall with the dryers. Opening one of the round glass doors, she dumped it in.

She was thin. Almost too thin to be a match for the other, but she would have to do. Her shorts were cut off sweat pants and they were high and tight. His eyes ran down the curve of her hip to her pale white legs. She wasn't wearing any shoes. That was good. Yes, very good. She was taunting him with her uncaring busyness; acting like everything was alright, acting like she didn't see him. She was begging for it.

The pressure in his pants was tremendous. He was throbbing. In his coat pocket he ran a finger down the cold blade. It was talking to him, telling him to calm down and not be such a damn sissy. The sweat poured down his face and neck.

A real man could do it.

He pressed his eyes shut. They were stinging and red.

Are you a real man, or just a little girl?

She sat down on a plastic chair and picked up a magazine. She flipped through looking at the pictures. He hated her.

Do it. Do it you little bitch, or I'll do it to you.

She was perfect. Sexy, barefoot, distracted, uncaring. She was the other, the one that watched it happen, standing at the doorway with glazed over pupils, laughing like a fucking hyena.

Do it.

He couldn't wait until she was finished. It could've very well taken another hour. He could not risk that. She was alone now. *You've got to seize the moment*, his good old dad used to say.

His thumb in the coat pocket was bleeding onto the sharp metal. He ran it down the blade once more, before opening the van door and sliding out. Stepping into the dark shadow of the tall vehicle, he peered into the night, looking to see if anyone had noticed him. There was not a person in sight, save the girl in the Laundromat, and she was unaware of his presence until he stepped inside.

The little bell above the door announced his arrival. On a small radio in the corner Steppenwolf's *Magic Carpet Ride* could be heard above the churning of the nearby washing machine. The girl was singing along with the music happily when she realized that she wasn't alone.

She turned, sending a smile across the noisy room. He did not reciprocate. He paused a moment, scanned the area until satisfied, and then walked around the long row of washing machines. His hands were no longer in the deep coat pockets. They hung limply at his sides, the right one leaving a trail of little red drips on the tile floor. He slowly made his way down the long isle.

She sensed an oddness about his manner as he got closer. He held his head down facing the floor, but his eyes were on her. His back was rigidly stiff, even as he turned the corner around the washer. Her smile faded into concern when she saw the blood on his hand.

"Jesus. Are you hurt?"

He looked down, "Yes, I've cut myself."

She was not as beautiful as he had imagined from the van. Up close, he noticed that she wasn't very attractive at all. Her lips were too small, her eyes too big. She'd have to do anyway. There he was, he couldn't stop it now. He just kept telling himself, *It's her*.

She took a step back, reaching for her purse.

"Do you need a Band-Aid? I think I have one."

Flexing his hands into fists he said, "You don't care. You never did."

His thick arms were around her before she could run. Her scream echoed off of the stainless steel and glass. She fought him hard, kicking and scratching. She was stronger than he had expected. He held tight with his arms bleeding from her long fingernails. He dragged her into the women's bathroom and dropped her onto the slick tile floor. She scrambled backward as he pulled the knife from his pocket.

Do it you little bitch. Do it.

It was her all right. He could see the other clearly. She was laughing at him like she'd always done. He was all grown up now. She couldn't hurt him anymore, but he could hurt her.

When the knife found its mark, he experienced it for the first time. The slick shine on his hands was amazing. It was more blood than he'd ever seen, ever *felt*. He stabbed her until she couldn't laugh at him anymore. He looked into her blank, dead stare while he raped her.

Her eyes had been blue when she was still breathing, but now they looked so black, like a tunnel, a void trying to suck him in.

Oh God.

He pinched his eyes shut, as tight as he could, finding a picture in his mind of the one he remembered. She was there. She was *always* there, looking at him with careless amusement. She was usually laughing, but not now. He, for the first time in his life, had shut her mouth.

Slowly, he opened his eyes. He was still thrusting into her, almost involuntarily. It was surprising how quickly her body cooled after death. He was disgusted and he kept going.

It is her. It's always been her.

When he was finished he realized that her lips were still too small, her eyes too big. She was way too thin. It was okay though. Perfection was in the eye of the beholder, and at the time, she had been perfect.

Still, he wished he'd found a closer match. Oh well, he'd just have to keep looking. He grinned down at her. She did not reciprocate.

"I'll find you," he whispered, gently caressing the blood-spatter on her cheek into a smear.

The silence was bliss to him. The laughter was gone, for the moment.

His arms were bleeding as he looked down at her bluing fingers. Blood and chunks of his skin were under the long, painted nails. That was evidence that he could not leave behind; he'd been too careless already.

He got up and went out to his van for the hatchet. If her hands were going to give him away, well then, he'd just have to take them home with him.

1:4

The table in the back of the restaurant was round with a bright red surface. The bench seat behind it was a curved semi-circle of hard plastic. Out in front sat two stools with high backs.

In the first stool, the one nearest the door and the big square trashcan, sat John. He ate his French fries heartily, as if he hadn't eaten in days. He dipped four and five at a time into a pile of Catsup smothered with pepper.

The next one over to his left was Cindy. She was a pretty girl with short, blonde, newly cut and newly dyed hair. She was eating a salad she'd brought from home. It contained broccoli, asparagus, a light sprinkling of bacon bits and fat free ranch dressing, on the side. She had sworn off fast food over a year ago, much to the dismay of her Quarter-Pounder with Cheese loving friends. She always kept a pre-made salad in a carefully sealed Tupperware container in her refrigerator and a clean fork wrapped in a sandwich bag in her purse, just in case.

She looked across the table at Bobby with a *please don't embarrass me in public* kind of look. He was paying no attention. He was too busy zooming in the lens of his video camera. The newsman's face on the television across the room was getting bigger in the viewfinder. He did not look down when he grabbed a handful of fries and stuffed them in his mouth.

To his left sat Sally. She watched him alertly with eyes lined with thick, black eye liner. She was used to Bobby's video camera addiction, they all were. But no matter how long they'd put up with it, it annoyed her just the same.

Her lips smeared dark red lipstick onto the sesame seed covered bun with each bite. She stopped in mid-chew to announce to the group what a moron she thought Bobby was. "God, you are a grade-A moron. Do you ever put that thing down?"

He lowered the camera down into his lap.

"If some psycho busted in here and started shooting the place up, you'd be thanking me tomorrow."

"Why? So next week on Cops we can watch John and Cindy diving under the table while that guy over there gets shot?"
The elderly man at the next table glared at Sally. She was talking too loud again. She was always to loud when she spoke to Bobby. She smiled at the old man, "No offense."
Bobby leaned over to her, "Maybe the killer would get away with it if I didn't get him on film. *Maybe…*"
"Maybe you ought to chew with your mouth closed. You're grossing me out."
Cindy added, "Yeah, Sal's right. Close your mouth. That's sick, dude."
He turned back down to his tray.
"Fuck you guys," he said, taking another big bite.
John swallowed, "If you guys are done Bobby bashing, can we talk about something else?"
"Fine."
"No problem."
Bobby said sarcastically, "*Yeah*," with a mouthful of half chewed fries.
Sally motioned to Cindy, "So are we going to watch a movie at my place or what?"
"Just not Star Wars again. I'm really sick of that movie," John said under his breath. "And what's wrong with Star Wars?" Sally asked in an annoyed tone.
She hated when John complained about her favorite movie.
Bobby got up to dump his tray, "Well, let's see. It was pretty cool the *first* billion times we watched it, but now…I don't know. Maybe it's getting a little *old*."
Cindy added, "Yeah, we should rent something we haven't seen."
Sally said, "Fine."

The weatherman on the television caught her eye. She soon forgot about the movie as she watched the small man in the oversized suit. He was practically swimming in it. She had to laugh. Nobody in the restaurant, including her friends, could figure out what she thought was so funny, nor did she tell them.

1:5

Jack walked out to the parking lot. The black Nissan was in between an old Dodge van and a Volkswagen bug that was parked too close. He squeezed through and ducked into the small car. On the passenger seat next to him laid a couple of Stacey's books: *Astrology for Lovers* and *Ways of the Wiccan.* He paid little attention when one of them slid onto the floorboard as he made the left turn out of the lot. With a right onto highway 50, he was on his way.

All of the snow they had gotten over the previous week had melted away, leaving dead grass along the median and in the yards beyond. Just behind the row of houses that lined East Main Street, Jack could see a huge metal building. It was tall and yellow, with a white roof. It looked more like a warehouse than it did a church. From Jack's current vantage point it looked like a building that would be much better suited at the Estes Model Rocket Plant in Penrose. The only thing about it that looked religious at all was the big wooden cross above the large glass double doors. Of course he couldn't see that from the highway.

Jack didn't need to see the crucifix above the doorway to know that it was the First Assembly of God Church. He had attended services there with his parents and sister as a child, only in a much smaller building. The new structure itself was less than two years old. It was enormous compared to the one he remembered.

He imagined the inside was mostly the same as his memories from childhood, except maybe the size. He'd bet it had rows and rows of pews leading up to a stage. The stage would have a stand up piano on one side and an electric organ on the other. In the center stood a large podium where the preacher would frequently speak of Hell, God's wrath and the rapture. He would, every Sunday, call for the sinners to come to the front to get prayed for and become filled with the Holy Spirit and what have you.

To a ten-year-old Jack, the idea of going up to the altar was terrifying. He felt like he should go, but never did.

He was quite sure for many years that he was a sinner, (not saved, that is) and if he were to die he'd drop down into the very hottest part of Hell's fire. He didn't know why he believed that.

Maybe it was because he could feel the eyes on him as the Reverend called out for sinners. He just didn't fit into the whole church thing and everyone knew it. It was like they could smell it on him, his dirty little non-Christian ways. He was the boy that questioned everything, without saying a word. It was easily seen in his face.

When everyone else stood and praised God with his or her hands held toward Heaven, he just watched. He looked all around the room, confused. He wondered what those people were feeling. What made them worship God? What compelled them to cry, to yell Amen? What did they have that he did not? Well, faith, he supposed.

Again he didn't understand. He could no more comprehend faith than he could achieve it. When he asked others about faith they said things like *you can feel it* and *you'll just know*. Of course that was his problem in the first place. He didn't feel it, couldn't feel it and had never felt it. He didn't just know anything.

For a time he'd considered the idea that he'd been born without a soul. Maybe by some weird accident, he'd been skipped. The supply had not met the demand and he was left to suffer the consequences. But without a soul, there'd be no consequences, would there? He could do whatever he wanted, good or bad, and the outcome would be the same. He toyed with the idea in his mind for a while but it soon became silly to him. He wasn't a freak of nature. There wasn't anything special or *anti*-special about him. If everyone else had a soul, well then, so did he.

This brought an interesting thought into his mind. Maybe he didn't have a spirit and neither did anyone else. Maybe it was all just some grand deception that the people were pulling over their own eyes. He wondered why they would do such a thing. Why would they want to believe a lie? He guessed they were afraid of death. It made sense. Certainly, the thought of going to Heaven would take the fear right out of being dead. It would be kinda like a reward for making it through the whole dying business.

He realized something at age fifteen. It wasn't a faith in God that was required to be saved. It was not asking Jesus Christ to wash away his sins that would get his name into the book of life.

Those things would come along by themselves if the true faith were achieved.

Jack figured that true faith was believing in the *existence* of God, the devil, Heaven, Hell and all the rest. A person had to know those things were real in the first place.

It was then that he knew why he had no faith. He could not believe in a religion with no proof. He refused to participate in a belief that had been given to him just because it had belonged to his parents. Jack had his own path to follow, his own questions to ponder and he was sure the answers he'd find would not be his father's.

So one Sunday morning he told his dad that he would no longer be attending services at the First Assembly of God church. That sparked quite an exchange of words, but in the end Jack stayed home while his parents sped off to pray for their son's immortal soul.

He watched a rerun of Gilligan's Island while they were in Sunday school. He listened to the radio while they sang *What a friend we have in Jesus*. He played video games on his Atari while they listened to the preacher go on about the rapture of the church.

It had been one of the best days he could remember. He had finally liberated himself. He was a free man.

Jack turned on Fifth Street. After another block he pulled into a space in front of the bookstore. He turned off the ignition and sat for a moment.

At thirty years old he was very much the same free man he'd been at fifteen. He had no more answers than he did at that age.

He worked on Sundays now and his parents hadn't asked him to attend church with them in over ten years. That's the way he wanted to keep it.

1:6

The old woman behind the counter watched Jack closely as he looked around the shop. It made him feel uneasy, the way she stared at him. Sure, he was the only person in the store, but why did her eyes follow his every move? Trying to ignore her, he walked slowly over to the bookshelf labeled *WITCHCRAFT*.

He hoped he could find a book with spells in it. Stacey would like that. She always read books about magic. The trick was, finding one she didn't already have.

"Are you interested in the occult?"

The old woman's raspy voice startled him, but he tried not to let it show.

"Um, no, not really." Jack turned around and saw that she wasn't behind the counter anymore.

"I'm looking for a present for my wife."

She took two steps toward him and stopped.

"That's nice. Do you have any children?" she asked smiling.

"Yes. We have a son," he answered, looking over the top row of books.

The woman took another couple of steps toward him.

"How old is he?"

Jack pulled a hardbound book down, looking over its cover. A thick, silver design of a circle and star extended from one side to the other. The bold letters at the top read *Wiccan Handbook* in red ink.

He looked up, "Oh. Um, Chris just turned six."

"What a wonderful age. Is that short for Christopher?"

Jack was getting annoyed with the old woman's questions.

"Yes, Christopher," he snapped off quickly. She could tell that she was getting on his nerves. It was quite obvious that he wanted to be left to alone to look around. She didn't care, nor did it stop her questions.

"Do you and your family live in town?"

"We live in Penrose."

He slid the book back onto the shelf.

"Oh," she clasped her wrinkled fingers and took another step closer, "So it's a present for your wife you're looking for?"

He gritted his teeth, "*Yes*. My wife."

She looked him straight in the eyes and smiled, "That's nice."

"Yeah, she's into all this magic stuff."

"What kind of stuff are *you* interested in?" Her smile got bigger.

"Oh, I don't know. I guess my interests lean more towards *reality.*"

That was not the response she was looking for, and Jack knew it.

"Oh, but magic *is* real." She turned and made her way back to the cash register. "Come here. Let me show you something."

She disappeared under the counter.

Jack could hear her shuffling through papers, moving small boxes, and cursing under her breath.

"It's got to be here *someplace…dammit…*oh *here* we go!"

She reappeared from the clutter below holding a very large jewelry case. It was dark purple velvet. The edges were lined with a decorative flower and leaf design made from silver metal. It was big enough to hold two baseballs, side by side.

"This might change your mind."

The look of excitement on her wrinkled face eliminated the uncomfortable feeling Jack got from her continuous staring just minutes before. He couldn't help but be amused. He was reminded of Christmas day, the way his son cried out *Neato!* as he tore the wrapping off a GI Joe.

"This will definitely make you believe," she said as she creaked the box open.

Inside sat a necklace made of gray stone. What kind of stone Jack couldn't tell. The centerpiece was a bird, a hawk, he thought, or maybe an eagle. Its wings were spread wide open, as if in flight. It was an amazing piece of work. The intricate detail was unbelievable, but the truly fascinating part wasn't the realistically carved out feathers. It was what the bird had in its claws that was so striking. Underneath the talons, it was carrying an oval shaped crystal vial full of some kind of fluid. It was clear, with a thicker substance floating all through it, very much like a film of oil swimming through a bucket of water. It made him think of a lava lamp.

"Go ahead, take it out."

Her vision was once again fixed on him. That time her staring went completely unnoticed by Jack. His eyes did not leave the necklace.

It looked very old, and more importantly, expensive, and he didn't want to break it. Nevertheless, he had to get a closer look.

Nervously, he took it in both hands and held it up so the light from the shop window showed through the vial. The oily lava substance was no longer dark and murky as it appeared in the case. With the sun standing behind it, the fluid was now sparkling red. Jack was amazed at its constant movement. He tried to hold the necklace perfectly still, but it circled and swam all through the vial, just as though he were gently shaking it up.

"How does it do that?" He couldn't take his eyes off the liquid.

"It's the power in the blood that stirs it."

"Did you say blood?"

The old woman held out her hands and Jack handed her the necklace. She raised it up between them so the front of the bird was facing her. Looking at the back, he noticed that it was as detailed as the other side. But that side was not carved to represent the shape of the bird. It was flat as if made to sit on a table or hang on a wall. The entire surface was covered with designs and some kind of lettering Jack did not recognize.

She laid it down on the table facing Jack. Pointing to the spiraling mixture in the vial she said, "The blood is from the offspring of an angel."

This lady is crazy.

Jack had to admit to himself that the constant movement was unbelievable. It seemed almost magical. But surely there was some explanation that he was not seeing. He must not have been holding it still. But as it lay on the counter it continued to move.

There must be some vibration in the counter.

He put both hands down on the glass, one on each side of the necklace. He felt no vibration.

She said, "Have you ever read the Bible?"

She placed her hands on the glass and leaned over close to him. He backed away from her and crossed his arms.

"Yes, I've read the Bible."

That was not entirely true. Sure, he had attended Sunday school all throughout his childhood, and yes, he knew all of the popular stories taught in mainstream Bible study. But, had he read his Bible from one cover to the other? No, not even close. He supposed few people had.

"Then you know the story of David and Goliath."

"Everyone knows *that* story."
"Not many people know the *full* story. Would you like to hear it?" She ran her hands along the stone bird's wings, caressing it.
Having no idea what the story could have to do with an old necklace, he started to wonder if the woman was totally off her rocker.
But, he thought, *this should be interesting.*
Before he could answer, she began to speak.

She told him a very strange tale that would be the beginning of a whole new belief system for Jack. He didn't believe in God, at least he didn't *think* he did. But that was the day it all changed for him. Of course, when he heard her words, he took it as a crazy story told by a crazy old woman.

But later that night, at 12:42 AM to be precise, his skepticism would be long forgotten.
At that moment, he would believe.

1:7

Sally puffed on her cigarette, holding the silver Zippo lighter in front of her face. She stared through the wafting smoke at the television. Darth Vader stood foreboding with his crimson sword, ready to strike. Luke was somewhere in the shadows of Cloud City.

Sally mouthed the words along with the actors on the screen. She knew every line. It was hard to say how many times she had seen The Empire Strikes Back. She had stopped counting at twenty-five.

Bobby, sitting down at the other end of the couch, blankly gazed up and the white painted ceiling. Cindy slurped a caffeine-free Pepsi, flipping through the latest issue of Cosmopolitan. John lay next to her, face down, snoring.

Bobby looked over, "Well Sal, it's been fun but, I gotta go."
She didn't hear him.
He leaned closer, "Earth to Sally. Come in Sally."
She managed a quick glance in his direction before the television sucked her back in. "What?"
"I'm leaving."

She exhaled a thick stream of smoke into the air and flicked the ash into the black tray on the table.

"Okay, Bob. See ya."

Bobby didn't say another word. He just stood up and walked out, shaking his head in disgust.

With her distraction gone, her world was once again filled with Vader's heavy, mechanical breathing. Even after as many times as she had seen the movie, she was still amazed at how perfectly evil the Lord of the Sith appeared. His huge silhouette through the steam in the carbon-freezing chamber looked as dark and menacing as any image she had ever seen. But, as she found out in the third movie, The Return of the Jedi, he was human after all. Underneath the armor and the cape, he was just a man who'd gone terribly wrong.

At thirteen-years-old Sally learned (whether she knew it at the time or not) that there was no ultimate evil in the universe threatening all that was good. It was only an illusion. Vader had shown his goodness and it was apparent that he loved his son. Even the dark side of the force itself was only one side of a power that kept balance in the universe. So it was in the real world.

It hadn't been until very recently that she realized the lesson she'd learned at thirteen. Her own dark side had shown her that evil equated to nothing more than sadness, fear, anger and awful experience. Every person who'd ever taken a breath had experienced all of those things, in one degree or another. They could not be avoided or denied. They were just part of life.

As she watched the two light sabers clash together, she thought about the parallels between Star Wars and religion. The force was definitely the equivalent to God and the devil. The divine and the damned. She imagined that there was probably some good and bad in both sides. God's Old Testament, wrathful nature showed the same true colors as any evil his adversary had ever shown. So, what goodness could be hiding somewhere within the devil? If he were as human as the creator was, then surely he had a divine side to him also. What did he care about? What was it that he held most dear?

Sally tried to picture what Satan's face would look like inside Vader's mask. She wondered what might cause him to risk everything and heave the emperor to his death.

Luke Skywalker's pain and fear were on display as the shadowy figure leaned out to him, telling him to yield to the dark side. He tried to take advantage of his son's most desperate moment.

Sally's own alcoholic and abusive father had tried the same with her when she was eleven years old. The path to Sally's dark side led her on a ten-year quest before she had to choose her destiny. She very nearly made the wrong choice. But something inside her, that had been there all along, helped her break free of the pain of childhood.

It had been her innocence that had been denied for so long, that saved her. It was the same sense of goodness that lived inside everyone. Fear and pain that had nearly eaten her alive. Those too, lived inside everyone.

As she stared at the corrupt, black silhouette on the screen, she realized that we were all just one choice away from going terribly wrong.

1:8

November, 1971

The paint on the concrete floor was chipped and dirty. A small round table sat in the center of the room. A piece of smooth red velvet covered much of its surface. All of the walls in the dimly lit chamber were lined with tall bookshelves. A green desk lamp was the only light source. It illuminated the pages of the notebook the man was writing in.

He always kept to a determined, almost religious routine with his writing. He wrote everything in the notebook daily. The words he linked together on the white sheets with the thin blue lines were to be his masterpiece. They would chronicle his rise to greatness, to power.

He was a man with a dream. It was as big and fantastic as any had ever dreamt. It was not a fool's dream. Oh, no. It may have been at one time, but not anymore, not with the recent acquisition of one very rare artifact. The only one of its kind, actually.

It had been unearthed at an archeological dig near the Dead Sea in 1960. Transferred to the University of Washington, it was stored for study and safekeeping. It baffled all the researchers that came in contact with it. It had amazing qualities to it that could not be explained. It was more than three thousand years old, and yet it showed no signs of wear at all. The stone remained as unblemished as the day it was carved. The glass enclosure containing the fluid was far beyond the capabilities of the time.

And the fluid. The dancing, magic fluid. Many tests were going to have to be done and some of the greatest scientific minds were called upon for the task.

But then, it just disappeared. A full investigation was still underway when the object made its way into the hands of the man sitting there in that darkened little library. The ancient talisman was lying on the red velvet under the light.

On a nearby shelf was a very old text. It was the forbidden scripture written by a man who had been damned by God long ago. Roman Catholic priests had translated it from Aramaic. The pope himself had deemed it blasphemy and locked it away. No one was supposed to ever see it again.

But one priest, a historian with access to the Vatican's highly guarded vaults, stumbled upon it most accidentally one morning while doing some research for a paper he was writing. He secretly wrote down every word by hand. It took him months of daily visits and long hours to make a complete copy. The book became his life's work.

It was the secret scripture of the Fallen Ones. It contained the spoken word of an angel, and instructions from Lucifer himself.

The man pulled it off of the shelf and set it under the light. He ran his fingers over the yellowing pages carefully.

It was a blueprint for the Devil's own messiah. The necessary components were scattered throughout the verses. They included the scripture itself, a certain talisman, and a willing receiver.

For the first time in over three thousand years, all three existed in the same place.

1:9

Stacey looked up from her laptop computer, noticing a chill in the breeze. It swept through the leaves that were left on the trees, and scattered the ones on the ground.

She raised her knees up to make her lap a more level platform to set the computer on. She had been playing a chess program. She didn't normally play video games, but she was bored, and wanted something to pass the time. What she really enjoyed was surfing the Internet. The phone cord just wasn't long enough to reach out to the porch.

Looking toward the back of the yard, she could see Chris playing under the old swing set. A shiver went down her spine and she pulled the afghan up over her shoulders.

A storm is coming. I can feel it.

That was a thought that always made her feel empty somehow. It seemed as though the whole world were dying. The grass, the trees, *everything*, had to endure the skies cold anger.

When she was a little girl she lived in Illinois and the winter there seemed to last forever.

Cold as a goddamn witches titty! her father would always say, fighting his way in from the snow.

Her dark blonde hair whipped her face. The faint lines at the corners of her eyes deepened as she squinted at the cold air. Her birthday was in a week, and she was positive they would have snow before then.

She would turn thirty next Saturday although she looked much younger. The smooth pale skin and faint freckles across her nose, her pastel blue eyes, always brimming with curiosity and her willing, warm smile embodied youth.

Most people who met her thought she was in her early twenties. She enjoyed getting carded at the bar and liked the way the college guys looked at her. She only wished that her husband would pay her the same attention. He hadn't in a long time.

The wind was picking up, and the temperature was dropping fast. She decided to let her son play outside a little while longer.

Looking back down at the small screen, she pondered which move to make next. Moving the roller ball mouse over to her rook, she slid it across the board, highlighting a black pawn. With one click of a button, the piece disappeared, and her rook stood in its place.

"Take that, you asshole."

This was her third game and it looked like she might lose again.

The little sapling they had planted in the spring rustled its leaves and shook at a cold gust of air. She hoped the tree would make it though the season alright. She was a bit worried, seeing how she couldn't keep any of the plants *inside* the house alive.

Stacey's mother always had lots of beautiful ferns and flowers all around the house. She was good with things like that, but Stacey hadn't inherited the green thumb. She liked plants all right, but always forgot to water them. Her mind was on more important things. That was the way she justified it. Anyway, it was Jack who couldn't accept the fact that every plant that entered the house was on death row.

He frequently would bring them home, set them on the table and say, *isn't it pretty?*

Not for long, Stacey would think, as she smiled and said, *yes, beautiful.*

A black car pulled into the driveway. Stacey looked up from her game, and smiled.

An enthusiastic "Daddy, Daddy!" sounded from the swing set.

Jack slid out of the driver's seat with a brown paper bag under his arm, "Hi, honey."

"Hey, whatcha got there?" His wife gave him an innocent, inquisitive look.

"Never you mind."

"Oh, come on, just a little hint?"

"Nope." Jack received a welcome home hug from Christopher.

Stacey closed the lid on the computer, "You were gone a long time."

"I had an interesting morning," He went up the porch stairs and opened the screen door. "I'll tell you all about it next Saturday."

She would have to wait until then to hear about Jack's conversation with a crazy old woman.

He disappeared inside the house, and went straight to the small spare bedroom at the end of the hall. Chris followed his daddy inside. Stacey stayed on the porch for a few more minutes to give him time to hide her gift.

When she went inside her family was watching television. Chris glanced over at her, and then back to the cartoon that was playing.

"Hurry up Mom! Cow and Chicken's on!"

They all sat on the couch and watched TV for most of the evening. They ate hot dogs and macaroni and cheese for supper. Part one of Stephen King's *The Stand* miniseries was on at seven O'clock. It was the second time they had seen it.

Christopher sat at the kitchen table. A big pile of multicolored blocks sat beside him on the floor. The red, blue and green castle he was constructing was coming together nicely. His imitation of heavy machinery sounds rumbled out of his mouth as he snapped each piece into place.

He decided against a long white block and sounded out slow beep-beep-beep sounds as he backed it away from the structure. Stacey smiled and nudged her husband in the side.

She whispered, "Hey, look."

Jack looked over from the commercial that was playing. Chris had his lips in a pucker as his invisible crane lowered part of the castle wall into position. He grabbed his uneaten hot dog out of a bun on his plate.

Holding it up in his fist he said, "I am the weenie king! Finish my castle or I'll kill you!"

Catsup flew in different directions across the table as he shook the processed meat vigorously. Stacey covered her lips to hold back laughing. Jack pursed his mouth together, looking away. Although it was hilarious they didn't want to encourage him.

When Stacey thought she could control her amusement she lowered her hand and spoke.

"Chris, don't make a mess."

Her son ignored her and tossed the weenie into the center of the building with his sticky hand.

"Chris!"

"Mom! This is the king's house!"

Jack spoke up, "You heard your mother. Put the king back in his bun."

Stacey couldn't hold back any longer. She laughed as she got up and approached the kitchen. The six-year-old grinned.
"Go wash up," Stacey said, trying to sound stern.
Chris wiped his hands on the front of his shirt before hopping down and heading for the bathroom. Jack's vision shifted from his wife, who was ankle deep in Legos, to the television screen. The movie was back from commercial.
"That's my boy," he said with a chuckle.
Stacey, with a wet wash cloth in hand, wiped down the table.
"He's *yours* alright."

Twenty minutes later Christopher proceeded to make another mess, on the carpet. The cleanup wouldn't be so easy that time. Multi-colored chunks of play dough were squashed into the fibers behind the recliner. He had been in bed sleeping for more than an hour before his parents noticed it. Stacey was so mad at the sight of it that she considered waking him up just to punish him. After much deliberation with her husband, she decided against dragging her son to the living room by his ears. All four open cans of molding clay however, did find their way into the kitchen trash can.

1:10

Journal entry- November 12, 1971

The group is almost complete. One more member will make seven, not including myself of course. Linda has someone she is going to bring to the ritual tonight. It is a young girl, twenty or so, named Elizabeth. She is the product of an unfortunate childhood involving physical and sexual abuse. She suffers from chronic depression and has attempted suicide on numerous occasions. She sounds *perfect.*

A confused and tortured mind always leads to a weakened spirit. In that state they are so *controllable.*

Just so we don't get another Robert. What a fiasco that was. I *told* her his soul was too healthy for it. But, we live and learn. There shall be no problems such as that tonight. I will make sure of it.

Now it truly begins. Everything up until now has been practice, just rehearsal for the real show. The forbidden scripture tells us that with a circle of seven it can commence. Their pain is a necessary step in my evolution.

I alone hold the secrets of the fallen ones. I am the master of their energy now. God does not stop me. He cannot. He shall sit by helplessly watching as I myself, become him. I will be the ruler that mankind kneels before. The transformation starts in just a few short hours. The ritual, the Black Communion. This is your body, eat of it. This is your blood, drink of it. This is your soul, I shall swallow it. Not in remembrance of God, but to *become* God.

Those that would condemn me are fools. Good and evil do not apply here. They are obsolete concepts for the weak. Let them damn me if they will. They shall all die before me. I will consume them. Their eternal power will be mine, and they will cease to exist. Where will their morality be then? It will disappear into the same darkness of nonbeing that they themselves shall occupy.

So come now, my sweet Elizabeth. Come share in the glory of my eternal feast. You play a very important part in my ascendance. You finish the circle. And in the end, you too will become a part of me. But don't worry dear, when that time comes, you'll be dying to go. Few can stomach what you're about to take part in. Power can be such messy business.

Soon it will be complete. I will then destroy the old god and a new genesis shall unfold.

In the *new* beginning, God consumed the heavens and the earth.

And it was good.

Oh yes, very good.

1:11

Sally was lying down on the head of John's faded Pontiac Firebird. With her back against the windshield, she stared up into the night sky. The low cloud cover only allowed a few stars to be seen. Shivering in the breezy chill of less than twenty degrees she pulled the fuzzy hood of her thick coat over her ears.

Cindy sat on the hood also, with her legs crossed in front of her. The sour look on her reddened face was telling her friend that she was ready to go. Bobby and John were inside the car with the heater on full blast. They'd been ready to go for nearly twenty minutes.

Cindy leaned over, "This cold air is going to dry out my face, Sal. You ready to leave yet?"

Sally's vision was tightly focused on the brightest star she could find.

"Just a few more minutes," she grinned, "I like it here."

Cindy slid over and stepped down to the ground.

"Well I'm fucking freezing," she chattered out, "I'll be in the car."

The vehicle jolted at Cindy's slammed door. Sally didn't notice; her mind was a million miles away.

Inside the flittered dot of light in the sky, she imagined her father's eyes. She remembered what a good man he'd been, when she was very young. They used to have so much fun together. Going to the park, homemade ice cream afternoons, he even played Barbies with her in her room. (Although he told her never to tell anyone about that. He said he had an image to uphold.)

But that was all before her uncle died. His tragedy became her father's tragedy. The sadness led to the depression. The depression led to the drinking. The drinking led to…well Sally didn't like to think about that. She still spent many nights trying not to think about that. Sometimes she was successful, sometimes she wasn't. But at least she didn't blame herself anymore. Her self-loathing days were over.

It had been a little girl in fuzzy pink pajamas that had saved her. Sally smiled, remembering the sheet she used to tie around her neck for a cape, pretending that she was a Jedi Knight, master of the force.

Her parents fought frequently, making her feel angry and sad. She spent a lot of evenings at the top of the stairs listening to them yell at each other. At the time she wished she really was a Jedi and could make them stop.

She expected them to get a divorce and they probably would have if her dad hadn't done what he'd done.

A single tear found its way down Sally's cheek as a cloud drifted in-between her and her star. She raised a hand and waved goodbye to her father for tonight. It twinkled slightly before fading away completely.

She slid down the cold hood and her feet met the ground. She no longer felt like a ten-year-old at the top of the stairs. She could feel the shivering ache in her lower back from lying against the windshield wiper. As the years since her father's death fell back into her she opened the car door. She leaned down, looking at her friends huddled around the heater vent. She grinned at them

"You guys ready to go or what?"

1:12

Jack found himself awake with the sheet twisted around his legs. Looking up at the ceiling, he noticed a shadow stretched out across the plaster. It looked just like the silhouette of a person. He imagined a face in the darkness. A tree outside the window shook in the breeze, and the shadow man came apart at the waist.

He rolled over onto his side and squinted at the little red numbers shining on top of the dresser. The clock read 12:28 AM. He got up slowly, and went to the bathroom. As he stood at the toilet, the dream he had been having came back to him. It was pretty hazy. He recalled strange images of people running, terrified. He saw a boy, and of course, a giant. He wondered how the woman's story could have affected him so much.

"Now I'm dreaming about this shit. This is ridiculous."

He couldn't get her words out of his head.

The offspring of an angel.

He walked through the darkness down the hallway. He stepped into the spare bedroom and ran his hand down the wall until it came to the light switch. He clicked the light on and closed the door behind him. Squinting in the light, he scanned the room. Everything was just as he had left it a few hours before. Scattered papers on the desk. The computer fan was humming. He and his wife smiled in a picture that hung on the far wall. The closet door was shut, and a large velvet jewelry box lay inside.

He opened the door carefully, tying to make as little noise as possible. He didn't want Stacey waking up and seeing her present before her birthday. A big cardboard box with a Marlboro logo on the side sat full of books. He kneeled down, felt around the back of the closet, and pulled out the velvet box. Looking at it for a moment, he thought about the lady's story.

Crazy old bat.

Reaching down, Jack turned the lid open. The stone necklace felt cold in his hands as he lifted it out, but as he placed it around his neck, he decided it was even colder against his bare chest.

It's so big and gaudy.

He wondered where his wife would ever wear it. But she would love it. Especially after he told her the tale that came with it. The liquid inside swam just as it had done at the store.

A buzzing sound filled Jack's ears, faint at first, and then louder and louder.

What the hell is that?

He couldn't tell where it was coming from. It seemed to be all around him. He began to feel hot. His whole body raised in temperature so fast it felt like he might burn up. He could feel the sweat running down his face.

And then the panic.

Jesus Christ.

He was shaking uncontrollably.

Fuck. Got to get out...

And then it started to move. His fingers and toes were feeling cooler and his arms and legs felt hotter. It made its way through him getting hotter as it went, until it all centralized in the middle of his chest.

Jack tried to stand up, but his body was too heavy. He could barely move his fingers.

Oh, god. I can't...

The heat pushed out of his chest. It felt like swirling water pouring through his skin.

Looking down with wide eyes, he could actually *see* it escaping him. It was forming into a small silver cloud. Very dim at first, and then it grew slowly brighter until it glowed as if a light bulb were floating in the center of it. Small shimmering bubbles began appearing and then popping inside of it.

This isn't real. It's not happening. This is no...

Jack's vision faded into a dark blur. The warmth was gone from him completely. He was no longer shaking. He felt groggy.
I feel…
Nothing.

His mind, like his sight, drifted into blackness. But the unconsciousness only lasted for a moment. When he awoke, he felt strange. He couldn't feel the carpet under his knees. The pumping of his heart wasn't moving his chest. No air was entering his lungs. And yet, he was feeling *something.* A tingling, a vibration, a…

Something started to come into view. Hazy light, and then a shape, a figure of someone. He watched, as it became clear. In that moment, many things became clear.

The old woman wasn't crazy after all. Her story was true. What he saw in front of him was the most amazing thing he had ever seen. It was himself, kneeling in front of the open closet, motionless, wearing a stone necklace.

It was his body, and he was no longer inside it.

And when the angels, the sons of heaven,
beheld them, they became enamoured of them,
saying to each other, Come, let us select for
ourselves wives from the progeny of men,
and let us beget children.

Enoch 1: Chapter 7 Verse 2

BOOK TWO: EARTHBOUND

2:1

The group of angels now in human form despised the earth, hated God, and vowed revenge upon mankind. They would seek out every human they could find and kill them. They traveled many days, walking through the desert. They came upon a man working in a field. The angel Samyaza told the others to stay behind while he approached. When the farmer saw the deformed giant nearing him he cried out to God.

"Lord God, please save me from this terrible demon!"

The prayer went unanswered, and Samyaza's smile was toothless and drooling. His black gums glistened in the afternoon sun. The man stood shaking, paralyzed with fear.

"Get back devil, for the Lord God walks with me."

"Nothing walks with you but death, little man."

When the angelic giant closed the distance between them to ten cubits the farmer turned pale and fell to the ground. Samyaza knew immediately that this was not from fear. He could see the man's spirit pushed out of its shell. The angel's power over man had shown itself. The human flesh, in the presence of an angel, could not hold its etheric matter. This was a strength the giants would take full advantage of.

As the helpless man's body lay before him, Samyaza took a sharp stone and cut the head away from the neck. They had been in the wilderness for many days and were feeling the pain of hunger. They gathered around the man and ate the meat from his bones.

One of the giants known as Zavebe could no longer submit to his earthly prison. He begged the others to kill him, and after much discussion, they agreed. They decided that he should go forth and tell Lucifer what had happened, and of their plans. They all took up large stones in their hands and beat him. His cries were heard for miles. It was not until his skull had been crushed that the astral energy left his body.

The remaining giants ate the flesh from the giant's enormous frame. When their bellies were full they continued on the hunt for mankind. Zavebe returned to Hell and told Lucifer all that had come to pass.

Lucifer, hearing what had happened, was pleased. His plan was coming together even better than he had hoped. Two hundred of his brothers now walked among man.

God knew that his remaining angels were growing unsatisfied with the little attention he gave them. They all yearned for the time when they were his only companionship and love. His compassion for them led him out of the mundane world, into the astral plane. There he attended to the angels, trying to make the lost time up to them. His guilt subsided as they formed a new relationship together. He remained in the ethereal realm with his brothers for a hundred years.

With God occupied, the giants were free to do what they liked among man. He would not interfere. So with God in the heavens, the giants killed all men, women, and children they came upon.

Tales of giants traveled quickly among the people. They were said to be invincible warriors, great demons of terrible strength. Many prayers went unheard during that time. It was thought that God had forsaken them.

Men gathered together their strongest champions to seek out and kill the giants. None of them ever returned. They could not get near enough to them to cause any damage. Spears and stones that could be thrown from a distance could not pierce their leathery skin. A small scratch on the surface was the most that could be achieved. That only served to anger them more.

After a time the killing became a great game to the giants. They quite enjoyed surrounding a village, so not to permit escape, while two or three of them stomped through, destroying all they saw. The killing was always so easy. As soon as the humans got within ten cubits they would fall helpless, their souls driven out. The fallen ones would then simply walk up and bludgeon or stab them to death.

Men tried to fight back from a distance, but their ineffectual efforts were always mocked, just before their deaths. When the last man was killed, they would have a great feast, filling themselves with the meat of their prey. They would then set the place afire and travel on to the next slaughter.

The angel named Azkeel happened upon a group of women bathing in the river one day. They were laughing and talking and didn't notice him standing in the nearby bushes. Before any of them realized what had happened, he ran into the water between them, huge waves splashing from under his feet. They fell immediately spiritless and floated limply beside him. He dragged each one to the sandy bank. Three of the six women drowned before he pulled them out.

He sat staring at the naked bodies that lay before him. His lust grew as he looked them over. He did not leave the riverbank until he had raped them all. Of the three that had not drowned, two were crushed under his terrible weight. Their broken ribs pierced through their lungs and they were left to drown also, in their own blood. The one remaining, bruised and with many broken bones, was now with child.

Many of the others began to give in to their lust for the earthly women. It was not long before nearly every female they encountered was raped and left to die or bear their children.

Because of the unusual size of the half-breed babies, all of the women died during the birth. The children were always male. They had the same leathery skin, sloped foreheads, and twisted black spines. Although they didn't grow to the extreme stature of their fathers, few stood less than three feet above the tallest men. Their strength went unmatched by all humans that came up against them. When they reached full maturity the angelic power to cast out men's souls developed. The magic of the fallen ones had become the magic of their offspring.

The new demi-gods.

The Nephilim.

2:2

Jack's astral energy floated lazily backwards away from his material body. He couldn't believe how utterly comfortable he felt. No clothes were hanging from his body, no itchy tags against his neck. He had no feet on the floor supporting his weight, and no pressure on his back from a chair. He was completely weightless and unencumbered.

Looking down at his motionless body in front of him, he noticed something that seemed impossible. He was seeing the wall and the window behind him. He saw the desk at one side of him and the other wall too, *clearly*, all at once. His eyes didn't hinder his vision anymore. He was seeing in 360 degrees. He could focus his attention in one direction, and still know what was happening directly behind him, without turning around.

Amazing.

He continued to drift backwards and he began to pass right through the wall. It felt like gently being lowered into a pool of water. Only *he* was the water being displaced by the wall. He could feel the sheet rock, the nails, the insulation and the metal siding as he went through. He found himself floating outside the house, in the yard. The grass was humming with a yellowish glow. A brighter, white fog surrounded the trees. A dog in the neighbor's yard barked, its red energy bubbled and spat as it ran.

Then he saw a silvery light, not unlike his own, shining in his neighbor's bedroom window. He wanted to take a closer look, and his astral body started across the fence, over the barking dog and directly to the bedroom. It felt slightly different going through that wall. They didn't have metal siding.

Jack's energy hovered at the side of their bed. His neighbors were Bob and Sheila Thompson. They were a twenty-something couple, and Jack and Stacey had been friends with them for almost two years. They both lay quietly sleeping in bed, Bob on his stomach, Sheila on her side. Bob had a purplish glow to his body, his astral self contained within. But Sheila's was quite different. Her spirit floated directly above herself, connected by a bright white cord. The cord was attached to her physical body at the waist, and her astral body at the chest. Her spirit seemed to be as unconscious as she was.

Jack looked down to see if he also had a cord connecting himself with his body. He did not.

Strange, he thought, *Must be something to do with the necklace.*

Stacey had a book about astral projection, and he had read a couple of chapters. It said during travel a person would always be attached to their body with a cord. This was because the astral matter would never entirely leave the body. Some energy would always stay behind. This apparently was not the case when you used a stone bird to exit your body.

He considered going to check on himself, but decided not to just yet. His physical body would be just fine. The old woman said so. And after experiencing what he had so far, he no longer doubted her at all.

He flew straight up through the ceiling, into the open night sky.

2:3

1971 AD

Linda sped up the winding dirt road in the tan Pinto. Its wheels spun against the loose gravel, kicking up a cloud of dirt that wafted through the surrounding trees.

Her young passenger stared into the passing blur of forest, wondering what to expect from the approaching evening. Her sweating hands were clenched together in her lap. She tapped her right foot nervously on the floorboard.

They came into a clearing where a large, old farmhouse sat. They were about a mile off of county road 185 now. The drive time since they left town had been at least forty-five minutes.

We are definitely in the country. A perfect place for a pagan ritual.

Elizabeth had never been to one before. She thought it might be interesting. Linda had told her that they would light some candles, maybe do a little meditating, nothing major. Of course, she was lying. She would have told her anything to get her out there. They *needed* her.

Linda smiled calmly as she pulled the car up next to the house and stopped. They both opened their doors and got out. The place was very rundown. The boards were coming loose and the paint had all but worn away. The front porch sloped down to one side due to a crumbling foundation. Weeds filled what used to be a front yard. A strong smell of something rotting caught Elizabeth's attention. She wondered if there was a slaughterhouse nearby. She looked around as far as she could see. The house was completely surrounded by tall trees. There was no livestock in sight.

A man appeared at the doorway. It was dark inside and what they could see of him wasn't much more than a silhouette. He was tall and thin. As they climbed the steps he came into view. He wore a wrinkled brown suit and lots of rings on his hands that were made of thick gold with multicolored stones. The wide bands seemed out of place on those long, sickly looking fingers.

His face was worn from age. Deep grooves of skin separated his cheeks from the corners of his mouth. His eyes were sunken and dark. He did not blink once as they neared the doorway, nor did he say a word.

He stared at Elizabeth, holding out his entire arm's length toward her. He cupped his hands together as if trying to catch water from a faucet. She stopped at the top step wondering whether or not to continue. The way he just stood there, completely silent with arms extended was odd, to say the least. *What the hell? This guy's creepy.*

Just as she was about to turn around and leave, *walk* back to town if she had to, he lowered his arms and spoke.

"Welcome my dear. Please don't be afraid. I was just feeling your energy."

Emotion entered him at the lips and his smile was big and toothy.

"Actually, I was thinking of changing my mind. I'm not sure if this is really my thing."

She was going to need some convincing, "Well, why don't you just stick around tonight and see what we're all about. Then, if you're not interested, no harm done, right?"

She looked past him, into the house. She saw a couch and a television on a small stand. Beyond that was the kitchen. Four yellow vinyl chairs sat around a wooden table. Everything looked normal enough. It looked almost *too* normal for a ritual. She had expected colored beads hanging from the ceiling and maybe a crystal ball. She didn't see anything that would indicate a spiritual atmosphere at all.

"Well, alright. I'll give it a go."

Her fear subsided and she walked past the tall man and went inside. They followed her in and the man shut the door behind him. Elizabeth watched as the afternoon sun was pushed out.

That was the last time she ever saw daylight. From that moment on her world would be illuminated by a sixty-watt bulb and dim candlelight. By midnight her throat would be raw from the screaming. She would be naked, surrounded by the harsh chill of concrete.

In that last moment of clarity, of *sanity*, she gave the odd man with the dark eyes a smile. He did not reciprocate. With the deadbolt locked, the emotion drained away from his face, leaving no sign of ever having been there. He whispered to her from across the room.

The words hissed off his tongue sharply, "Now the circle is complete."

She gave him a puzzled look, crossing her arms in front of her. The confusion ended when the sharp thrust of the syringe entered the back of her neck. She tried to scream, but the drug took effect too quickly. The terror faded away, along with her vision, in one swirling moment.

2:4

Jack ascended up into the starry sky. He realized that movement in the spiritual world was simply a matter of will. After a few minutes he saw that it was no more difficult than controlling his physical body.

He looked down at his glowing arm. The energy was spiraling, silvery blue, transparent. It glowed with ever drifting colors. It retained the same shape as his mundane body. He could see the veins in the top of his hands, the thick fingers. When he flexed he watched the skin push out as if there were still muscle underneath. The spirit had been inside the flesh so long it knew the body's every movement. It imitated the shape of Jack's physical arm perfectly.

It doesn't have to look like me, does it?

He focused on the transparent mass, concentrating. The surface of his hand began to ripple like a pool of water. The fingers stretched out like snakes, thinning as they went. His entire forearm bent and twisted in front of him. It spun slowly around and around, forming an astral corkscrew.

Unbelievable.

He stretched it far out in front of him. It pulled away like an extended rubber band. He realized that the mass remained the same, he had only changed the shape.

Jack's focus shifted up to a bright dancing flicker in the in the distance. His arm snapped back into the original look of his physical form. He had not willed that to happen, it just did. It was the soul's self image that had pulled it back, the energy's default position. He would soon learn that he could transform himself into any shape he wanted easily, but he had to be constantly willing it to happen. If attention were lost he would revert back to his true form.

The distant blue light raced across the blackness like a firefly.

What is that?

He slowly gained speed toward it, watching the earth behind him get smaller in the distance. As he approached he saw that it was at least five times the size of his own astral mass. It did not have a human form. It was more like a churning ball of light. Its bright blue glow faded slightly darker as he got close.

Jack was amazed at the powerful, tingling energy he could feel emanating from it. He was close now, right in front of it. It had stopped to look him over. They both hovered for a moment, staring at each other. Jack reached out his hand to touch it. The charge made his astral fingers vibrate and pop. It backed away quickly, speaking to him in a language he'd never heard before. He understood every word.

You do not belong here. Go back. The world you know is waiting.

Jack didn't move.

Are you an angel?

It sat silent. Jack tried again.

Can you understand me? Do you know who I am?

A harsh grinding sound surrounded him with a yellow film, pushing him back. He strained against the liquid wall of light, testing its strength. It held steady in front of him.

The spirit spoke again, *Go and reclaim the flesh.*

He pleaded with the entity that was pushing him away, *Please, I have so many questions.*

The spirit said nothing more. It flew away from him quickly, its speed creating a bright white jet trail. Jack followed its path as fast as he could. The shining blue light's velocity was too much for him. He watched it shrink into the distance.

Why won't it talk to me? Why is it running away?

The ball of energy was soon gone completely. There were no other astral beings in sight.

He looked back toward Earth. The whole planet glowed in a multicolored ethereal haze. The swimming oily glow was a giant beacon in the middle of the starry universe. He took one more look around, scanning the sky for other living things. He saw only stars. It was hard to tell how long he'd been gone. His sense of time was lost. Getting back home seemed like a good idea.

His spiritual instinct led him down through the atmosphere, below the clouds and into the yellow streetlights of Penrose. He buzzed over the neighborhoods exploring his home in a way he had never done before. He flew low, just over the roofs of the houses.

Through the windows he saw the glow of souls inside each one. The yards were covered with sheets of soft white and green fog. The trees' surrounding haze was yellowy white. He saw the glow of numerous small animals in the yards and fields, in the trees and under brush. Rabbits and cats, dogs and mice and even a coyote who had wandered over to fifth street from across the highway. Each one's energy had a different color, brightness and movement. Some vibrated almost violently and fizzled with excitement, anger or fear, while others looked calm and serene.

A group of sleeping horses in a nearby field stood huddled together. Their spirits melted in and out of each other, creating a brighter illumination.

Jack soaked it all in with the wonder and amazement of a child. It was like opening his eyes for the very first time. He dived down lower, skimming the ground. The astral mist of the grass parted as he soared through it. His spirit created a slight wake of displaced light and then it slowly re-gathered itself over the yards. It felt so much like swimming that he took to kicking his legs behind him like a frog.

He zipped past a large brown house at the intersection of Eighth and K Streets. He leaned to his right and made a sharp turn around the corner of the house.

A huge dog stood raging just in front of its physical body. Its presence had taken Jack by complete surprise and he had no time to stop. He plowed right into the animal's energy. It jumped, spun around and bit at him. The dog's mundane teeth clacked together against themselves with nothing to grab hold of. Its astral teeth on the other hand did find something between them, Jack. His glowing arm flashed dark yellow when the sharp, electric pain entered. Jack pulled away screaming.

Tiny little dots of light expelled out of the spiritual wound. He pushed himself back, up into the air, end over end. The animal barked excitedly as its ethereal self screeched in blinding anger. Small streaks of lightning popped over and across its translucent skin.

Jack held a hand over the gritty, stabbing pain. It was glowing with florescent intensity. He backed away, higher into the air. The dog and its astral self stayed at ground level, frantically barking and growling. Jack drifted above the trees, terrified. The bite felt like his arm was asleep with pinpricks running all through it, except this pain was much more intense.

Looking down at the crackling bite mark, he saw that it didn't take long for the dots of light to stop pouring from the wound. It still glowed dark yellow, but the pain quickly subsided as he watched the haze diminish.

It hadn't occurred to Jack that he could be harmed in any way in his current form. It had never entered his mind. He had always thought that souls were immortal, forever. He guessed that's why he thought that they were indestructible. It was then that he realized that he was not Superman, buzzing around a world that couldn't hurt him. Danger was as real here at it was in the physical world. Perhaps even more so, due to the fact that he was a pilgrim in uncharted territory.

Sure, this time had only been a dog, but what was waiting around the next corner? Jack started to feel like a river fish that had just washed out to sea. An uneasy fear came over him and deep orange illumination took over his previously blue glow.

He looked out over the rows of houses and cars lining the streets. The angry dog's barking below him seemed distant now as he found home's direction. He'd seen enough for tonight. It was time to go back.

2:5

The concrete felt like ice underneath her naked body. She could see a dim light coming from somewhere.
A window maybe?
No.
The door behind her. Beyond the iron bars was a hallway. The light was coming from another room. She tried to push herself up from the floor. Her muscles felt like lead. She was shivering. Her mind was spinning. She remembered something...a face.
Those dark eyes.
A sting.
Her hand slowly reached back and felt her neck. She ran her fingers over a lump on her skin just under her hairline. Thoughts swam through her head like a surreal story with a forgotten ending.
My clothes.

A clanking noise could be heard down the corridor. And crying. Someone was *crying*. Her whole body was stiff and sore. Her hips were badly bruised and scraped. She sat up. She felt pressure between her legs, swelling. The insides of her thighs were wet and sticky.
Blood?
Yes. And something else.

Tears were running down the dark bruises on her cheeks. She had been raped before, but never when she was unconscious, until now.

She remembered her father's sweaty body on top of her, his smothering weight and foul breath. She was twelve years old in her darkened bedroom. A talk show could be heard in the next room. The volume was turned way up. It was always too loud. Every few seconds the studio audience would laugh concurrently, taunting her. They were cheering him on. He was the star of the show, and she, his unwilling guest.

The more she struggled, the more violent he became. He would hold her down and hit her over and over. But not in the face.

Never in the face. If anyone saw the damage he'd inflicted she might not be back for the next night's encore performance.

Mom was at work. Her graveyard shift provided the regular opportunity for him. Of that he took full advantage. Her cries for help went completely unheard in a house far from town, not unlike the place she was in now.

One thing was different though. Her parent's house didn't have a cold basement with locked cells. She had been free to go to school every day, carefully hiding her pain. It's hard to even walk straight and normal like the other girls, having been raped the night before. But she did conceal it, for almost a year.

There would be no hiding it now. Her whole face was swollen. Both eyes were purplish black. She could barely see out of the left one. They would not be letting her out for school or anything else. She was there to stay.

She knew that the door with the metal bars was locked tight. That didn't stop her from desperately pulling on it with all the strength that was in her. Her screaming echoed throughout the whole basement. Nobody answered her. Nobody came. All she could hear was *them*.

Laughing on and on.

2:6

Jack woke up with his right cheek lying against the carpet. A thin line of drool led from the corner of his mouth into the tan fibers. He was face down on the floor with his arms stretched out away from him, palms up. He immediately felt around for the necklace.

Where is it?

He should have still been wearing it, but he didn't feel it beneath him.

He got up slowly. It felt like he hadn't gotten any sleep at all. He was very tired and had a pounding headache. Looking around the room, he couldn't see the stone bird anywhere. Sliding over to the velvet jewelry case, he popped it open. There was the necklace, safe and sound.

How did it get in here?

Jack didn't remember putting it away. He supposed in all of the excitement, that he'd forgotten setting it back in its box. In any case, there it was, and that was all that mattered. He sat in front of the closet wondering if what he'd experienced could have possibly been a dream.

It was as real as anything I've ever seen. It wasn't a dream.

So many questions he'd lived his whole life with had been answered in a few short hours. But there was so much more he wanted to know. He would travel again tonight. He didn't just want to, he *had* to. He'd been let in on the secrets of the universe and he was going to learn all there was to know.

But why me? Why do I get to know?

There had to be a reason why the old woman, out of all the people she could've sold the necklace to, chose him. It couldn't be just random luck. He couldn't imagine why she would've sold it in the first place. It had *real* power. He was quite sure it was worth far more than the fifty bucks he'd paid for it. She knew something that she hadn't told him at the store. He decided to call her from work later and have another talk with her.

He thought about what Stacey would say if he told her.

My god, she'd think I was fucking nuts.

She wouldn't believe him. No one would. He could barely believe it himself.

It really happened. It was not a dream.

He would prove that tonight. And this time, he'd go even further. He would come back with the truth about life after death, God, and everything. At least he hoped so.

Jack carefully opened the door and padded down the hallway to their bedroom. He peeked in and saw that she was still sleeping. He hoped that she hadn't woken up in the night and wondered where he was.

Looking down at his watch, he saw that it was almost 6:30. He thought he'd better get ready for work as he smiled to himself.

The X-Files is right. The truth is out there.

Walking into the bathroom, he grabbed a towel off the shelf.

Way out there.

Still grinning, he stepped into the shower.

2:7

Stacey was still sleeping when Jack left the house at 7:30. It usually took forty-five minutes to get to work. His drive took him out of Penrose, twelve miles west through Canyon City, another eight miles to the turnoff, and four more up the mountain. He worked at the Royal Gorge Bridge. It was Colorado's premiere scenic attraction. That's what all of the brochures said. At a thousand fifty-three feet above the Arkansas River it was the highest suspension bridge in the world.

Jack thought about how high he was above the earth the previous night, without the help of any man made structures.

On the way to work he passed by a group of tourists feeding the deer. The father, mother and two children had handfuls of what appeared to be popcorn. The three animals ate their breakfast enthusiastically from the palms of the Texans. When the food ran out the deer wondered off into the nearby forest. The father frantically dug through the trunk of his car, looking for a camera.

Jack drove on to the parking lot and pulled into a space. He locked the door and walked over to the wooden gate at the back of the visitor's center. It was the largest building in the park. It mainly served as a gift shop, but also had a restaurant and an information booth.

He went inside and poured himself a cup of coffee. He peeked in at the time clock. It read 8:21. He still had a few minutes before he could punch in. He waited outside the back door.

The gate opened and in walked Jerry Davis. He was a tall man, well over six feet. He carried a large blue lunchbox, whistling as he strutted in.

"G'day Bruce," he said in his very best British accent. He'd been watching reruns of Monty Python's Flying Circus again.

"Good morning," Jack answered back, knowing full well that his accent wasn't as good as Jerry's.

They worked together on the aerial tramway, the cable car that carried people across the span, just east of the bridge. The view was quite beautiful out in the middle, but after three years Jack barely noticed it. It had become just a background for his daily routine.

Other employees started filing though the gate, wearing all different colors of uniforms, according to which department they worked.

A line formed at the clock, meaning it was time to punch in. Jack and Jerry sipped their coffee, waiting for the others to finish. When the line was gone the tram crew slid their cards through the bar code slot. The machine beeped and flashed OK on the screen. Jerry looked at his co-workers weary face.

"Damn man, you look like shit."

"I didn't get much sleep last night."

Jerry was smiling and sarcastic, "Oh, I thought maybe you got hit by a train."

Jack couldn't help but grin back, "Thanks man, you really know how to brighten a guy's day."

"I do what I can," he said in the most serious voice he could muster.

The two of them walked out to the tram building and got to work.

2:8

Stacey was standing in the bathroom wearing a pink robe. Her hair shook back and forth against her face as she brushed her teeth. She stared into the big mirror above the sink, watching herself. She remembered waking up last night. Well, *this morning,* really.

Was it two O'clock, three maybe?

She couldn't remember. What she did recall was that Jack wasn't asleep beside her. She looked around the bedroom, but he wasn't there. Then she heard his voice. Not in the room with her, somewhere down the hall. He was talking to someone.

Was somebody here last night?

She hadn't heard any other voices, just his. He must've been talking on the phone. She doubted that anyone called them. She always woke up when the phone rang. It had one of those high pitched beeps that was impossible to sleep through.

He must have made a call. But, to who?

She walked out to the kitchen with the toothbrush hanging out the side of her mouth. She picked up the green receiver, looking down at the glowing buttons. She pushed the one labeled REDIAL. When she lifted it up to her ear she heard it ringing. After five rings, they picked up.

"Hello?"

It was an older woman's voice. Stacey recognized it immediately.

"Hi Mom."

She hadn't expected her mother to answer. She didn't quite know what to say. She decided to ask her if she wanted to have breakfast at Village Inn on Monday. They talked for a few minutes and then she said goodbye and hung up the phone. She realized that her mother had been the last person *she* had talked to, not Jack. They had spoken the previous afternoon.

Okay, so he used the cordless.

She went into the spare bedroom and removed it from its charging cradle. She again pushed the redial button and waited for a response. That time it only rang once.

"Paradox coffee and books, can I help you?" The voice was female.

Stacey paused and then said, "Sorry, wrong number."

She set the receiver down on the desk. She walked back to the bathroom to wash the toothpaste out of her mouth.

He called a bookstore at 2:00 AM?

That was very strange. But what was even more strange to Stacey was that there was actually someone there at that hour to answer the phone. She thought it might have something to do with her birthday, but he had already brought her present home earlier that evening. It made no sense at all.

"What the hell are you up to Jack?" she said out loud, as if he were standing right there with her.

2:9

The cable car was parked in the dock. Jack was just finishing up putting on his safety harness. It was made of yellow and black nylon straps. He made a final length adjustment to the one that wrapped around his upper leg and then clicked it shut.

It was definitely the best attraction in the park. The view was breathtaking. He looked out across the canyon. The span to the other side was nearly a half a mile. The distance he'd be above the Arkansas River was about a quarter mile.

Jack would not be riding inside the cable car. It was the first of the month, and it was time for a visual inspection. He'd be riding across on top of the carriage.

He climbed up from the catwalk at the north terminal. Once sitting in position, he wrapped his safety rope around the top rung of the ladder. Turning around, he gave the thumbs up to the man in the control booth. The Aerial Tramway started across. Once Jack cleared the terminal he sat up straight and looked around at the amazing view. Scattered clouds hung over the mountains to the west. The sky was deep blue behind them. To the east it faded into a soft white haze. A bitter cold breeze could be felt on his skin, pushing away the sun's heat.

He was far above everything now. Tourists from all over the world walked over the suspension bridge. An ever-growing line of people waited at the South tram terminal for their opportunity to ride. The whole park was brimming with vacationers. But, if Jack looked out to the east, he could ignore all of it.

For a few minutes, out in the middle of the canyon, it was just him and the sky. Jack remembered his nervousness the first time he rode on top of the car. That had been more than four years ago.

At the time he'd thought that would be the closest he would ever get to really flying. As he thought about his previous night's experience, he realized that he'd been wrong.

2:10

It was almost dark. The sun had finished its afternoon labor and had sunk down below the horizon. Not that it mattered in the basement. Time effected nothing there. It was always the middle of the night in the cells.

Elizabeth was leaning up against the cracked wall with a wet green blanket around her shoulders and across her lap. She had found it wadded up in the corner. It smelled like urine.

She'd given up screaming hours ago. She sat staring through the bars into the chamber across from her. Her current pastime had taken up about forty-five minutes. There was no sound or movement at all in the shadowy cell across the way. Banging, crying, and screams of every kind were heard from the other rooms, but not from that one. She had tried to speak to them earlier, but none answered her. She thought that the cell she was staring at was probably empty. Or maybe there *was* someone, sleeping or...possibly dead.

Nevertheless, she kept looking; hoping a face would appear in the doorway. She hated feeling so alone, so terrified.

After another thirty minutes passed by, she saw something. Movement...coughing...a girl. She crawled over to the bars. She had blonde hair. Her hands were shaking as she grasped the iron, pulling herself up onto her knees.

Elizabeth sat up. The girl was probably about her age, maybe twenty years old, maybe more. It was hard to tell in the dim light. She nervously bobbed back and forth; her vision blankly fixed on a crack in the corridor wall. Elizabeth scooted closer to the front of the room.

“Hello?” Her throat was dry and raspy.

The girl's eyes did not move. She gave no indication that she had heard her at all.

“Please talk to me. I need you to...”

Elizabeth stopped. There was no telling how long the girl had been there. Weeks, months, *years,* maybe. She was sure the girl was crazy. Elizabeth knew that would happen to her if she didn't find a way out.

She quickly found out that she was wrong about the girl. There was a spark of sanity left inside her mind. She opened her mouth slowly, and spoke.

“You are the last,” she said as her eyes jumped over to the one with the green blanket.

“What? What did you say?”

“The beginning of the end is here.”

Elizabeth was desperate to keep her talking, "The end of what?"
"Everything."
She began to laugh nervously, but it quickly turned into tears. A year's worth of torment was pouring out of her face.
"What's your name?"
"I have no name," she choked out in a raspy whisper.

A long pause lingered between them. A hand slowly emerged from under the blanket. It stretched through the bars. Her upper arm's thickness filled the space between the iron. Her face rested on the cold metal as she held out her comfort to the other girl. A dirty hand extended out of the opposite cell. The two clasped in the middle of the hallway.
"My name is Elizabeth," she said with a sympathetic look.
"Not anymore," The unnamed girl pulled her hand away, "We're all dead, you know."
"What?"
"I was alive once. I had a mother and father. I lived in a nice house in town. My dad just bought me a car," She was swaying back and forth again.
Elizabeth was crying. She had to find a way out of there.
"We're all dead and this is Hell. Didn't you know that?" Her eyes found the crack in the wall.
"Stop it."
"It's true. We're all sinners here."
Elizabeth sobbed, holding her face down in her hands, "He raped me."
"*Rape?* I've been raped more times than I can remember. Do you actually think that's the worst of it? You don't know *anything*."
"Please *stop*."
"No matter how strong you think you are, they're always stronger."
"No, don't..."
"It's the most terrible thing you'll ever do."
"You're crazy. I don't know what you're talking about. Just stop it, *stop*."

2:11

At noon Jack made the phone call from the break room.

"Hello, Paradox books, can I help you?" It was not the woman who had sold him the necklace. This voice was much younger.

"Yes, I need to speak to the woman who was working yesterday afternoon."

"I'm sorry, she's not here right now. Can I take a message?"

Damn it. I need to talk to her.

"Can you tell me when she'll be in?"

"She has the next couple of days off. Is there something I can help you with?"

He didn't think he should discuss it with her. She probably didn't know anything about it anyway.

"Do you have a home number I could reach her at? I wouldn't normally ask, but it's terribly important."

"I'm sorry. I can't give out that information. But if you call on Tuesday, she should be here."

"She didn't give me her name yesterday, could you tell me so I know who to ask for next time?"

"Sure. It's Ms. Holland." She did not offer a first name.

"Okay, thank you." He hung up.

Shit. I guess I have to wait. I have no choice.

The microwave beeped four times. His lunch was ready. He ate the soup thinking about his spirit flying through the sky. It was all he could think about the whole day.

2:12

Jack drove the black Nissan into the driveway. He had been thinking about the old woman's story the whole way home. He couldn't get it out of his head.

Is it true?

What she had said about the necklace sure was. But his logical mind still fought the validity of the story. He thought that maybe she had found out about its power and made the story up to go with it. Or maybe, it *was* true. Would God really have allowed those things to happen? Would God himself have done the things she said he did? And if so, if it were all true, where was he now? With such an active role in the world in the beginning, why didn't he show himself now? What was he doing up there? Even with what he had experienced so far, he still had so many questions. He was determined to find the answers.

He was so anxious to go again. The comfortable weightless feeling was like a calm bliss. All of his problems seemed so far away. He could *definitely* get used to that.

He wished he could tell Stacey. She wouldn't believe him. She didn't listen to him when he told her *believable* things. It was like she had just woken up one day and decided that she didn't trust him. His opinion meant nothing. At least that's the way it felt to him. But he knew that he hadn't been the best husband either. It was just that it was so easy to get caught up in work and money troubles and...

Who cares about any of that shit now? It seems so pointless.

He could barely stand it. He wanted to go right now. But, he couldn't just yet. Not until they had all gone to bed.

He got out of the car and walked into the house. His wife and son could be heard in the back bedroom laughing. Jack flopped down onto the couch staring into the television. He pulled the remote out from underneath a cushion and changed the channel. He stopped at the local news just before it cut to a commercial. An image of a cross appeared on the television screen. The voice of a calm toned man spoke as the picture faded into a couple smiling and talking to a well-dressed man in a suit. The narrator continued talking about God and Jesus and the First Nazarene Church, located in Canyon City, as the pictures changed from one to another.

The entire commercial seemed to have been shot with a home video camera. The colors were all wrong, the images were grainy and the brightness was way to high. Jack figured he'd get a headache if he had to watch it very long. He was soon relieved as the final screen came up indicating the name and address of the church.

Another advertisement popped onto the screen as Jack remembered the time the faith healers came to his church, when he was ten years old. He first found out they were coming when brightly colored flyers were passed out before the service on Sunday. At the top of the page stood stylized graphic of a man

with is arms stretched up towards heaven. Cartoonish outlines of clouds filled the paper behind him. Underneath the picture it read in Italics,
Come share the worship and healing power of God's love.
Just below that it stated,
Don Lovejoy, deciple of God, has been blessed with the gift of healing minds and bodies. The service will be a celebration of out lord Jesus Christ and God's will for us all! Let God heal you through Brother Lovejoy's hands!
At the bottom the text said,
Wednesday, July 14th, First Assembly of God Church, Canyon City.

Jack had to read over it three times to be sure of what he was reading. His eyes were wide as he read the words, *gift of healing*. He thought that might be what he'd been looking for. He wanted so badly to believe in God but he just hadn't been able to. Everyone else seemed to have faith and he wanted to also.
Actual proof of God. Wow.

He asked his parents a total of eight times in the next three days, if he could go on Wednesday night. They said yes each time, tiring of his persistency. It was the first thing he thought of when he woke up Monday and the last thing in his head when we went to sleep. By Tuesday he'd become so excited he thought he might bust. When Wednesday finally came Jack could think of nothing else.

He rushed home from school on his bicycle and ran into the house. The service was still hours away but he went to his room to pick out what he was going to wear anyway. He pulled his Easter suit off of a hanger, laying it out on his bed. He wanted to look like a good Christian tonight. He couldn't have Brother Lovejoy thinking he was a slacker.
No siree Bob.

When his mother asked him why he was wearing his best suit he simply said, *Oh, no reason.* She promptly told what kind of trouble he'd be in if he got it dirty and he responded with a promise that he wouldn't.

Jack walked into the church excitedly and sat up front. He wanted to be able to see everything without anyone blocking his view. The service began as usual with a prayer and the singing of songs. The Reverend then turned it over to Brother Lovejoy. He asked everyone to stand and then he said a prayer of his own. Holding his arms up to the sky he asked God to bless him once again with the power of healing. People in the congregation started to say *Amen* as he danced with the Holy Spirit. He told them that anyone who was sick or crippled or had any health problems whatsoever should come up to the stage to be healed.

Jack's eyes were fixed on brother Lovejoy as a line started to form at the front. One man was limping holding himself steady with a cane. Another had a large dark patch on his face that looked like a huge mole. There was a woman with a neck brace and last but oh so far from least, was a man in a wheelchair. Jack wondered what Mr. Lovejoy was going to do for him.

Surely he can't make a crippled man walk, can he?

Now, Jack had seen some pretty amazing things in his ten years. Just last summer he'd seen Jason Conner swallow an earthworm whole. He remembered it squirming as the boy lowered it onto his tongue. At the time Jack had said it was the most amazing (and disgusting) thing he's ever seen.

Then there was the strong man on television who lifted concrete blocks with is pierced tongue. It really looked like it had to hurt. But then something came along that had taken over the number one spot on the list of most amazing things Jack had ever seen, hands down.

Ronny Johnson brought a deck of playing cards to school with him. Not just any old cards, but cards with *sex* pictures on them. The glossy black and white photos showed people doing it in every possible position. Some of them even had a *dog* in them. Jack had never seen anything like it. They were mostly poor quality photos that looked like somebody's brother had taken but they were astonishing just the same. Some of the pictures (mostly the ones with the dog) made Jack feel sick to his stomach, but no matter how ill they made him feel, they definitely topped his most amazing list.

As Jack sat in the front pew of the Pentecostal church with people yelling *Praise God* all around him he waited for the new amazement to shove its way into first place. He watched with his mouth gaping open as the limping man made his way up the ramp.

Brother Lovejoy cried out to Jesus as he laid his healing hands on the man's forehead. Jack was sweating and his shirt was soaked completely through. He wanted to believe so badly that he could feel it pulling at him from the bottom of his stomach.

"Be healed!" Lovejoy commanded and he slapped the man's head with the palm of his hand. The cane fell to the floor and the newly whole man cried and danced around the pulpit. Jack almost swallowed his gum.

The woman with the brace on her neck stepped up. With a slap from the Holy Spirit, she was healed too.

Wow.

The large blotch on the next one's face was easily rubbed away by Lovejoy's magical fingers, but what topped everything, what won by a landslide was waiting at the bottom of the ramp.

The old man's wife struggled to push him up onto the stage. The wheelchair came to a stop and she locked the wheels. Lovejoy kneeled down to the man praying, laying hands on him. Jack's eyes didn't blink for a full twenty seconds. He was frozen in place staring at the miracle in front of him. The elderly man received his holy swat and he firmly placed his hands on the arms of the chair. Unsteadily at first, he pushed himself to an upright position. When he let go of the wheelchair he raised his hands into the air. He was standing all by himself. Jack's gum rolled down his tongue, falling onto the carpet.

Praise God. Hallelujah.

He was dumbfounded. What he had just witnessed blew the playing cards completely out of the water. He believed. For the first time in his life he could feel his faith filling the emptiness inside of him like warm water.

The healer's wife passed the basket around as he told the crowd that God would bless all those who gave unselfishly. When it was full of dollar bills she emptied it and passed it to the other side of the church. The newly healed people filed down the aisle happily, and out the front door.

When the service was concluded the Lovejoy's promptly left. Jack, still in awe of the things he'd just seen, stared at the quiet stage. He felt a hand on his shoulder and he looked up. It was his dad.

"Wait here Jack. I'm going to talk to pastor Gibbons for a few minutes."

Jack didn't notice the anger in his father's face. He was too busy thinking about God and brother Lovejoy's magic hands.

After a few minutes he looked around and noticed that he was the only one left in the front room of the church. He walked to the back, past the bathrooms and into the hallway. He heard voices behind the Pastor's office door. He could hear his father faintly. He didn't hear everything that was said but he did hear a few words very clearly. Words like *ridiculous* and *carnival sideshow*. He didn't care what the conversation was about.

Still caught up in the whirlwind of God's power he went outside and sat on the curb. It was another ten minutes before his parents came out. Jack whistled enthusiastically, sitting on the sidewalk in his best suit and tie. They said nothing when they came out. They just walked straight to the car and got in.

"Hurry up Jack," his mom said with an annoyed tone.

They pulled into the gas station at the corner of Ninth and Royal Gorge Blvd. Jack's father got out to fill the tank. A large fifth wheel camper sat across the lot attached to an old pickup truck. Jack recognized the man pumping the gas.

It's the guy in the wheelchair.

Jack said, "I'll be right back," to his mother.

She paid little attention looking through her purse for her checkbook.

As he walked around the back of the large camper he noticed that the side door was open. A voice sounded from inside. It was Brother Lovejoy. Jack listened, standing back in the shadow.

"Goddamn, Podunk cheapskates!"

Jack took a soft step forward.

"We barely pulled in a hundred bucks! God, I hate these small town losers!"

Lovejoy's wife shuffled through the stack of dollar bills.

"Shit," she said, angrily.

Looking under the table by the door, Jack saw a neck brace. The woman who'd been wearing it earlier was sitting in the cab of the truck. Jack's faith fell out of him as quickly as it had appeared. *It was all a scam.*

He started to cry. He couldn't believe anyone would do such a thing, using God to rip people off. The so-called healer stuck his head out the door, peering down at the ten-year-old, crying in his best Easter suit.

"Shit," the man said under his breath before saying, "Get lost kid."

Jack trudged slowly back to the car. His elation had melted into disappointment. He flopped down on the back seat and slammed the door. He figured the worst thing about it was that the number one spot on his list of the most amazing had reverted back to pornography.

If he'd known the concept of irony he would've thought just how ironic it all seemed, but he did not. So instead he thought that it sucked, *bigtime*.

2:13

"Do you want to know my secret?" The girl with no name was grinning.

Elizabeth shifted her weight to the other leg. The floor was making her sore, "What?"

"I found a way to beat them. Wanna know how?"

"I don't know what you mean."

"Look, all of the others are crazy now, but not me. They didn't know the secret."

She was rocking in place again, her hands wrapped around the bars. The banging and crying continued down the hall.

"What is it?"

"I outlasted all of them. I've been here longer too, but they didn't know what I know."

"What?"

"It's this," she held out two little rolled up pieces of cloth. 'Make sure to clean the wax out of your ears every day and wipe it on. That way it makes a better seal."

"What *are* those?"

"Homemade earplugs. Cool, huh?"

"What for?"

"It's the screaming that will drive you mad. Block that out, and you'll be like me."

Elizabeth thought about what the girl had said earlier.
It's the most terrible thing you'll ever do.
She was completely nuts. They all were.

There had to be a way out of that place. And she was going to find it. She could only hope she could escape before *he* came back. She got up and ran her hands along the back wall of the cell. She was feeling for a hole, or a vent, anything that might lead her to freedom. What she didn't realize was that they were already coming. It was too late.

2:14

Jack lay in bed quietly, staring up at the ceiling. His wife had been asleep for a few minutes now, but he waited a little longer just to be sure.

She rolled over onto her side, facing him. The dim moonlight shining through the window reflected off her face. Jack studied the little lines at the corner of her eyes. He saw the way her hair gently rested across her neck and over her shoulder. He listened to her breathing. The rhythmic little tufts of air moved in and out of her slightly open lips. In that light it was impossible to see the dark red lipstick that remained. The mascara lining her eyes was all but invisible now too. The blush that was on her cheeks had been wiped away hours earlier.

It was the makeup she had put on just before he got home from work. It was the makeup that had been put on for him. It went completely unnoticed, as did the silk blouse with the small white flowers. The top three buttons had been left undone. Jack was sitting not more than five feet away when she bent down to pick up the magazines off the floor. Anyone who had been paying attention would have seen the black lace bra underneath.

He was not. Almost anyone at all would've picked up on the way she looked at him across the table, the seductive glare and the little grin. Anyone but Jack, that is. His mind was not at the dinner table, nor was it anywhere in the house. He was in the heavens, soaring among the stars.

He only glanced back at earth once, when his son spilled his milk. Stacey got up to get a towel and Jack's imagination immediately took off again. After dinner he stared blankly into the television.

She even went as far as to sit next to him on the couch and kiss the back of his neck. She ran her fingers through his hair softly. Jack looked over at her and gave her a short kiss and went back to his staring, and thinking.

Like so many nights before, her futile efforts left her crying in the bathroom. She pushed the towel across her face, looking at herself in the mirror.

What's the use?

After a couple of minutes she dried her eyes and checked them closely to see if they were still red. She didn't open the door until she was sure the signs of her crying were gone. She didn't want his pity. It was his passion she longed for. It had been months since they had made love and months before that since he had spent more than five minutes talking with her.

They didn't share anything anymore. She missed him more than she had ever missed anyone. She hoped that he would come back to her and love her the way he did when they first met. She didn't know what was bothering him. He wouldn't talk to her. He wouldn't talk to anyone. It was like the fire that used to drive him had burnt out. Something inside of him had died, and even he didn't know what it was or where to begin to fix it. And yet, he did not want her help or support. He was determined to do it his way, in his time.

If he hadn't been so overwhelmed with himself and everything that was happening, he might have seen his wife across that table. He might have noticed that she was sitting there all alone.

As he laid there in the dark next to Stacey, he wished he could tell her how much he loved her. He wanted her to know that his feelings for her hadn't diminished. He still cared as much as he ever had. He had just lost *himself* somewhere along the way. He needed to find out who he was and where his life was going.

He remembered a time when they could sit and talk for hours about anything. It didn't matter what, as long as they were together. But things change in six years. She didn't seem to understand him anymore. The anything they used to talk about had turned into nothing. Most of the time when they looked at each other they just couldn't think of anything to say.

Jack couldn't help thinking that maybe everything that was happening now would change things for them. If he could just find meaning it all somehow. He'd had no luck in this world. It was possible that he would find himself in the stars.

He considered waking her up right then and there and telling her everything. But she wouldn't believe him. They would just get into another fight. No, he couldn't tell her just yet. He had to find out more himself first. Waking her up in the middle of the night was not the answer. But he knew that he would have to talk to her soon. He had to find a way to communicate with her. She was losing faith in him quickly.

Jack squinted up at the clock on the dresser. It was eleven forty-eight. He took in one last image of her peaceful face and carefully got out of bed.

Jack went to the spare bedroom and closed the door. He laid down flat with his back against the carpet. The cold chain and stone were once again in place on his chest. The buzzing in his ears got so loud it felt as if his head was vibrating. He took a deep breath into his lungs and tried to stay calm. His eyes were fixed on the rough textured ceiling above. The blood inside the glass swam faster. The heat entered him and centralized just as it had done before. Jack remained still. The watery swell pushed out through his chest and his consciousness went with it. He watched himself pour out of his body like mist. He could see each breath the soulless flesh took in. With closed eyes it lay there sleeping.

Jack's matter flew down the hallway and into the bedroom. His wife's spirit was mostly contained inside her unconscious body, although a slight edge of her light showed just above the covers. It was a brilliant blue haze that lit up the whole room. It was stunning. Jack thought that it was like looking into the very heart of beauty. He felt its warmth all around him.

But then he saw floating in the center of it, sadness. It was a darker blue just above Stacey, spinning hard against itself. As the smoky light collided in mid swish it created a kind of unfulfilled circle that made Jack feel afraid. The brilliant color of beauty soon faded into the darker, and the entire room fizzled and boiled.

Jack's soul felt empty. He couldn't stand to stay there a moment longer. He shot up through the ceiling, into the open air. The darkness had a frigid bite to it that would've made his mundane body shudder. But it was no less comfortable to his ethereal self than the temperature inside the house.

He focused most of his attention on the full moon high in the sky. He began racing toward it. A small part of him kept his home below in view as it got smaller and smaller. It just took a moment for it to be out of sight completely.

Other astral bodies soared and danced all around him. The higher he climbed the more of them there were. Up ahead in the distance he saw a blazing white storm. Lightning popped inside the enormous exploding cloud. As he got closer he realized that the explosion never ended. Smoke just kept piling out and circling around, feeding back into itself. As he hovered next to it, he saw huge patches of color drifting inside. Florescent reds and blues and greens crashed into each other, creating new colors. It was beautiful.

He saw souls entering through the cloudy haze effortlessly. When they crossed its billowing white border they would turn bright yellow, bright as a sun.

Mortal eyes would have been blinded, but Jack's vision stayed with them. The spirits immediately went limp and floated inward. With unhindered faith they all willingly went inside and fell into a kind of trance like state. Jack was amazed.

He stretched out into the storm. The white fog took him in and surrounded his energy. Everything in his being became peaceful as the color embraced him. His fear washed away. All of his mortal cravings and curiosity disappeared. His life no longer existed. Nothing did now, except the calm caress of love. It was a more complete and satisfying love than he had ever felt. It came with no confusion; there was no doubt. He was swimming in a universe of perfection, surrounded by bliss.

Just as he decided that he wasn't going to leave, that he could *never* leave that place, it spat him out. He was shot away from its euphoria in a jolting wave. His spirit was clear of the exploding storm of piece and all of his confusion and desire fell back into him like thunder. It was an emotional comedown like nothing he'd ever felt. The bliss was gone and Jack's withdrawal was devastating. He bolted toward it but he could not get back inside. It was pushing him away. It was telling him that he did not belong there. All he could do was scream. His ethereal cries echoed across forever in darkened red flashes.

To touch Heaven was the superlative of everything the human spirit strove to become. Being rejected by it felt like emotional drowning. The life giving substance was so close and yet he was helpless to rise into it. As he took in desperate gulps of reality, the pain washed in all around him. End over end he drifted back toward earth.

His soul was crying.

2:15

Footsteps were coming down the hallway. The click clack of hard soled boots echoed off of the crumbling walls. The two girls had been sitting in silence across from each other. The little cloth plugs were in place now. She had stuffed them as deep inside her ears as they would go. She was shaking in terror.

Elizabeth quickly slid back into a blackened corner.

Oh God, please make them go away.

She heard a whisper. Her neighbor had taken an earplug out so she could hear herself.

"It's happening now. Just try to find a place in the back of your mind, and *stay* there. It's all you can do."

She quickly replaced the plug and rocked back and forth, nervously crying. Elizabeth had no idea what was going to happen.

God, please...

The loud boots stopped in front of her cell. She couldn't move. She couldn't breathe.

"My sweet Elizabeth, You are about to witness the power of Azazyel," His yellowing teeth were clenched together in a horrific grin, "Be proud, tonight *you* get the honors."

He turned and walked further down the corridor in a stride of confidence. She closed her eyes tightly.

Go away go away go away...

A strong loud voice sounded out from a distant room. It was female. It was Linda.
"Hail to the dark ones, once divine, now condemned!"
Why Linda? Why?
"We call to thee and ask thy presence. Ready thy receivers and bring them unto you!"
The stone bird was vibrating in her hands. The fluid swam faster with every word she spoke.
What's happening?
"Let thy power be known!"

Elizabeth stood up. The dirty green blanket fell from her shoulders. She walked over to the door. The girl with no name stood silently at her entrance also. They did not want to be standing there. Given the choice, they would've been hiding in the pitch black at the back of their cells. But they had no choice. Free will had been taken from them. They were being *controlled.*

Elizabeth tried to cry out. She could not. She tried to turn around, it wouldn't let her. She could feel it inside of her, in her body.
Oh god, oh god, oh shit...
They stood there together, perfectly still, waiting.

Linda walked to each cell, unlocked it, and went on to the next one. Something, some force, had taken them all. All six prisoners were now completely helpless inside themselves. The fallen ones had possessed them. While their bodies performed the ritual, their minds would scream in defiance.
Please God. Make it stop.
Elizabeth was going to see, hear, and feel everything that was about to happen.
No no no...
Her cell was unlocked. Her body stepped out into the hallway.
I...can't... stop....
She was walking now, following the others. They were on their way.
Please...
It was time for the Black Communion.

2:16

After everything Jack had seen and felt that night, he just wanted to get back. He descended down through the starlight into the street light of home. Everything looked so quiet and peaceful. As he neared his house the dog in the neighbor's yard sprang alive and barked. It watched him closely as he floated across the street and up the driveway. Its energy boiled and popped in excitement.

Doesn't that thing ever sleep?

He entered through the wall and found himself floating in the hallway. He passed through the closed bedroom door. The computer fan was humming like always. The screen saver shined multi-colored reflections on the opposite wall. He drifted down to the floor where he had left his body. He wasn't there.

What the...

Jack looked around frantically. Nothing.

Oh, god.

He shot out through the house, searching. He wasn't in bed. Not in the bathroom.

How could this have happened?

He stopped in the living room. His body was lying on its side on the couch. It looked completely comfortable, like it had fallen asleep watching television.

I wasn't here. How could I...it, have moved?

Jack needed answers and he knew where to get them. She hadn't told him everything. She had left out some very important information that he had to know. He couldn't have his soulless body traipsing around the house when he was gone. What if his family woke up? What if it hurt itself? Without a consciousness, how could it move in the first place? He wondered if his brain alone could control his body without him. And if so, what the hell was it doing? Jack thought that maybe, when he re-entered himself he would have access to the body's memories. He'd know what had happened.

Gently lowering down into the flesh, he was once again part of the material world. His vision narrowed, and centered in front of him. Everything behind disappeared. The immortal became mortal, and he sat up.

Concentrating hard, he tried to find the memories of the past few hours. He searched for an image, a feeling, anything that might be a clue to what he had been doing. But there was nothing. *Not a goddamn thing.*

It took him a few minutes to realize that what he was looking for wasn't in his head, but on his hands. He leaned over and clicked on the lamp. It was dry, crusting. It was blood.

Shit.

He was sure that what he had feared had come true. He'd hurt himself somehow. He quietly hurried to the bathroom. He wasn't in any pain but there had to be something. A cut, or scratches, something. He closed the door carefully, so not to make any noise. Standing in front of the large mirror, he started to remove his clothes. The T-shirt.

I wasn't wearing this earlier.

And the jeans.

I didn't have these on either.

Fear was setting in.

What the hell happened to me? What did I do?

Jack was totally naked now. He looked himself over thoroughly. Other than the dried blood on his hands and arms, he appeared normal. There were no cuts, not even a bruise. He felt through his hair, running his hand over his scalp. Nothing.

If this isn't my blood, then who...

He turned off the light, opened the door and headed down the hall. His son's room was illuminated with the soft glow of a yellow night-light. Jack stood over Chris for a moment, examining him. He was fine. He slept quietly with the covers pushed down around his ankles. When he was satisfied, he took off down the hall, toward his bedroom. Stacey slept unharmed also. Relief came over him as he sat down on the edge of the bed. He was completely baffled. Had his body possibly gone outside? Had he gotten into it with that barking dog? Maybe. He'd have a good look at it in the morning.

The old lady had kept things from him and he wanted to know why.

If my soulless body is going to wander around where it likes while I'm gone, wouldn't she think that was an important piece of information to include?
He would take a sick day tomorrow and ask her that question.
He went back to the bathroom to wash up.

2:17

Elizabeth's body continued, following the others. At the end of the hallway it opened up into a large room. Tall, slender candles lined the walls along the floor. A thick concrete platform stood table height in the center of the chamber. It was littered with dark stains. The dried designs covered almost the entire top surface. There was a symbol painted onto the concrete in thick black lines. From where she was standing she couldn't make it out.

Her eyes were elsewhere now. She could only watch as her hands lifted a long garment off the rack. Swinging it around, she pulled it over her shoulders and laced the front.
Each scratchy brown robe had a symbol on the back, stitched with black thread. It was a circle with an inverted star crossing over it. At each intersecting point of the star was a smaller symbol carefully embroidered into the fabric.

All of the garments had dark stains splashed across the front. The putrid odor from them filled the whole room. It smelled like rotting meat. If Elizabeth had been in control of herself she would have gagged, and possibly vomited. But the power over her kept her rigidly still. She appeared to be calm and emotionless. Just underneath it all, she was screaming.

She tried desperately to turn around and run. She could not.
For the next hour, she would be free only in her mind.
Free to pray. Free to silently cry out for help.
Free to watch herself participate in unspeakable horror.

2:18

"Jack?"
Stacey shook him awake. It took a moment for him to realize where he was.

"What? What's going on?"
She was looking at the clock. She had an annoyed tone in her voice.
"Jack, you're late for work. Get up."
He sat up, rubbing his eyes.
"I called in."
He had left a message on the Royal Gorge answering machine hours earlier.
"Are you sick?"
"Well, no not really..."
She stopped him, "What's going on with you Jack? This isn't like you."
He put his hand on hers, "I'm just going through something right now. I need some time to figure it out."
"Come on, that's been your story for *six months*, and I've gotta say I'm getting pretty sick of it."
"No, you don't understand. This is different."
"No Jack, *you* don't understand. It's always the same. *Always.*"
"Look honey, listen to me. I'll tell you everything..."
She got up from the bed, Where were you last night, huh?"
"What? I..."
"This is the second time in a row that you took off in the middle of the night. I'm not *stupid* Jack."
She knew he had been gone. He wondered what else she knew. He couldn't hide it any longer. He had to tell her.
"Stacey, if you'll just sit down I'll tell you everything."
She was on the other side of the room digging clothes out of a drawer.
"You know, I'd love to stay, but I don't have time. I'm meeting my mother this morning, and I'm already late," she was steaming with frustration and anger, "But when I get back we *are* going to have a talk, and you'd better have a *damn* good explanation of where you were."

She walked out of the room and slammed the door. Jack laid back down. He stayed in bed for another half-hour. He listened to the shower running. He waited until he heard her leave to get up.

He walked out to the living room and sat down in the recliner. Out the window he saw his neighbors outside in their yard. Tom was kneeling down beside the dark haired dog. Sheila was standing on the porch.

Jack jumped up and went outside wearing only his boxer shorts. He shivered in the bitter cold. It couldn't have been more than twenty degrees. He walked over to the chain link fence that separated the two yards. The bleeding dog immediately growled and barked at jack.

"Hey Tom, what's going on?"

Tom looked up, and over at him, "It looks like my dog got into a fight last night. He's scraped up pretty bad."

A feeling of relief came over Jack.

That's where the blood came from. I must've tried to stop the fight.

"We're gonna take him to the vet. I'll see you later Jack." He led the animal into the house.

"Okay, see ya." Jack hurried back inside. He was freezing.

The origin of the blood had been discovered. It still didn't explain how or why his body was able to move while he was gone.

He was trembling from the cold. It was time for a hot shower. Stacey would be gone with her mother for two or three hours. That would give him enough time to go into town and find the old woman. She wouldn't be back to work until tomorrow but surely he could get someone there to call her at home. He would tell them that it was an emergency.

She knows about the necklace's power. That means she knows about its side effects, and what happened to my body. She'll have to see me.

Jack had to hurry. He needed to be back when Stacey got there. He had an awful feeling that his marriage depended on it. She was mad. *Really* mad. He was sure that she would calm down when he told her. She'd have to believe him after she saw what the necklace could do.

He turned on the radio in the bathroom and stepped into the shower. As the hot water flowed over him he remembered the colors caressing his astral body. They had been so comforting and calm. He had done what no living being had ever done before. He had touched Heaven and returned to the material world.

His thoughts easily drowned out the weather report that was playing on the radio. They were calling for a storm. The three-day forecast expected lower temperatures and snow toward the weekend. The voice was covered in static due to poor reception. *Break out those scarves and mittens, it's gonna be cold!*

Jack was in and out of the shower in five minutes. He padded into the bedroom to find some clothes.

Out the window he could see the darkening sky. The storm was coming. Cold gray clouds had taken over the domination the sun once held.

It was a warning. The overcast sky was telling him to stay inside tonight.

He wasn't listening.

And, behold, I, even I, do bring a flood
of waters upon the earth, to destroy all flesh,
wherein is the breath of life, from under Heaven;
and every thing that is in the earth shall die.

Genesis: Chapter 6 Verse 17

BOOK THREE: DELUGE

3:1

Upon his return to the Earth God saw that the Giants' war on mankind had been devastating. The few people whom they had not slaughtered were left to starve as the earthbound angel's insatiable appetites had consumed all of the livestock and produce man had. The Giants had even taken to eating one another to calm their unending hunger. They consumed the flesh and the bones and drank the blood, leaving nothing to waste.

The powerful leader Samyaza and the one known as Armors were the only angels left who stood over 200 cubits. The smaller fallen ones had taken to attacking the larger giants in groups, eating them alive. Just as Samyaza had feared, their original intentions had changed, giving way to the physical needs of the mundane world. Lucifer's mighty army had become ungovernable savages, caring only about feeding themselves.

In a thundering rage God descended down to them, gathering the giants together in a violent storm. He could not let them corrupt the few humans left who still worshiped him. He needed a place where the giant's blasphemy and killing would have no effect on his children. There was such a place, where men were godless, having no fear or love for their creator. The raging storm carried the giants across the waters to the land of the heathens, beyond the Mediterranean, in the middle of the great ocean. There he banished them all, leaving them to do what they pleased.

The angels looked out over the new landscape, seeing that wildlife and trees baring fruit were plentiful. Samyaza called out to the angelic army. Their remaining number was thirty-two. "My brothers, fill your bellies with all that you see! But heed this; any one among you that turns on his own kind shall be dealt a painful death."

A few did go on to meet their earthly ends by the hands of Samyaza and Armors. The rest agreed to follow their leader's commands.

The angels, now twenty-four in number, along with thirty-two of their sons, came upon a small village of humans. Instead of slaughtering them, Samyaza decided to rule them. They would be worshiped as Gods among the men.

Azazyel oversaw the teaching of knowledge. He taught the humans of architecture, metalworking and the use of energies such as electricity and fuel burning. The giants and men built great machines to make their work not only possible, but also easier. The erection of tall buildings and structures became commonplace. Temples and statues in honor of the new Gods were many. Humans learned secret arts such as astronomy, herbal medicines and the creation of weapons and armor, readying themselves for war with the worshipers of the God of Israel. Samyaza led the men in constructing huge ships that would carry them over the waters.

It took hundreds of years to create an intelligent civilization with great cities and advanced technologies. It took thousands of years before their war would be possible.

For God would not allow the ships near the shores of any lands but their own. Terrible storms sank many vessels that got too close to Egypt, Judah, and Israel. They were free to explore the seas as they liked, but always had to return to their homeland, the kingdom of secret knowledge.

God's angels Michael, Gabriel, Raphael, Suryal and Uriel went to him and told him that it had been Azazyel who'd overseen the forbidden teachings of technology to the humans. The creator traveled down into the mundane lands, looking over the great structures, the temples and walls of heavy stone, the homes filled with weapons and gold.

He saw women who had adorned themselves with shimmering jewelry and colorful garments. Their faces were painted with dyes to invoke the lusts of men. He saw some watching the heavens, recording the movements of the planets and stars. He saw others forging metals to create weapons of war and armor.

He watched men casting spells and chanting for better crops, good health and control of the weather. The same men gathered herbs and mixed them together for medicines. The people made wine and became drunk. They danced and celebrated in their fornication.

The Giants were worshiped as gods for their power and knowledge. They acted as deities over men, accepting prayers and sacrifices.

None were as pleased as Azazyel, the blasphemer and teacher of men. His betrayal had become an entire society of heathens.

God returned to the astral plane and instructed Michael and Raphael of Azazyel's punishment. His death was to be slow and torturous. They descended to Earth and scooped the giant into the air. He struggled and growled in defiance as he was carried across the great sea and into the land of Israel. In the desert a pit opened up in the ground and Azazyel was cast into his grave. His screams echoed inside as they covered him over with heavy stones. There he would remain alive for hundreds of years.

Though the pains of hunger and thirst would take him, they would not kill him. His throat would become as dry and parched as sand in the hot sun. The cool touch of water would not be felt over his lips until the time of the great flood. The refreshment of the waters would only be enjoyed for a few short hours, until the depths overtook the land. The substance he'd cry out for (over many excruciating decades) would come finally, and kill him.

The giants had corrupted the entire world. The few people that were left despised God for abandoning them. All except one man. He alone had kept the faith. His name was Enoch.

God heard his prayers and went to him. He fell to his knees before his creator.

"My Lord, you have listened to my prayers!"

"Yes, my son."

"Evil devils plaque your kingdom. What would you have me do?"

God knew that he would need to begin again. There would be no saving the remaining inhabitants of the planet. The fallen ones had seen to that. They had ruined everything.

He swept the man up into the sky and carried him to the astral plane. He showed the human the legions of angels devoted to him. He took Enoch to Hell and they gazed out over Lucifer's realm and the ones that had defied his will. God gave him visions of their eventual punishment and the forthcoming disaster of flood upon the Earth. Enoch was in awe of his creator's power and asked what God would have him do.

God told him to record all he had seen into a book and warn others of the coming wrath. All that believed and worshiped him would be spared. Enoch returned to the mundane realm to spread the word of God.

He wrote everything into two books and told his sons to have people read his warnings. God then took Enoch from the earth forever.

When the time of the flood finally came, only one man held faith in his heart for God. His name was Noah. God descended to him and spoke.

"Noah, you shall build a great ship, for the land will soon be covered with flood."

God left him to his work. It took Noah and his sons a hundred and twenty years to build the vessel that would keep them above the icy depths of God's wrath.

On the day they were finished it began to rain. At the end of the second day the entire ground was soaked through. At the end of the fourth day the water covered the men's feet and they took to higher ground.

The angel giants and their sons knew that God's anger was upon them. They welcomed death as it grew closer. The mighty Samyaza knew that some would need to stay alive to continue the destruction of creation. He and his son Goliath would remain, along with five others: the angels Tamiel, Armors, Asaradel and the Nephilim sons, Amazarak and Barkayal. They filled five great ships with as many people as they could hold. Nearly six hundred humans, along with the seven fallen ones took to the seas.

On the tenth day all of the valleys were filled and by the twentieth the flood was deep enough to lift the great arks out of the mud.

Most of the people in Israel and Egypt were already dead from drowning. The few that remained were dying of starvation. All of the animals had fled or drowned. The trees with fruit were far beneath the surface now. By the thirtieth day only the highest peaks could be seen.

On the night of the fortieth day the rain ceased. The following morning the clouds parted and the sun blazed brightly in a clear blue sky. The terrible storm was over. Many days passed before the ground in the valleys could be walked upon again. Noah and his family thanked God for sparing their lives.

The trees grew new bountiful fruit. Animals from distant lands repopulated the countryside. God returned to the highest of the astral planes to rest. Much of his power had been spent over the past few weeks. He was unaware of the ships that sailed the distant waters of the great sea.

The Angels and the Nephilim quietly waited for instructions from their master, Lucifer. He went to them and commanded that they set a course for Egypt. There they would settle, to begin their new civilization of knowledge. They were not to make their presence known to God. Lucifer promised that he would devise a plan to destroy the earth and steal God's strength. He returned to Hell while Goliath, Samyaza and the others waited.

3:2

MURDER IN RED CANYON

Police and Sheriff investigators are currently examining the terrain surrounding a badly mutilated body found in a dry riverbed just south of Red Canyon Road. Coroner Lyle Simmons said the deceased was a girl in her teens. Her name has not yet been released, pending notification to her family. Simmons said the victim died sometime around 1:00 AM this morning.

"This is one of the most horrific things I've ever seen," said Officer Brent Danielson of the Canyon City Police Department.

According to the police report the girl had gone with three of her classmates to the area to drink alcohol earlier in the evening. The others in the group noticed her missing at about 12:30 AM. They began to search the woods and found her body only two hundred yards away from where their car was parked.

Few details have yet been given about what has been determined as foul play. It has been stated that the attacker used a knife or other extremely sharp object.

Sergeant Lunderman of the Fremont County Sheriff's Office said that a manhunt is currently underway as the scene is being studied. He went on to say, "We are appalled at such a terrible crime and are dedicated to finding this person's attacker."

Although Canyon City police officers were the first on the scene, the crime falls under Fremont County Sheriff jurisdiction.

3:3

The tall man stood at the front of the platform in the center of the room. He was anxious to get the ritual started. He very much enjoyed the tasks involved in what he considered to be his life's work. It was a feeling of control, of power. To feel the body shudder as the life was snuffed out of it. It was better than any drug. The slickness of the blood on his hands was entrancing, the way it glistened in the candlelight.

He had developed quite a taste for the killing. But tonight would be even better. Tonight would be the first *complete* ritual. He had the scripture. He had the talisman. And *now,* he had a circle of seven. Everything was in place. He was ready to begin his transcendence. That day would mark the rise of a new kingdom. He would destroy the earth and rattle the heavens.

It would all start with one. That one lay before him, tied down to the altar. She would be the first.

Not the first to *die*. The first to be truly *consumed.*

3:4

Stacey's anger subsided as she drove into Canyon City. She was still mad at Jack but at least her hands had stopped shaking. She knew he was up to something that he wasn't telling her. It wasn't like him to call off of work when he wasn't sick. It wasn't like him to sleep in past eight in the morning. Even on his days off he always got up by seven. *Always.* He was tired because he'd been up late doing something. He was *hiding* something.

Stacey took a couple of deep breaths trying to calm herself down. She didn't want her mother to see how mad she was at her husband. Her mom wasn't that fond of Jack to begin with. She had always hoped that her daughter would marry someone with more ambition. Although Jack hadn't been out of work a day since they'd been together, he'd never had what Marion considered a *career* position.

Christopher sounded from the back seat, "Are we there yet Mom? I'm hungry."

Stacey turned into the Village Inn parking lot.

"We're here."

He son leaned forward, "Good, cuz I'm hungry."

"Alright, baby, alright."

She saw her mother's car parked in front of the building. She looked down at her watch. "Shit. We're twenty minutes late."

Chris looked in the rear view mirror at his mother's reflection.

"Don't say shit, mom. It's not nice."

Stacey held herself from laughing, "Okay Chris. Sorry."

When they entered the restaurant she peered into the non-smoking section. Her mother sat alone at a booth in the corner. Stacey took her son's hand and walked quickly.

"Sorry mom," she said approaching the table.

"You're late," her mother said looking up at the clock on the wall.

"*I know mom*. That's why I said sorry."

"Well, sit down. I've already ordered our drinks."

"Hi Nana!" Chris said excitedly, hugging his grandma.

"Hello, young man. Shouldn't you be in school?"

"He got a three day weekend. Teacher's conference."

Marion noticed the redness in her daughter's eyes.

"You look tired dear. Haven't you been sleeping well?"

"I'm okay," she said attempting a smile, "I was just kind of restless last night."

"Money problems again?"

"No mom, we're fine. We've got everything we need."

Marion sat back in her seat, "I'm telling you, there's nothing like financial stability to help you sleep."

"*Please*. Don't start."

"I'm just saying that if that husband of yours would get a better job…"

"What?" she interrupted, "I'd *sleep* better?"

"Well…*yes*."

Stacey looked Marion in the eyes with a tense glare, "Jack's employment doesn't bother *me*, mom. It bothers *you*."

"But if he got a better job, you'd be happier."

"We have enough money. He likes where he works. Don't worry about it."
"He likes his job? More that he likes his family? Is that it?"
Stacey lifted up the menu so she didn't have to look at her mother.
"I'm not doing this with you today. Can't we just have a nice meal?"
Marion rubbed her left arm with the palm of her hand. Her skin had become pale.
"I'm just saying…I'm…"
Sweat dripped down her brow. The muscles in her face seized, "I…"
With a clenched fist over her chest she gasped. Stacey lowered the menu.
"Oh my God!" she yelled as Marion fell over and down to the floor.
Christopher screamed, "Nana!"

A waitress ran into the kitchen and picked up the phone. She dialed 911, keeping an eye on the dining room through the open door.

Stacey kneeled down beside her mother, holding her hand. Marion was unconscious. Christopher cried, hiding under the table. He stayed there, watching his mother and grandmother, until the ambulance came.

3:5

Jack pushed the door open and stepped inside. A cold gust forced its way past him, into the store. The tinkle of the little bell above the entrance went unheard in the icy howl. He closed the door quickly, blocking out the weather.

Sally was sitting behind the counter reading a book. She looked up with a smile.
"Hi, let me know if you need any help," Her words were upbeat and friendly.
He walked over to her, placing his hands on the glass counter top.
"You can help me actually. I'm the one who called yesterday. I need to talk to Ms. Holland. It's really important."

Her face got serious, "Grandma won't be here until tomorrow, she..."

"She's your grandmother?"

"Yeah. We run the shop together. What's so important?"

"It's something that I really should discuss with *her*."

She could see that he was genuinely upset.

"Is she in any kind of trouble?" She paused for a moment; "You're not from the state hospital, are you?"

"What? Hospital? Um, no. I'm just a customer."

"Oh, okay," She was embarrassed for asking. She didn't want it to get around that her grandma was until recently, a resident in a psychiatric ward, "I'll tell you what, I'll call and see if she's home, okay?"

"That would be great. Thanks."

She dialed the number and held the phone up to her ear. She let it ring ten times before giving up.

"She's not answering, but if you tell me what the problem is I'm sure we could work something out."

Jack looked her over for a moment. She was in her early twenties. She had jet-black hair. Her face was definitely too pale for that color. She wore thick eyeliner and bright red lipstick. She was very attractive, although Jack thought her sense of style left something to be desired. She seemed kind, honest. And she *was* the granddaughter. Maybe she knew something about all of this.

"Do you know anything about the necklace your grandmother sold me? It's a big stone bird with an oval glass container in the center of it," he held up his hands to show her its size.

"No. I haven't seen anything like that."

She didn't know anything. Jack's frustration was building.

"Damn," he said under his breath.

"What's wrong? Did it break or something?"

"No. It..."

He didn't know how to begin. He felt like an idiot standing there, trying to find the words to explain the most unbelievable truth he'd ever known. He was sure that she was going to think he was nuts. He told her anyway.

"Ok, here goes."

He told her everything. The necklace, the story, the travel, *everything.* It took him almost a half-hour. When he was finished, he waited for a response. She didn't speak.
"So, what do you think? You think I'm crazy, don't you?"
"No. Not at all."
She could see that he believed all of it. Of course, she did not. She figured that he believed it so much that he had been having dreams, sleepwalking, and...
Hell, who knows?
She didn't think he was crazy. Just *confused.*
"Well, that's quite a story. If it works like you say it does, I'd like to try it out myself."
"Yeah. I'll have to bring it with me next time."

She slid a pen and a piece of paper over to him, "If you write down your name and number, I'll have her give you a call when I talk to her. I'm sure she'll be home soon. She's never out very long."
"Thanks."
She watched him writing, "Your name is Jack? I'm Sally."
He smiled and handed her the paper.
"I know you think I'm nuts, but I'm really not."
"No *really*, I don't."

He turned and walked to the door. He could see that it was starting to snow. Little flakes were melting on the glass. He opened the door, stepping out into the frigid air. It was time to go home and tell Stacey what he had just told the girl. There would be a difference in his wife's reaction though. She wouldn't just *say* she believed him. She really would.

The necklace was at the house. He would *prove* it to *her.*

3:6

Sergeant Lunderman was leaning over his cluttered desk looking closely at the top page of the file. He flipped through, finding the pictures. He spread them out across the mess of papers and McDonalds wrappers. They were photos of the scene from every possible angle.

The girl was young, seventeen years old. She had been a junior in high school.

In the pictures she was naked with her back to the ground. She had been completely disemboweled. Her organs were strewn around the field where she was found. Also a symbol had been cut into her chest with a very sharp knife. It was a circle with an inverted star overlapping the edges. There were smaller symbols at each intersecting point, five in all. He studied the design carefully. He had definitely seen it before.

Another man walked in carrying a large manila folder.

"Got it," he said, setting it down on the corner of the desk, "What are we looking for?"

Lunderman stood up and turned it open. There were piles of pictures. Crime scenes, victims, weapons. He thumbed through quickly. He stopped at a black and white photograph that showed the inside of a room. In the center stood a large concrete platform. What he had been searching for was painted on the top in thick black lines. He put his finger onto the glossy surface.

"This."

"Shit. It's the same goddamn thing."

Lunderman was pleased with himself; "I knew it."

"Do you think these crimes are connected? This picture is twenty years old."

He held up the image of the dead girl, "Yeah, and this one is twenty *hours* old. But, guess who got released from the Colorado State Hospital six months ago."

"Who?"

Pulling another black and white out of the stack he announced, "Linda Holland."

"Who's she?"

"She is one of two survivors of Howard Killien's cult."

"*Jesus*, you think she did it?"

"Why don't you ask her to come in for a few questions, and we'll find out."

He grabbed his jacket off the chair; "I'm on it."

As his partner left the office he shuffled through the stack. He found the cult members' bios. Linda was three down from the top.

If she was thirty-five in 1971, that'd make her, um, sixty-four now. Damn, that's a bit old for a murderer. But, lord knows I've seen stranger things.

3:7

Elizabeth's eyes were focused on the squirming naked girl on the altar. She had been tied down with duct tape and rope around her wrists and ankles. She was pleading with the man that was leaning over her.

"Please let me go. *Please.*"

Her screams echoed through the basement in sharp bursts. She tugged as hard as she could against her restraints. They held tight. Her legs jerked from side to side, kicking.

Every robed person in the room stared blankly at her panic. They all appeared to be as unfeeling as the cold steel blade each one held in front of them.

The daggers had been sharpened to razor perfection. There were seven in all, but only one would be put to practical use tonight. It glimmered in the twitching candlelight. Elizabeth held it steady in her right hand.

This isn't happening. It can't be.

She tried to find a place in her mind, a memory, an image, anything she could hold on to. But the here and now had her in its grasp. She was looking right at it. There was no turning away, she was totally helpless. Her ears were ringing from the high-pitched fear echoing off of the walls. The begging. The *shrieking.*

It's the screaming that will drive you mad.

Looking up, she saw Linda standing at his side. The fallen ones had taken her too.

Why Linda? Why?

The man was speaking now. He read scripture from a large black book. Elizabeth couldn't hear what he was saying. He was just a voice in the background. All she could hear was the girl. He called out a few phrases in a language she'd never heard before.

He took a moment to look down at his victim. He smiled and caressed her cheek. She screamed and tried to pull away. Her fear pleased him. He leaned down close.

"Say goodbye, my sweet."

He sat down in a chair behind him. Linda turned and hung the necklace around his neck. He closed his eyes and leaned back into the thick cushion. His body remained motionless throughout the rest of the ritual. Linda took over the reading as Elizabeth stepped up into position beside the altar.

I have to stop this. I have to...

She looked down. The girl looked up. Their eyes met.

"Please don't hurt me. *Please.*"

The steel blade was held in two hands with the point down toward its victim.

God, no. I can't be here. No...

The screams were deafening.

Not happening. Oh god...

The point was over the sternum.

This isn't real...not real...

Over the abdomen.

God make me stop.

When the edge pierced the skin the girl jerked upward, driving it deeper.

No...no...no...

She shrieked in pain, fear. It filled the whole room, the house, the entire universe.

A large oval was cut into the skin over the stomach. The bright red blood poured down the sides and onto the icy concrete. She pulled, jerked, cried. Elizabeth's hands peeled away the skin, exposing the muscle and fat. A deep slit was cut through the tough abdominal wall. With the knife carefully set aside, her hand entered.

The screaming stopped. The girl had passed out from shock.

Elizabeth's hand was under the ribcage now. She could feel it *moving.* When her hand emerged from underneath it was grasping the organ tightly. It was held upwards for the group to see.

It was still pumping.

Somewhere far back in the dark recesses of Elizabeth's mind, she could hear them.

They were cheering her on.

3:8

Sally couldn't help thinking about the odd story that Jack had told. She was amazed at how strongly he believed it.
"Astral travel. Yeah, *right.*"
Still, she felt sorry for him. He seemed really worried. What an outlandish tale her grandmother had him believing. Sally hadn't heard anything like it from her, or anyone.
Would she really make up that nonsense to sell a necklace?
She didn't really know her grandma that well. All the memories she had of her were of the last few months. Up until then Linda had resided at the Colorado State Hospital. Sally's mother visited her once in a while, but never took her along. She wondered why her mother didn't want her to go.

They hadn't been together in more than twenty years, when Sally was very young. All that time she had been locked up in that institution. A third of her life had been taken away because of that terrible man.

Sally hadn't asked Linda about any of it. She didn't want to drudge up painful, perhaps horrifying memories for her grandmother. She'd talk about it in time, if she wanted to.
What an awful thing to go through, the cult, the murders.
Sally was sure she wouldn't have been able to handle it either.

She didn't have many details, just newspaper clippings that her mother had kept. She couldn't figure out for the life of her why her mom would've had them stashed away in that box.

She found them one day when she was fifteen, looking in the attic for a Halloween costume. They said that he had held them all prisoner. He raped them. He killed them, all but Linda and one other girl whose name Sally couldn't remember. He had left them alive, locked up in the basement of a house in the woods.

They would have to live the rest of their lives with the pain of what had happened to them. Both survivors experienced mental breakdowns and psychotic episodes. That's why they had spent all those years in the asylum. That's why Sally had grown up without her grandma.

But finally, after two decades, they had let Linda out of that place. And Sally thought that she seemed all right. A little odd, but all right.

Sally's mother had left the bookstore to her when she died, three years ago. She took it over and added the metaphysical stuff, tarot cards and such, and the cappuccino machines. It became a popular hangout for the high school and collage aged kids. The business had really picked up since she became the boss. That was why she could afford to give her grandma the job.

Years ago, Linda had been a nurse at the local hospital. She had assisted in numerous surgeries. Sally wasn't a bit surprised when her grandma told her she didn't want to return to that kind of work.

She was really working out great at the store. She was always so friendly and helpful with the customers.

Sally just couldn't imagine Linda telling that fairy tale to people. Maybe it was something that awful man had told her all those years ago.

Picking up the phone, she dialed the number again. There was still no answer.

3:9

Jack pulled the Nissan into the driveway. The engine coughed and jerked to a stop as he turned off the key. Stacey's car wasn't there. It had been more than two hours since he had left the house.

He got out and stepped up the porch stairs. Unlocking the deadbolt, he could hear the phone ringing inside.

It rang three more times before he could get to it.

"Hello?"

"Jack! Oh god, where have you been?"

"I had to go to town. Honey, what's wrong?"

"It's Mom. She had a heart attack," her words turned into tears.

"*Shit.* How is she?"

"They don't know yet. She's not good Jack."

"Where are you, Saint Thomas Moore?"

"Yeah. She's in the emergency room now, but they're taking her into surgery."

"I'll be right there."

"Hurry Jack. I need you."
"I will honey. I will."

Stacey hung up the phone. A small hand was pulling at her fingers. She kneeled down and looked him in the eyes. Christopher was confused. He didn't understand what was happening. She picked him up, hugging him tight.

"Is Nana gonna be okay Mommy?"
"I don't know honey, I don't know."

3:10

The familiar humming filled his head as the heat took him. Moving up his arms and legs, it gathered in his chest. The swimming energy forced its way out and formed a cloud in front of him. It glided up to the ceiling. The astral mist peered down at the girl holding the twitching heart. Dark red blood ran all down her arm. The one beneath was still shaking in a violent spasm. He waited as the dying body gave out and became still.

He could see her now. Her living eternal essence was ascending. As she left her mundane body, her spirit retained the same shape. It glowed dark yellow, fizzling and popping. It drifted upward slowly.

Back in the material world, the scripture rolled off of Linda's tongue in an emotionless monotone. With the last magical word spoken, his attack became possible.

He pounced like a lion on top of the girl's energy. Her soul struggled against him. He surrounded and imploded into her. His expanding light suffocated her. The ethereal cries were heard only by him. She was trapped inside his spiral. He began to absorb her. The searing heat made her shudder in pain. For a second time, she was dying. His light grew brighter as hers faded into nothingness. He had eaten her whole and could feel the power surging through. The power of the Black Communion.

3:11

When Jack entered the hospital Stacey was sitting on the far side of the waiting room with her back to the door.

"Honey?"
She turned and rushed over to him. They stood there in each other's arms trying to make the fear and sadness subside. He was with her now. She no longer had to hurt alone. He would be there for her, no matter what happened.
"How is she?"
"They took her in to surgery. They're going to do a bypass."
Jack looked around the room, "Where's Christopher?"
"I called your parents earlier. He's staying with them for awhile."

They sat down. The television bolted to the wall was on. The weatherman was pointing at Colorado Springs on the map. He was talking about snow. Neither of them was even aware it was on. Stacey held Jack's hand tightly looking over at the receptionist.
"They said it didn't look good, that she might not make it through the operation." She lowered her head down onto his shoulder, "I'm so scared Jack."

He wanted to tell her that everything was going to be all right, but those words would've felt like a lie. He didn't know what to say. He didn't know what to do. All he could do was hold her close and hope.

He did know one thing. It was something that had been spinning around in his head ever since he got the news. If her mother didn't survive there would be only one way for Stacey to see her, to say goodbye. The purple velvet box bulged in the side pocket of his thick winter coat. He needed to tell her about the power of the necklace before it was too late.
But she wouldn't listen to me now, would she? With her mother in surgery? How can I tell her now?
It was too important. He had to try.
"Stacey?"
She looked up at him with teary eyes.
"Yeah?" she said faintly.
"I've always been a skeptic when it comes to all that spiritual stuff, you know that, right?"
"Yes, Jack."
"You were always the one the believed in those things."
"Well, I'm not sure what I *believe*. I like to read about it."

She looked down at her hands on top of his, "I like to believe in the possibility."
"Something's happened to me Stacey. I *believe* now. It's not just a possibility. It's *real.*"
"What are you talking about?"
"This."
His hand went into his coat pocket and emerged with the velvet box. He sat it down in his lap and creaked it open. The necklace caught Stacey's eye for the first time.
"What is it?" She ran her fingers over the feathers carved in stone.
"This is what I'm talking about. It's an ancient talisman. It has real power."
"What kind of power?"
Jack looked at his wife and smiled, "It allows you to leave your body."
"What?" Their eyes met. Hers were filled with disbelief.
"I swear to you, it's *real.*"
"Oh, come *on*, Jack."
"I'm not asking you to take my word for it. I'm asking you to *try* it."
Stacey's eyes drifted over to the emergency room door. "It's not really the time for this. My mother…"
"No. If ever there was a time for this, it's *now*."
She could see that he was serious. She'd always thought of herself as open minded about that kind of thing. She was the one with three kinds of tarot cards and stacks of metaphysical books. She even had one on astral travel. She'd been searching for meaning just like everyone. "So what, am I just supposed to put it on?"
"Yeah, that's it."
She held out both hands. "Give it to me."

Jack couldn't believe it. He had actually convinced her to try it. He didn't know how he'd done it. She was going to see for herself now. His job was done. He hung it around her neck carefully.
"Go be with her. I'll be here when you get back." He gave her a kiss and took her hand.
Stacey sat looking down at the stone bird against her chest. The humming filled her head. The heat was rising in her arms and legs. The pressure was building.

"Jaaackk…" Her eyes were wide.
She was afraid.
"Don't fight it. Just stay calm and soon you'll see everything."

Her spirit pushed out through her chest in a twisting whirlwind. She was hovering over them. She was glowing a brilliant blue. She could see the soft haze of her husband's soul surrounding his body. He was sitting quietly, watching her body sleep.

Oh my God. It's really happening.

Her vision was in every direction. She saw the television, the main entrance, the door to the emergency room…

Mom.

She flew over and passed through the metal door easily. Her mother was in one of the rooms beyond. She had to find her. She could only hope it wasn't too late.

3:12

Linda was sitting at the large dinning room table. The book with the yellowing pages was open in front of her. The phone was ringing in another room. She did not get up to answer it. She didn't have time for such things. Everything was happening quickly and when the time came, she would have to be ready.

She studied the words carefully, saying them over and over in her head. It had been more than twenty years since she'd had them all memorized. Some phrases were familiar while others seemed new to her. It was going to take some long hours to get all of it down. What had ended so abruptly two decades ago wasn't over. Not by a long shot. Not as long as she had something to do with it. Her work was just beginning, finally.

It had taken what seemed like forever to convince those bastards at the hospital that she was fit to re-enter society. She was an old woman now, not in the best shape for what needed to be done. She hoped that she would have the strength required to continue the task.

There was a knock at the door. A man in a gray suit was looking at her through the window.

Damn it.

She got up and walked over. He was wearing a long dark coat. His hands were deep in the side pockets trying to stay warm. She opened the door. "Yes?"
"Ms. Holland?"
"Yes."
"My name is Tom Randal. I'm with the Canyon City Police Department. Can I come in?"
"I suppose so." She pulled open the door and backed up. A frigid blast of air entered with him.
"It's really getting chilly out there. It's gonna be a heck of a storm, doncha think?"
"Yes. It looks like it."
"What I'm here about Ms. Holland, is this. We had a homicide in town last night."
"*Oh, my.*"
"Yes, we were hoping to get you to come down to the station and answer some questions for us."
"I'm not a *murderer,* Mr. Randal. I'm an old woman."
"Well ma'am, no one is saying that you are. This situation has some similarities to a case in 1971, a case that I believe you remember?"

She knew full well what he was talking about. She hoped that her lover was not getting too careless. She hoped that the police didn't know too much. She knew that she would have to be mindful of what she told them. She did not let any of her concerns show on her face.

"I'm sure I'll never *forget it*, Mr. Randal."
"I'm sure. So we thought that you, having the unique insight that you do, might be able to help us."
"I don't know how much help I'll be, but I'll tell you what I know."
"Great. You can ride with me if you like. My car is already warm."
"That sounds fine. Just give me a few minutes to get ready."
"Absolutely, Ms. Holland. Take your time."

She went in to the table. Looking back to where the policeman was standing, she quickly closed the book. He was busy watching it snow out the window.

The storm was getting worse. It was close now. Very Close.

3:13

Journal entry-November 13, 1971

The ritual was a success. It was like nothing I've ever felt. I am twice the man I was yesterday. I am denser, stronger, and more alert. Her power melded with mine completely as her will and consciousness faded away.

I could *taste* her fear. It was more satisfying than any death I have caused before. She *became* me. It was beautiful.

I am now more powerful than any human that has ever walked the earth. I believe that puts me in the demi-God category. And this is just the beginning. Soon I will be more powerful than the creator of the world. When that time comes, I will then eat him up and snuff out his consciousness. What a glorious day that will be. *The death of God.*

I will taste his fear as I consume him. Perhaps he will beg for his life. Wouldn't that be something? And, just maybe I will leave him alive. I could absorb all but a tiny, little powerless puff of dim light. I could leave his existence inside of it. I would then make him suffer the way I have. The dominator could see what it was like to be dominated. *What comes around, goes around.* Yes, that would be something indeed.

How art thou fallen from heaven,
O Lucifer, son of the morning!
How art thou cut down to the ground,
which didst weaken the nations!
For thou hast said in thine heart,
I will ascend into heaven,
I will exalt my throne above the stars of God:
I will sit also upon the mount of the
congregation in the sides of the north,
I will ascend above the heights of the clouds,
I will be like the Most High.

Isaiah Chapter 14 Verses 12-14

BOOK FOUR:
BLOOD

4:1

The angel giants guided the heathens from the Mediterranean to Israel and settled along the western coast. To the local Israelites they became known as the Philistines, the people of the sea.

The Philistines established trade with the people of Egypt and Israel. They sold fabrics and dyes, pottery, metal ornaments and jewelry. The local rulers allowed them to remain in their countries for trade purposes. Roads were built, connecting the routes they used to sell the wares.

The Philistines began to take over cities along the Mediterranean coast by force. They took Ashkelon, Ashdod, Ekron, Beth-shan, Tell Fara, Gath and Gezer, among others. Great stone walls were built around the city-states and a Government counsel was appointed. Samyaza and the other angelic giants remained in power over the Philistines, hidden within the walls of the cities.

Once their fortresses were in place and their armies were ready, they declared war on Israel. God's people were unprepared for such an attack and they fell in great numbers to the warriors from the sea. They continued inland toward Beth-lehem and the Judean Mountains. Israel was forced to endure Philistine rule for many years.

God appointed a king over his people. The new king, Saul, had an army trained to defend them from the Philistines. The battles became increasingly difficult to sustain and many lives were lost. Samyaza and Goliath watched from afar and did not interfere. They were pleased at the war they had begun with God's faithful. Their original task upon the earth was now complete. They were no longer needed, or so they thought.

The giants yearned to join their brothers on the astral plane. God's failure was in full fruition and they tired of the mundane realm.

And then Lucifer went to them. God was unaware of his presence, for he was delivering his wrath to the cities of Sodom and Gamora. As men's lust was punished with fire from the sky, Lucifer gave the giants his instructions.

"Go to the Philistine named Karradel. His hatred for God is strong. He will provide the human element needed to destroy him. Only one that is part of God's energy can be victorious over him." Lucifer went on to explain his plan to the giants. The powerful magic to be used against the world's creator would be carried out by human hands. A ritual with a joined gathering of seven earthbound souls and an open receiver would provide the energy of God. The scripture of the fallen ones would set the magic in motion. And one more element, the key piece of the puzzle, was something that had been created by God himself in his own rage. The mundane flesh that bound the angels to the earth. The enchanted fluid that pumped through their veins. It was the blood that held the power to cast out the souls of men. It alone contained the strength of the angelic energy that had been passed down to their offspring.

The death of God would begin with the push of the Nephilim.

4:2

Linda and Detective Randal tried to shake off the bitter cold as they entered the police station. He led her to the elevator at the end of the corridor and pushed the up button. The stainless steel immediately slid open and they stepped inside.

He watched her closely as they ascended to the second floor. She calmly stood staring at the glowing numbers above the door. He was just behind her trying to notice anything in her manner that indicated nervousness, agitation, guilt. She remained perfectly at ease and motionless.

The chime sounded, announcing their arrival at the upper floor. The elevator opened with a clunk and they stepped out. He walked down three doors and knocked. She followed slowly.

When she entered she saw the two men whispering to each other at a large wooden desk at the far side of the room. She took one step past the threshold and stopped. The older man sitting at the desk raised his voice to speak.

"Ms. Holland, please have a seat."

His outstretched hand was motioning to the wooden chair across from him. He closed a large manila folder as she sat down onto the hard oak.

"Did Detective Randal give you any details about last night's crime?"

"No. Not really."

"But, he did say that there was a definite resemblance to it and crimes you witnessed in 1971, right?"

"Something to that effect, yes."

He looked into her face, trying to read her emotion. She stared at him blankly.

"Do you know of anyone that would wish to continue were Howard Killien left off? Anyone at all?"

"No. Every person I knew that had anything to do with it is either dead or in the asylum."

"He had no dealings with anyone outside of the cult?"

"Not that I know of."

"Did he ever speak to people on the phone when you were there?"

"No."

"Have friends over?"

"No."

"Talk about any bars he went to or restaurants he liked?"

"No."

The questions were going absolutely nowhere. It was time to change the subject.

"What was the other woman's name, the one in the state hospital?"

Linda pretended to think hard and look concerned and the same time, "Lisa…something."

"Yes. Lisa *Stockard*, that's right. You were the only two survivors."

"That's correct."

"I sure commend both of you. Making it through something like that is quite a feat."

"Humans are resilient creatures. We do what's necessary to survive, *if possible*."

"You know what's so odd to me Ms. Holland? It's that to this day Lisa still maintains that you weren't a victim like the others. She says that you were his accomplice."

He waited for a second to see if any emotional response showed up in her face. There was nothing.
"Do you have any idea why she would feel this way?"
Linda cleared her throat and looked the detective straight in the eyes, "Howard Killien was a very sick man. I don't know why, but he liked me more than the others. I suppose he fancied me to be his girlfriend. The other girls were locked up in the basement. I stayed with him upstairs. Therefore it would've been easy to think that I was in on it, but I was not."
"You slept with him? Upstairs?"
"Yes."
" Were you tied up or bound in any way?"
She looked down at his desk, "I believe that you've got the answer to that question sitting there in front of you Detective, in that file."

She was becoming irritated. Even a fool could see where that line of questioning was going. They hadn't brought her in because of her unique insight into the case. They were trying to determine whether or not she was a murderer. They wanted to accuse her.
"It's a big file Ms. Holland. I haven't had a chance to read all of it."
"No, I was not tied up or bound in any way. I did not attempt escape because of fear. If I had tried anything, he would have killed me. I'm sure of it."
He decided to change the subject before she became uncooperative. He handed her a line drawing. "Do you recognize this picture?"
"Yes, it represents the fall of the Christian God and the rise of Lucifer and his messiah."
"Could you explain the smaller symbols to me?"
"The two at the top are Lucifer himself and the dark messiah. The two lower ones are the physical body and the soul. The one at the bottom is God."
He looked closely at the inverted star, "The body and the soul?"
"Yes, it is how Killien believed he would gain power. By killing his victims and consuming their spirits."
"He believed that he was eating their spirits?"
"That's what he thought, yes."
"How did he claim he was doing that?"

"I'm sure I don't know. He just said that's what he was doing. He didn't explain it."

The two policemen looked at each other. They both knew that they didn't have any evidence pointing to Ms. Holland. She had admitted nothing. Still, it seemed as though there was much she wasn't saying. Sgt. Lunderman thought that maybe he wasn't asking the right questions but in his logical assessment of the interview he was pretty sure that was not a murderer sitting across from him. She seemed too frail and harmless. He had to ask anyway.

"Can you tell us where you were last night, about one A.M.?"

The question didn't surprise her in the least, but she was angry at his words just the same. She gave Lunderman an icy glare.

"I was in my bed, sleeping."

He smiled, "Of course you were. Thank you for your time, Ms. Holland. If we think of anything else, we might need to talk to you again, if that's alright."

She knew that they didn't have anything on her. She hadn't committed any crimes, yet.

"Fine. I'd like to go home now please."

Detective Randal escorted her out of the office, and back down the hallway. Lunderman dialed a number on his telephone.

"Yeah, Frank? I'm gonna need surveillance on Linda Holland. I need to know names of every person she comes in contact with."

A pause.

"No…No, I don't think she's our perpetrator. But she might know who is…Yeah. Thanks."

He hung up.

4:3

The streets were packed with snow and ice. The slick surface made the squad car slide as it turned onto her block. The tires found clear pavement and the vehicle straightened out.

The officer was a bit embarrassed, "Looks like its gonna be a rough storm."

"That it does."

He pulled over in front of her house.

"Do you need help up to the door ma'am?"
"No, thank you. I can manage."

Her front steps were extremely slick. She held tight to the handrail on her way up. She saw a light on in the dining room. Someone was inside. Linda looked out at the street. Sally's car was parked a couple of spaces down. She hadn't noticed until now. Sally quickly closed the book when she heard her grandmother's footsteps on the porch. The door creaked open and in went a big gust of wind and snow.

"Hi grandma. What are you doing out in this weather?"
She smiled in her granddaughter's direction, "Oh, just trying to catch my death."
Sally helped Linda remove her coat and hung it in the closet.
"I came by because there is a man looking for you. He said you sold him a necklace. His name is Jack."
"Oh yes, *Jack*, of course."
"He seemed pretty worried. I told him I'd have you call."
"Sure, I've got his number on the desk over there. But first I'm going to make a hot pot of coffee."

Sally wanted to ask her about the necklace and the book. But she didn't want Linda to know she'd been going through her things. It was none of her business anyway, but Sally wanted to read more of the book.

It was the same story that Linda had told Jack, and he had told her. Only it was written in more of a biblical kind of speech, but the same story nonetheless. Sally knew there had to be a lot more to that book than just that one tale. She had gotten through most of the Nephilim story in the first fifteen pages. There were lots more pages she hadn't read yet. She wondered what other bizarre writings could be hiding in there. Maybe she would ask her grandmother about it sometime.

But not now. She wanted to get home before the road conditions got any worse. She made no more attempts to find out where Linda had been that afternoon. She was just glad that she had found her.

"So you'll remember to call Jack, right?"
"Yes dear. I'll call him."
"Ok. I'll see you later," she said putting on her coat.

"Be careful. The streets are getting slick."
"I will."

She pushed her way out into the icy darkness. Her car was completely covered over again in a thick blanket of white. Inside, Linda watched Sally clean off the windows.

"Nosey little bitch."

She was sure Sally had been reading the book. In her earlier haste she had forgotten to put the scripture away. She would have to be more careful. But the police coming by was quite unexpected. She didn't think those fools would catch on until it was far beyond too late.

Things needed to happen quickly or they might not happen at all. The police suspected her, Jack knew something was wrong, and now Sally had been reading the forbidden prophecy. It was impossible to know how much she'd read.

Linda looked up into the black sky. Little swirling pellets glistened in the porch light.

"Hurry my love. The time is short."

4:4

Stacey was hovering over the operating table. Her mother's chest open wide and the surgeon was leaning in close. A nearby machine beeped with metronome regularity. Two nurses and another doctor stood by close. A tray of shiny metal instruments lay on a tray beside the table. Long black tubes wound around it and into her mother's chest.

Stacey couldn't hear what was being said. It all sounded like distant mumbling in a long tunnel. All of the people's bodies had a faint glow to them, a slight indication of a brighter light inside.

Except for her mother. Her illumination was halfway out of the still flesh on the table. Its shining gave the whole room a brilliant yellow haze. The energy swam quickly all throughout her spirit.

The tension was rising. Instructions were being called out forcefully, with more volume. The nurses were rushing now. Something was very wrong. The dark yellow essence was rising out slowly. The frequent chiming of the machine had become one long continuous tone. Stacey watched as they tried to restart her heart.

The dark yellow light was almost black now. It had become less smoky, less transparent. It looked almost like liquid. Her mothers' mundane body was dying. In another few seconds she would be free. No longer bound to this dimension. The light was completely out of her body on the table. They were still attempting to revive her. Then she saw her daughter.

Stacey?

Yes Mom, it's me.

She floated over and embraced her mother. As they hugged they could feel themselves drifting into each other. The edges of their energies were mixing. Marion could feel her daughter's sadness and fear. Stacey began to feel her mom's love for her. It was simple, unwavering and eternal. She was starting to understand her on a spiritual level. Even with all the mistakes that had been made between them, the misunderstandings and petty resentments, love's connection had never wavered.

Stacey, I don't know how, but I know you don't belong here. I have to go on without you. The embrace ended and their energies returned to them.

I love you, Mom.

The dark liquid yellow had changed into a bright white vapor.

I will always love you dear. Always.

She gently passed through the ceiling and was gone. Stacey knew there was a better place waiting for her mother. The doctor pulled a sheet up over Marion's face. They couldn't save her. What they didn't realize was that she didn't want to be saved anymore. The pain of that world was behind her now. Heaven was waiting.

4:5

Elizabeth woke up screaming. Cold tears streamed down her swollen face. The morning was pitch black in the back of her cell, as was every morning. A dim bulb illuminated the hall, carving thick, bar shaped shadows through the doorway, onto the floor.

The green blanket hung over her naked body. There was only a piece of dirty cardboard between her and the freezing concrete. Shivering, she pushed herself up.

A tray of food sat in the middle of the room. Someone must've set it there while she slept. It had pork chops, mashed potatoes and gravy, two slices of buttered bread and a glass of water. It made her feel sick to her stomach to even think about eating, but the water was eagerly accepted. She guzzled it down so fast it hurt her throat. She wiped her dripping chin with a forearm, nervously scanning the corridor.

The constant crying from the other cells echoed in the hall. The girl with no name was somewhere unseen. Elizabeth couldn't see her, but she knew the girl was there. She had to be.

"Are you there?" she whispered.

No answer came out of the darkness, nor could any movement be seen. Elizabeth stared into the thick shadow at the back of the cell. It was the blackest void she had ever seen, overflowing with death. Somewhere inside it was a pair of frightened eyes. They were pleading with her, begging her to stop.

Oh Jesus.

The reflection in the polished steel of the blade was her own eyes, staring back at her. They too, were desperate for Elizabeth to make it end. There was no stopping it until the girl's voice ate her mind alive.

It's the screaming that will drive you mad.

The stained blanket slid off her shoulders and down to the gritty floor. She was right behind it, falling into the blackness of her own shadows. The back of her head hit the concrete hard and the blood flowed. She laid on her back, her whole body shaking. Her shrieking cries ricocheted through the basement, up the crumbling stairs and against the door.

Only the faintest, distant wail could be heard in the kitchen. Even a person with his ear pressed against the door could not have recognized the sound as human. It could have just as easily been a loose alternator belt or a squeaky wheel on a toy wagon.

Elizabeth's anguish seemed miles away from the man who had caused it. He sat serenely at the table eating his lunch. He looked over at the closed entrance to the basement. Taking a big bite of mashed potatoes, he cocked his head as if listening to a whisper entering his ear. He knew what he was hearing was not a squeaky wheel. He knew what it was and who it was. It was the only part of her that would ever escape.

He stopped his vigorous chewing to say, "Welcome to the club, my dear."

4:6

Jack sat quietly in the waiting room with his arm around his wife's body. He had removed the necklace and placed it back inside the velvet box, which was now resting safely in the pocket of his thick winter coat.

Stacey gasped. She was back. Her eyes were full of tears when they met Jack's.

"Mom's gone." she choked out.

Jack took her in his arms and held her tight.

"I got to say goodbye to her. I *saw* her. Thank you jack, thank you."

It felt like a part of him was being crushed. His tears came out freely and they embraced each other in the waiting room for a few minutes and then walked out to the car. They didn't wait for the doctor to come out and give them the news they already knew. They just wanted to go home.

Jack called his parents on his cell phone. When his mother picked up he could hear his son playing in the background.

"Hello?"

"Hey, mom."

"What's happening? Is she alright?"

A silence lingered in the receiver. He didn't know how to say it.

"She didn't make it," he said it in a solemn whisper.

"Oh god. I'm sorry. I'm so sorry."

"Yeah."

"Tell us if there's anything we can do, okay? Do you want us to keep Christopher for awhile?"

"No. That's all right mom. We're coming to pick him up. We'll be there in a few minutes."

Stacey listened as Jack said goodbye to his mother. She sat in silence, wondering how she was going to tell her six year-old son that this Nana had passed away.

Stacey waited in the car when Jack went in to get Chris. She gave him a sad smile when he ran out into the front yard. She opened the door and he climbed on her lap and gave her a hug.

"Is Nana home now, Mommy?"

Jack was on the porch with his father, talking and looking out at Stacey. She squeezed her son tight, crying.

"No baby. Nana passed away. She's gone to a better place."

He leaned back, confused. "Nana didn't get better?"

"I'm sorry honey. Nana's in heaven now, with Grandpa Frank."

"Oh," he said weakly, with his eyes red and full of tears.

They embraced again. Jack was at the car now. He put a hand on his son's back.

"You okay, Chris?"

He didn't answer. He cried on his mom's shoulder most of the way home. As Stacey held him in her lap she thought about her mother's bright blue spirit hovering over the operating table.

She had not been sad to be leaving. While Stacey was going to miss her mom, she felt a sense of happiness for her too. Death was not the end, it was a new beginning. A wondrous journey was starting for Marion. She would be with her husband soon.

He'd been waiting for her almost five years. Mundane life was such a distant memory to him. His afterlife had far outshined anything he'd experienced on Earth. There were some things though, that he would never forget. His wife Marion, whom he's spent thirty-five years with, was the love of his life, and beyond.

4:7

Stacey lowered the tissue away from her red eyes. Looking at the windshield she could see the snow collecting on the glass. The side mirrors were frozen over with thick ice. "Jack," she said softly, "Where did you get that necklace?"

He glanced over at her quickly and then over to the icy street.

"A women at the Paradox bookstore sold it to me."

"Did she know what it could do?"

"Yeah. She knew."

"Why did she sell it to you?" Do you know her or something?"

"No. The first time I ever saw her was the day I bought it."

Stacey remembered how mad she was at him that morning. She has started to think that he was cheating on her, but now she knew what he had been doing late at night. I still didn't explain the phone call to the bookstore at 2:00 a.m.

"Did you call the lady at the store in the middle of the night on Sunday?"

"I don't know."

My body's been walking around at night, I have blood on my hands, and now I'm making phone calls? What the hell is happening to me?

"What do you mean you don't know? You either did or you didn't"

"The thing is, my body's been, um, doing things while I've been travelling. I don't know why."

"Doing things? Shit Jack, she didn't tell you that would happen?"

"No. I've been trying to get hold of her but, she's not home."

" Maybe you should lay off using the necklace for awhile, until you talk to her."

She put her head on his shoulder, "Just to be safe."

"Yeah."

"How does it work?" Did she tell you that?"

"Yeah, she told me," he was so happy to finally be able to tell her about the story.

He knew she would eat it up. She loved that kind of thing.

He cleared his throat and began, "It's quite a tale."

She smiled at him excitedly, "Tell me."

Jack drove carefully down the highway. It took them almost thirty minutes to get from Canyon City to Penrose. It was twelve miles of blinding snow and ice. Jack talked the whole way there.

When they pulled into the driveway he was telling her about his experience with heaven. He turned off the key and opened the door. Stacey sat quietly, not moving. She was staring down at the necklace. Her face was full of wonder as she watched the swirling crimson fluid.

"Honey, are you coming inside?"

Surprised, she looked up. They were home.
"*Oh.* Yeah, I'm coming."
She smiled up at him. Jack went inside and made a pot of coffee. His wife sat at the kitchen table gazing at the unbelievable motion of the blood. It had her mesmerized. "What else have you seen?" Tell me more."

They drank coffee and talked the entire evening. It was the longest conversation they'd had since before they were married. They found themselves interested in each
other. They laughed. The love had made its way back into their hearts. Stacey was so happy when they went to bed she was in tears. Jack caressed her, held her, and made love to her. It was the best either one of them could remember.

He had finally found himself. The happiness he'd lost years ago was there, inside her. She'd been holding on to it, keeping it safe for him.

He fell asleep with his arm resting across her naked body. She lay awake for hours staring up at the ceiling. She was wondering where her mom was now. She imagined her parents soaring hand in hand through the center of Heaven.

4:8

Jack was floating above the trees. He could see his car parked along side the dirt road. It was dark. He saw them around the bonfire, laughing. Two cardboard six-pack containers were lying on the ground by the cooler. The empty bottles were in the fire.

He could feel it in his hand, the ice-cold knife. He swooped down and into his body. It had been hiding in the shadows behind their truck. He watched them drinking and dancing and kissing. The song on the radio was *Every Breath you Take*. The boom box was on the open tailgate. It was loud. Jack could feel the truck vibrating from the sound.

The girl was young. She had long dark hair. The wavy strands reflected the yellowy firelight. She pushed away from the boy and stumbled backwards. She steadied herself, laughing. He smiled at her.

They were drunk, all four of them. The other couple sat in each other's arms with their backs to Jack. They couldn't see him.

The girl walked unsteadily into the woods by herself. Her boyfriend stayed behind, talking to the others. Jack carefully walked around the truck and into the trees. She was out there and he was going to find her.

He circled far around the fire. His heart was thumping as the sky turned bright red. It lit up everything around him. He saw her. She was walking back to them. She didn't see Jack. It was still nighttime to her. She did however, hear a stick snap under his foot. She jumped.

"Billy?" she said, "Is that you?"

Jack's pounding in his chest rattled his whole body. He was behind her. He covered her mouth before she could scream. They were in a large clearing not far from the road.

He had her pinned to the ground, covering her mouth with his left hand. She was squirming violently under his weight. He waved the blade in front of her face. She passed out from the fear. Her body went limp. He got up and held the knife above his head. The red sky faded into black. The crimson haze absorbed into him. His whole body was glowing with it. He looked down.

Where is she?

Something on his hands. Wet, sticky. He looked up. She wasn't gone. She was everywhere. Every blade of grass, every rock and tree, was coated with her. She wasn't a girl anymore. She had become liquid.

Blood.

Jack was no longer a man in the woods. He had become the pounding of his own quickening heart. He had no hands covered in red. He was only a mist hovering over the clearing. He realized that he wasn't really there at all.

And yet…somehow…he was still holding the knife.

BOOK FIVE:
SCRIBE

5:1

They found the Philistine scribe in the city of Gath. He willingly took on the project that would make the god of Israel's destruction possible.

The man wrote every word the Angel spoke onto three scrolls. The first was the story of the beginning. It described the creation, God and the angels. The second was an explanation of the rise to power. It told how a man could become a god through ritual and astral projection. The third part consisted of incantations, definitions of spells, and ritual format. It was a step by step blueprint for the end of the world.

Karradel wrote it all down carefully and in great detail. The entire project took them four months to complete. It was thought that Karradel himself might be the one, Lucifer's messiah. But his part would end with the gathering of the blood. His death would come swiftly after that task. The sun would rise and set three times more before his mortal flesh met its end.

The power to destroy the God of Israel was almost complete. Only two more things were required. The death of Samyaza's mortal body at the hand of God, and the death of Goliath at the hand of an Israelite named David.

5:2

Jack woke suddenly. The muscles in his arms and chest seized in a jerking spasm. The room was glowing deep red. It was freezing and he could see his breath forming faint clouds and then dissipating in front of his face. It felt as though his body was under water. The pressure was against him and it was getting tighter. He desperately tried to raise his arms. They were pinned to the bed, as were his legs. The most he could do was turn his head.

Stacey was asleep next to him. She hadn't woken up from the cold. There were no visible clouds of breath escaping her mouth. She wasn't covered in Goosebumps and shivering. It was like he had entered another reality right there in the same room with her.

A bone chilling dimension of fear. It was all around him. He could not speak and could barely move.

What's happening to me?

A swimming ocean of liquid hate spun in large circles above him. Jack could feel it. Powerfully, it shoved him down. His spirit was sinking into the mattress below. It pushed him under the bed as it filled his body.

God, no.

The crimson mass had him in a strangle hold. His soul panicked and fell further down into the floor. Away from its grip he darted around to the other side of the room. It had grown into a blood red bubble that Jack could not penetrate. He could only gaze through its bright window from a distance. He flashed dark yellow as he beat on its barrier. The energy would not budge.

God, please.

It started shrinking. The smaller it got the thicker and darker its density became. The light was like water, and then oil, and then almost solid. It was taking a human form, *his* form. The condensed energy settled into Jack's body and the muscles and bone vibrated at the pressure. He rushed at his body but it was like hitting a brick wall. He bounced backward in the air.

No...

His body now contained another and it sat up with a smile of satisfaction. It looked up at Jack hovering in the shadows. It gave him a wink as if to say *thanks Slugger. I'll take it from here.* It leaned over close to Stacey and gave her a kiss on the cheek. She woke up and rubbed her eyes.

"Jack?"

"Yes dear?"

No. Stop.

She smiled and gave her husband's face a soft kiss in the mouth. She kissed *it* on the mouth.

No.

Jack dove on top and strained to get back in side his body. It was no use. Whatever, *whoever* had possessed him was strong. *Very* strong.

It looked at Jack's spirit with a grin and whispered to his wife, "I can't sleep. I'm going for a walk."

"Everything okay, Jack?"
Looking over at her it hissed, "Everything is perfect my sweet. Just perfect."
She closed her eyes and lowered her head back into the dent in the pillow. It got up and walked out the door and down the hall. Jack followed closely.
Who are you?
It kept going, making its way to the front room. His body sat down in the recliner and put its feet up. Jack's spirit was in front of it now.
I know you can see me, so you must be able to hear me too. Speak to me you son of a bitch. Who are you?
The face was calm and pleasant, "The question *is*, who are *you*? You see, *my* name is Jack Sawyer. That's *my* wife asleep in bed. This is *my* house..." it put its hands on Jack's chest, "...*My* body." The spirit floating in front of it fumed dark yellow.
No. Get out!
It ignored him, "And *you*, well you are a faint vapor, an ineffectual little twist in the shadows. Just a figment of my imagination, really. But soon, *very* soon, you'll be nothing at all."

5:3

Jack was completely helpless as he watched his body get dressed. There was absolutely nothing he could do when it left the house. The entity that has taken over walked with a purpose out to the car. The kitchen knife that had been removed from the drawer was placed on the passenger bucket seat of the Nissan.

Jack followed the car down the street as it sped out to the highway. There was no hesitation in the possessor's actions. It knew exactly what it was doing and where it wanted to go. Jack had a pretty good idea that the crusty substance on his hands the other morning was not dog blood. He feared that it was something else.

What do I do? What can I do?

He knew why his body had been moving around while he was gone. He knew why the necklace had been removed and set back in its case. That spirit had been using his body.

He hoped against hope that what he feared was not true, that somehow there could be some other explanation for the dried blood. But looking down at the car below him, seeing the knife blade reflecting the moonlight, what else could he think? The energy that had taken his flesh was evil, with the most terrible intentions.

Jack could only speculate what his mortal hands had already been forced to do. His astral self paced the car all the way into Canyon City. It turned on Fourth Street and parked in the alley behind Main Street.

The bars had been closed for almost a half-hour and the sidewalks were mostly deserted. It climbed out of the car and started toward Fifth Street, carefully staying in the shadows. The long blade of the knife remained hidden under the flannel shirt. It stopped at the end of the alley and waited patiently behind an overflowing Dumpster. The aroma from the garbage was sweetly rotten. The muddy slush on the sidewalk across the street reflected the red neon light of the Budweiser sign.

Inside, the bartender was finishing up counting her cash drawer. It had been a good night at McClure's. Sandy's tip jar contained more than eighty dollars. Most Wednesday's she was lucky to get twenty. But the more her customers drank the more they tipped, and tonight had been quite the party. From pool leaguers to bikers, it was an eclectic mix of intoxication.

With the money locked away in the safe she made her way around the bar clicking off the neon signs. She turned off all of the overhead lights except the one above the door.

That time of night the darkened empty tavern always seemed so lonely. A deathly silence filled the void rock music on the jukebox and the talking and laughing of the numerous patrons had left behind.

Sandy's boyfriend Roy was supposed to stay to help her close up and walk her home. But he had too many shots of tequila on top of a belly full of beer earlier in the evening. He only made it to midnight before his slurring speech and unbalanced grip on the bar indicated to Sandy that it was time for him to go. The cab picked him up more than two hours earlier. His drunkenness had left her to make the walk home alone.

At least she thought so. But she would soon find out that she wasn't alone at all. It was waiting for her.

Jack was terrified, watching from a distance. In his current form he was completely ineffectual to the physical world. He could do nothing. Whatever had stolen his body had an iron grip that would not let go.

Please God, help me. Tell me what to do.

Sandy was outside now. She was locking the front door. Crossing the street she hummed a tune from a song on the jukebox. When she neared the alley entrance it stepped out of its black shadow. She only caught the slightest glimpse over her shoulder. The faint padding of soft-soled shoes on wet blacktop quickly became the heavy pounding of a screaming heartbeat. A thick arm around her neck pulled her into the stench behind the Dumpster. A heavy hand over her mouth kept her cries from alerting the passing police car.

On the ground now.

The long winter coat was soaking up the surrounding slush and mud.

A knee wedged into her throat. Panic.

Can't breathe.

Jack racing.

The knife.

The soft flesh of the stomach.

Over them now.

No. Please, no.

Muffled shrieks and kicking.

Jack blasted into his body and the presence inside with as much force as his astral self could summon. A vibration of condensed power knocked him backward end over end. It was too strong.

The blade found its purpose and the wet snow ran red with death. It looked back for a second to make sure Jack was watching. He was.

Noooo…

The grin on its face was cold and satisfied.

The thing that had stolen Jack's voice hissed, "Watch closely now. This is the best part." The slick steel sliced its way under her rib cage. Sandy's body was giving up. Blood filled her chest cavity and lungs.

Jack sped away as fast as he could. He couldn't be there anymore. He knew that it was all his fault. His carelessness and selfish curiosity had caused that poor woman to die. His own body had provided the vehicle for her death. All Jack had wanted was answers, to find the truth. What he'd received was horrific consequences he could have never imagined. He raced toward the horizon screaming.

Sandy's eyes were still now. The torture was over for the time being. Only the powerful energy inside Jack's body knew what was to come next. The beginning of the end was near.

The powerful spirit allowed a whispery laugh to escape Jack's lips as he walked back through the darkness to the car. Things were going exactly as the scripture said they would. The plan was flawless.

5:4

The girl woke from her restless sleep in the deep shadow in the back of the cell. She peered out of the cold darkness, across the corridor. The one she had met the previous day, the one who was still named Elizabeth, was busy with only her hunched back showing in the dim, yellow light.

Her arms moved quickly, her elbows jerked up and down, and her head hung low over the project in front of her. The unnamed one didn't know what Elizabeth was doing. She could only see the animated movement from behind. She scooted closer to the front of the chamber, trying to find out what her neighbor was doing. In the patch of illuminated concrete, in between the rigid shadows of the bars, she saw it reflecting like a mirror.

An ever-growing pool of blood lazily flowed around bumps in the uneven floor, searching for cracks to drain into. Elizabeth was kneeling in it.

The confused girl crawled closer. Hearing that she was awake, Elizabeth's head swung around to greet her. Her hair matted with bloody, drying sweat, she spoke.

“Hey,” she said excitedly, “you’re awake.”
Her ears were crusted with dark, congealed blood. They weren’t bleeding anymore. They were not the source of the shiny pool below her. The edge of the crimson pond found the nearby blanket and soaked into the fibers, creating a dark stain.

Two small pieces of cloth had been recently ripped from the side of the wool. They had been rolled up into tiny little cylinders that were lying at Elizabeth’s side. They were just the right size. All of the wax in her ears had been raked out with Elizabeth’s sharp fingernails. But that wasn’t enough, not to make a good seal. More had to be done if she was going to block out the sound of tonight’s ritual.

She turned to face her unnamed friend. Looking down, the girl across the hallway could now see everything. She began to bob back and forth frantically. With her mouth wide open, a wheezing, cracked scream escaped her.

The nightly hell they experienced was no longer limited to the ritual chamber. It had made its way down to the new girl’s cell.

Her long, middle fingernail had been broken on two sides, leaving a sharp point in the center. Of course, the girl with no name couldn’t see that. It was deep inside Elizabeth. It made for a useful tool to scrape the soft tissue. Blood ran down her legs and dripped heavily into the pool on the concrete.

Elizabeth was smiling. A nervous, heaving laugh pushed through her twitching mouth. The girl with no name could see that her neighbor was happy. Of course she was. Her earplugs were almost finished.

5:5

Jack’s astral self flew hard and fast over the buildings. His energy was boiling with fear. No one could help him now.

Linda hadn’t called him. He didn’t know where to find her. He suspected that she had set him up. She was in on it somehow. For what other reason would she have given him the necklace?
But why? What did she stand to gain?
It didn’t make any sense. The thing that has possessed his body wasn’t letting go. Jack was trapped in the spiritual dimension

while it used his body to terrorize the physical world. What would it do to his family?
Jesus.
He couldn't let anything happen to them, and yet there was nothing he *could* do. He stopped his flight and started back to the alley. There had to be a way to stop it. He didn't know how or what he was going to do, but one thing was sure. He couldn't do anything if he was running away. He would have to face it head on. But he also knew that he was much weaker than the enemy. Trying to fight it was completely futile. He would need another way.

All of this started with a temptation presented to Jack in a pretty velvet box. They had tricked him with promises of knowledge and truth. Sure, he had received much knowledge along the way, but the price hadn't been revealed until now. He had been used and manipulated. Jack's anger burned red hot. It was time to find out what had stolen his body, and how to make it stop.

5:6

Jack was high above the dark alley now. Looking down he saw the Nissan's headlights come on. He followed the car as it turned on Fourth Street and made a left onto the highway. Killien drove quickly past the E-Z food stop. The usual gathering of three city police cars sat in the parking lot. All of the officers were inside the convenience store talking and drinking coffee. None of them watched the black Nissan as it sped by.

Jack nervously looked in the windows as he flew. Canyon City's finest were totally occupied laughing at the latest blonde jokes. Relieved, he increased his speed to catch up to the car.

He knew that if anyone were caught for the girl's death it would be him. His *body* anyway. If that happened the only way he could return to the physical world would be in prison. He would probably get the death penalty. He hoped there was no evidence pointing to him in that alley. Jack thought that no matter how much he hoped there was most likely something there that would send him to the electric chair. The FBI didn't need much to find out criminals. A piece of hair, scraped skin under a fingernail, saliva, blood, the list went on and on.

Jack didn't even know if they still used the electric chair. Maybe it would be the gas chamber or lethal injection. Not one of them sounded any better than the others.

He wasn't afraid of death anymore but he couldn't imagine missing his son growing up. He had so much more that he wanted to do.

So many things he needed to say to Stacey. In the whole world she would be the only one who believed him about tonight. When everyone else screamed murderer, she would be the only one that knew the truth. That is if he could find a way to get back into his body to tell her. Jack was beginning to think that was not going to happen, that the game was over and he'd lost.

The car pulled up in to driveway. Jack's body ducked out of the driver's seat and out the open door. It walked slowly. His face was pale and sweating. The spirit was vibrating.

The soul's place in the universe had been vacant for three hours now and it was pulling him back. The bright red glow struggled against the magnetic force, but even Killien's powerful grip was not enough. He was jerked out and up into the black sky. Searing heat boiled all around him as he shrieked in defiance.

Jack's body dropped lifelessly to the ground and hit with a thud in the wet grass. He darted across the yard and re-entered himself. He was lying on his back looking up at the stars. Getting up quickly, he went into the house. With the necklace retrieved from the pocket of his coat, he sat down in the recliner. His shivering body sank into the soft cushions. It was warm inside and he was sure his body would be fine now.

Placing the chain around his neck, he lowered the stone bird onto his chest. His energy exited quickly and he was free of his flesh once again. He took off in the direction he'd seen the powerful spirit pulled.

5:7

Jack's soul raced to catch up with the spirit. A faint vapor trail of pain led the way across the black sky. He could feel the anguish washing over him in the ethereal stream. Whatever had ripped the murderer away from the material plane was full of hate. The anger boiled stronger with each moment he got nearer to its destination. The span between the material world and his current destination seemed like forever. Jack followed the ever-reddening astral residue for more than an hour.

He quickly zipped by many varied entities on his way. Some were larger, some were smaller, some hovered in place and others darted around hurriedly. He saw bright energies, multicolored mists of every kind and dull, almost invisible variations of light. Each one held its own consciousness, its own life force and power. And Jack knew as sure as he was seeing all of them, they were seeing him. They knew as he did, that he didn't belong there. His place was in the mundane world. It was only by chance that he was ever there at all. A twist of circumstance that had put his soul in danger. Yes, they knew who *he* was. They could feel it in his essence as he flew by. They could smell it on him as easily as perfume in stagnant air.

He was the *one*. Chosen by fate. Trapped in chaos. Lured by the devil. But it was God himself who now depended on him. He needed to be strong, to overcome.

But how?

Can a mortal man take on invincible power and expect anything other than failure?

But it's not invincible.

Whatever force that had ripped it out of his body and carried it screaming through space had proven that. It wasn't without flaw. Jack was beginning to realize that now. He also was aware that there was no way he could match its strength or the terrible energy that had whisked it away. He would have to find another way.

Another way to what?

He didn't have a clue of what to do to stop him from...

Oh God, that poor woman.

It had been Jack's own hands that had hurt her, made her scream and forced her to die. Even if he wasn't in control at the time his body was still a murderer. If he were caught back home for the crime *he* would be punished, not the entity. The responsibility would be his. The *consequences* would be his.

But what about out here, on the astral plane?

Would the same hold true? Would his soul be condemned for earthly actions not performed by him? Jack wondered if God saw him as a murderer. After all, it was his recklessness that had led to the powerful spirit's opportunity.

Something was coming into view. A giant tornado of shimmering light. It was as if the ground were in two directions. Both top and bottom were cone shaped and faded away into nothingness. But there was no ground above or below it. It just hung there in space like a great galaxy of fear. Constant bolts of lightning snapped across as it spun its crimson storm.

This was the place were murderers spent their eternity, paying for their crimes. Jack could feel it. The path he'd been following led directly into the center of the tornado storm. The possessor was somewhere in its core.

Even from that far out he sensed the torment swimming all around him. He was afraid. Jack couldn't help thinking about how Heaven had spat him out. Maybe Hell would welcome him home.

Jack's soul hovered for a few minutes, staring into the circling storm. He was still as least a half a mile from its border. Tiny dots of light buzzed around the spiral like distant flares wobbling and changing direction. Flares like an SOS signal from a distressed ship. He was sure that no one would see their cry for help. No one would show up to save them. It was much too late for that.

The dancing lights were actually entities; large, powerful spirits whose purpose it was to keep the storm's inhabitants inside. They were the guards at the most elaborate prison ever conceived. For most, escape was a distant memory long given up on. But some, the new ones mostly, would try to get out, frequently testing the angelic patrol. Momentarily success was always punished with a push into the core. The center of the violent swirl was the most hated place of all. It contained the origin of the tornado's power. The torment was at its very worst there and the pain was most dense. A soul passing through the core couldn't cry or call out for help. They could not desperately swim for the edge. The agony at the eye of the storm was so great that the most an astral body could do was shudder. It was like electricity entering directly into the spine and sending out a steady stream of ripping thunder to every nerve. The core was the thickest, blackest, and most feared place in Hell.

It had swallowed the dark one whole, and he was drifting slowly through its power. Even with all of the strength he'd shown that night, he was still as helpless as any of them in the core. He would have to wait until he reached the other side before escape would be possible again. There at the outer rim, the strong spirit *could* break free from the storm.

He would escape, sometimes for hours, before Hell pulled him back. Upon each struggling return he would be sent into the eye of the storm, punishment for his arrogance.

Jack wondered if the angel guards were working for God or the devil. According to the story, Hell was a place created by Lucifer for his followers. They despised the human race, yes, but why wouldn't they let the beast out freely? Wasn't he part of the devil's own plan? And if they were God's angels what were they doing *there*? Did the divine take over Hell at some point? None of it made any sense.

He slowly flew closer to get a better look. He stopped at about fifty yards. He couldn't go any further. His whole being ached with the stabbing pain that emanated from inside the cloud. The tiny spots of light he'd seen from a distance were now identifiable as huge masses of ever shifting energy. Through the bright white outer haze a multicolored dancing power could be seen in the center of each. They were extremely strong and fast and they all rumbled with etheric might. The angels paid no attention to Jack as he looked them over. They knew he was from a mundane reality but somehow, it was not within their power to help *or* hinder him. There was no way at all to tell if they were evil or divine. They only performed the task at hand.

Jack could see the huge presence through the hazy circling storm. The spirit blazed like a super nova out-shining all other's around him. He struggled, helplessly drifting across Hell's core.

The power inside that place seemed infinite, eternal. It was definitely more than enough energy to subdue the powerful spirit's ethereal strength. Hell was the only thing Jack was aware of that exceeded the murderer's might. What other powers might be able to conquer one with such spiritual fortitude? He needed to find out quickly. At the rate the beast was drifting he would be at the other side in just a few short hours. Jack feared what would happen when it got there. His mortal body lay completely unprotected back in the mundane world.

He turned and raced back to Earth. The angelic guardians didn't give him a second look as he jetted away. Following Hell's trail of wrath, he made his way home. Even back in his body there would be no defense against the entity. It could just push Jack out once again. At top speed it took almost an hour to reach his house.

It was 6:15 A.M. Stacey was in the shower. Christopher was playing in his room. The soulless flesh lay quiet in the recliner just where he had left it. His family was completely unaware that they'd had a monster in the house, a murderer.

The local news was playing on the radio in the bathroom. Stacey listened as she lathered her hair. They were talking about a homicide last night. A murder that had happened right there in Canyon City, no less.

Jesus Christ.

Found in the alley a man said. Brutally stabbed to death he said. Stacey had no idea that they were in danger. She couldn't have known that the hands that had performed the killing were coming down the hallway that very moment. The same power that had allowed her to say goodbye to her mother had stained her husband's hands with death. Jack was opening the door. She'd soon know everything. She was about to find out just how close she'd gotten to it. She would realize that she had kissed death on the lips and smiled.

5:8

A tall, dark figure appeared at the doorway. Pushing it open, he entered the dark room. It was eleven O'clock and her mother had left for work more than an hour earlier. The television set was on channel 13. The audience was enthusiastically clapping at Johnny Carson's monologue. The living room was roaring with laughter.

Elizabeth began to sob when she saw her father. He looked especially angry tonight, even more so than usual. He did not say a word as he approached her. There was nothing that needed to be said. She knew what he was there for. It was the same thing he wanted every night. And daddy always got what he wanted.

He didn't pretend to care about her. He'd given up on those lies months ago. The simple fact was, he hated her. He had wanted a son so badly before she was born. When he found out his wife was pregnant he prayed every night that God would bless him with a boy. He'd wanted to teach him to shoot, play catch; maybe he'd even become a professional baseball player. But, as his miserable luck would have it, the expectation and the reality did not go hand in hand.

His wife had a little baby girl inside of her and that was the way it was. What he always referred to as "female problems" kept them from having any more children. She had a hysterectomy at the age of twenty-seven.

So the son he'd always wanted turned out to be the daughter he couldn't stand. He spent as little time with her as possible, until very recently. She just turned thirteen and her young body had started to blossom.

Her straight, boyish figure had begun to curve at the hip and her small breasts could be seen underneath the cotton t-shirts. She was developing into a woman.

Her father only had two uses for women. Cleaning and fucking. Her chores were done for tonight and that left only one more obligation to fulfill. His forbidden lust for his daughter was laced with a contempt that would stay with her the rest of her life. Long after he went to prison for his crimes, the hatred for Elizabeth remained. She had taken over where he left off and her own self-loathing ruled her entire world. She had short stints at hating others but most of the time she found herself too busy despising herself.

The audience cheered as her daddy rammed his way inside of her. As his sweat dripped down onto her face she tried to find a safe place in her mind she could live in until he was finished. She could not. The here and now, as always, was everywhere. It would not let her go tonight, or any night. Elizabeth was forced to endure.

It had been years since her father had so forcefully taken her virginity away. As the man with the cold rings on his fingers pounded on top of her, it seemed like only yesterday.

5:9

Stacey heard the door open when Jack walked in. She pulled the shower curtain back and peeked out.

"Hi honey, you must've got up early."

He was shivering. His clothes were still wet from melted snow and mud. His fingers were crusted with blood and dirt. The shaking wasn't from the cold. It was from the strongest fear he'd ever felt. His mind was swimming with images of Hell and the woman who'd died in the monster's grasp. *His* grasp. Jack had been completely helpless to stop it and he felt responsible for everything that had happened. Tears ran down his face as he looked into Stacey's eyes. She could see the terror on him. When they embraced she felt his body shaking.

"God Jack, what's wrong?"

"I couldn't make it stop. It was too strong."

"I don't understand."

He pulled his face up from her shoulder, "Something terrible has happened," he paused rubbing the tears out of his eyes, "I'm so afraid. Please Stacey, don't hate me."

Her naked body was dripping water into the pink rug.

"I could never hate you. Please tell me what's wrong."

"Something took over my body last night, *possessed* me." It was too strong. I couldn't do *anything*."

The newsman had come back from commercial. He was talking about the murder again. Stacey looked down at her husband's hands. The blood was dry and dark.

"Oh my God, Jack. *Oh God*."

She pulled away from him, "What are you saying? *Jesus*. Tell me you didn't…"

"I couldn't stop it. I tried but it wouldn't *stop*."

Stacey's breath was short and fast. Her face turned pale.

"The thing that took over my body…It, it…killed someone."

She knew it had not been a dream. He hadn't imagined it. He wasn't lying. The magical necklace had shown her its power in the hospital. It was real.

The news on the radio had moved on to weather.

The storm was upon them now. It would last for two days. But long after it was gone it would stay with them. It would be the bitter storm that lived in their minds forever.

5:10

Stacey was staring at her husband. She was dripping wet and cold. Her eyes never left him as she pulled a towel off of the shelf.

"How did it happen? What's going on?"

"I don't know. I wish I knew, but I don't."

"Who was it?"

His frustration was building, *"I don't know."*

She put her arms around his neck, "I'm sorry honey."

The shower was still running. She turned to shut it off.

"What do we do now?"

"I don't know what to do, but I do know that I can't be here. It's coming back. I'm sure of it."

"Do you think you can hide from it?"

"I doubt it, but I won't put you or Chris in danger. When it comes again I'll be far away from here, or…" Jack had an idea.

He remembered watching an old movie. Lon Chaney played the wolf man; the scene where they locked him up before the full moon. He couldn't recall if they put him in a cage or chained him. It had been years since he'd seen it. But nevertheless, it was something that might work.

He'd have to act quickly. He imagined that the evil spirit was probably about to reach the other side of the core by now.

Stacey wanted to know what he was thinking, "Jack?"

"Give me your cell phone. I have to go *now*."

"*Please*. I think we should…"

"There's no time. I'll call you. I promise."

They walked out to the living room. Christopher was playing with is Legos on the floor in front of the television. Jack kneeled down to him.

"Chris?"
"Yeah daddy?"
"I love you. I just wanted you to know that, okay?"
"I love you too daddy."
He hugged his father tight. Tears rolled down Jack's face.
"Do what your mother tells you. Be good."
"Okay dad," he said with a smile.

He quickly got back to work on the colored blocks. Jack held his hand against the side of his son's head and thought about how much alike they looked. At that age he'd had the same straight brown hair, the same faint freckles. The same smile, dimples and all.

He had a feeling that might be the last time he'd see him. He hoped to God he was wrong, but the emotion was so strong. The *fear* was so strong. He forced himself away and stood up. Stacey was waiting with a black phone she'd dug out of her purse.
"Call me the second you get in the car. You got me? The very *second*."
"I will babe, I will," He looked around, "do we have any rope?"
"Rope? Um, I don't know…wait. In with the camping stuff, I think."
He opened the closet and started searching. He found it. Fifty feet of yellow nylon rope neatly rolled up. And, on the floor next to the flashlight, duct tape. He grabbed that too. Stacey followed him out to the car. He closed the door and rolled down the window. She leaned in and kissed him.
"I'm afraid, Jack. What if the police think it was you? What if…"
"It *was* me. My *body* anyway."
He paused, taking time to study the shape of her face, the color of her eyes.
He forced a smile, "I'm scared too, but I'll figure this all out. I promise."

She stood freezing in her pink robe and her bare feet on the driveway as he backed out. She didn't go inside until he had made the corner at the end of the block. When he reached the highway, he dialed the number. Stacey picked up in half a ring.
"Jack?"
"Yeah. It's me."

"Tell me what happened. *All* of it."

He talked all the way to town. She sat in the kitchen, horrified at what she was hearing. By the time he reached Canyon City it was snowing. A big gust of wind pushed against the little car. He turned on the windshield wipers to clear the collecting mass. The air's temperature was dropping fast. Even with the defroster on full blast, the ice was forming at the edges of the front glass. The freeze was moving in slowly toward the center. He knew he should've had the heater fixed months ago. But it was not something he thought about when he didn't need it. He couldn't go back and change things now. What was done was done. As he sped toward his destination his fear grew, and his vision got smaller and smaller.

And there went out a champion out of the camp of the Philis'-tines, named Go-li'-ath, of Gath, whose height was six cubits and a span.

Samuel: Chapter 17 Verse 4

BOOK SIX:
WRATH

6:1

The army of the Philistines marched into Ephesdammim, overlooking the valley Elah, where a settlement of Israelites camped in the mountains of Judah. The king's army had gathered there expecting an attack from the nearby godless troops.

With swords and shields raised, the Philistines charged into battle. The conflict ensued and the ground became soaked with blood.

King Saul watched from a distant vantage point with his most trusted soldiers. As the battle raged on, it appeared as though they would be able to hold off the enemy.

Back at the temple of the Philistines in Gath, hundreds of miles from the war, Samyaza stepped out through the arched doorway, into the morning sunlight. He took in a deep breath, expanding his gigantic chest.

With arms outstretched and muscles flexed, he called out into the sky with his mightiest voice, "God of Israel! God of the dimensions of light! Betrayer of your own brothers, I call to you! Show yourself!"

God could hardly believe it. The voice he was hearing was one who should have been dead long ago in the flood. At that moment he knew that he had been fooled. What he was not aware of was that the trickery was just beginning.

God's energy was charged with a fiery rage that thundered across the sky in crimson bolts. The clouds became dark and the winds howled. His divine anger carried him over the land to the temple of false idols. Samyaza knew that God's punishment would be terrible and swift. He was counting on it.

With Israel's deity gone, a signal was given from the nearby forest. The Philistines immediately retreated west, to make way for their champion. King Saul watched from a distance as Goliath stepped out from the trees. The giant said nothing. He only smiled as he raised his great hammer of wood and stone into the air. The Israelites scattered with fear at the sight of him. They had all heard the tales of the invincible giant warriors that had pillaged the countryside. They were the men of old, with renowned strength.

Goliath went running hard into the God fearing valley swinging his mighty hammer as the men cried out to God. One brave warrior ran toward him with spear in hand. His spirit was pushed out when he neared the giant. Goliath smashed his skull before the human could hit the ground. It was an explosion in mid air as the thick stone found its target. The giant stopped and lowered the bloodied weapon to his side. The humans cowered with fright at the deformed threat.

“Whosoever among you that would challenge me, step forth.”

He looked them over carefully, smiling. The humans stayed far back from the monster, cowering in fear.

“Will none of you come forward to smite me?”

Not one of them wanted to fight him. Many dropped to their knees in the dirt and prayed. Others turned and ran for fear of death. The King looked up from his prayer and said, “Surely the Lord has abandoned his children.”

Saul looked over a group of men who had recently arrived with provisions for his army. He called out, “Run for shelter and stay there until this battle is done. This is no place for you.”

All five took to the forest. David, a man of little more than twenty years, stopped behind the others and called to his creator. He refused to accept that his God would not help them.

“Please Lord, show us your wisdom in this dark time!”

Lucifer, who was waiting nearby, descended down to David. The human was in awe of the energy floating in front of him. He could feel its pure power like an electrical charge biting at his skin. He was sure it was God.

He dropped to his hands and knees, “Oh Lord, you heard my cry!”

Lucifer, the liar, was pleased with his reaction. “Rise boy, and meet your master.” Trembling, David got to his feet. A small circle of light formed in the center of the energy. It compressed smaller into itself until it glowed red-hot. A smooth stone lifted off of the ground from David’s feet and entered the light. There was a brilliant flash when the two met, and David fell backward onto the grass. The light subsided and the stone dropped down. It rolled over to the human. The devil spoke again.

"Take this stone, my son, and cast it at your enemy."
"I am not a soldier, Lord. My aim is not true."
"The vessel has been anointed with my power. Use the sling and you shall smite the enemy!"

David picked up the stone carefully and held it up in the palm of his hand. Staring at it, he saw it looked like any other. He lowered his hand, holding it tight. Lucifer said one last thing before leaving the forest.
"Go now. The God of Israel commands you."

Samyaza was standing in front of the temple when the whirlwind of wrath arrived. The air's whipping punishment carried with it the sting of earth and stone. The fallen angel held rigid in his tracks, waiting for the inevitable.
Laughing, he mocked God, "You are the creator of all we see and yet your enemy's presence goes unknown? Perhaps you have divided your energy too many times. Your power is weak."

The exploding cloud did not respond. Slowly it formed into a great tornado. Lightning danced around the twisting dirt and stone. The accompanying thunderclap dropped the giant to his knees, his ears bleeding. His screams of defiance went unheard in the deafening wind. The great storms' pull lifted the giant from the earth and into its barrage of swirling pellets. The nearby temple crumpled into flying sand and wood, as did the other buildings.

The angel who had been earth bound for more than four hundred years, without the power to soar through the heavens, found himself flying. Round and round inside God's own hate, he was slowly being beaten to death. His leathery skin had given way to the blasting of sand and rocks. The magical blood flowed out of every pore in his skin. And then, in an instant, God ripped the mortal flesh apart. In a thousand different directions went a thousand pieces of meat.

Samyaza's soul screamed in agony as it escaped. He was finally free of his mortal prison.

God looked down at the remains of his betrayer. He wondered how he could have gone unaware for so long. He wondered if there were any others hiding from him. His anger grew as he looked up at the fleeing angel. He cast Samyaza's spirit out of the mundane world. The fallen one couldn't wait to get back home, to Hell.

Goliath stood in the hot sunlight mocking the pathetic humans. He laughed heartily and swung the gigantic hammer. All of Saul's soldiers stayed far back, away from the monster. A young man came running up through the crowd.

Saul, seeing that it was David, called out to him, "Get back! Keep away from the devil!"

He paid no attention to his king and ran out to face the giant. He stopped when the distance between them was fifteen cubits.

Looking down, Goliath smiled with his black gums dripping, "I shall swallow you whole, boy."

David trembled, gripping his spear.

Goliath laughed mightily, "Am I a dog, that you would come at me with staves?"

"The Lord God has spoken to me. He has given me the power to smite you, devil!"

David dropped the wooden shaft to the ground and fished the rock out of the leather pouch. He pulled it tight in the sling.

Goliath lowered his weapon and called out, "Well, so be it. I beg you, cast your stone."

The son of the fallen ones stood ready. He knew that his time on this wrenched earth would end when the Israelite loosed the stone. David stood swinging the leather above his head in large circles. He swung faster and faster until his arm ached.

He heaved as hard as he could and let the rock fly. As soon as it left the sling he knew he had missed. The stone was too far off the giant's left shoulder. It was going to fly right past him. But as Goliath turned his head to watch it soar by, it began to turn. It circled far around behind him and began to increase speed. It was glowing like a star when it came around the other side and hit Goliath right between the eyes. His skull smashed in the impact and he fell face forward into the hard ground, shaking the nearby trees.

The soldiers cheered at the sight of the giant's death. The opposing army who had temporarily withdrawn ended the celebration quickly. They charged in once more and the battle continued.

One man unnoticed by the others went to the dead monster lying in the dirt. A large stream of blood ran out from the giant's face and down the hard packed soil. The man gathered the magical substance into a vial that had been forged by the devil himself. When enough was collected he stood and ran into the woods.

The king of Hell was waiting for him. Lucifer cast the impurities out of the fluid and sealed the vial. A small dust cloud rose up from the dry ground. It spun into a whirlwind of sand and rocks. The fragments' collisions glowed bright red in mid-air as a small mass of earth and stone began to collect.

Karradel's eyes widened, watching it get bigger, forming the shape of a bird. Some of the elements were swooped up from the surrounding area while others seemed to appear from inside the cloud. When the talisman was complete the dust settled and Lucifer then bound the oval vial into place, under the bird's talons. A clap of astral lightning exploded around the necklace, sending Karradel to his knees.

He looked up, shaking with fear and excitement. He saw what he had helped create clearly, for the first time. The gray stone had striations of a white mineral running through it in jagged, sharp lines. The sculpture was a hawk and had been formed beautifully. The magic blood in the glass vial swam entrancingly, glimmering in the sunlight. A panting, nervous laugh pushed through Karradel's lips. He alone held the power to destroy the God of Israel in his hands. He was the only man alive who knew of the creator's weakness.

Karradel ran his fingers over the stone, assuring himself it was real. He was amazed at the blood's constant movement, the way it danced in the sunlight.

The magic of the Nephilim was in the hands of a mortal. God's failure was now tangible. It was something that could be seen and touched. His wrath had made way for his own death.

Lucifer couldn't help but be amused.

6:2

Sgt. Lunderman ducked under the yellow tape and stepped into the crime scene. He carefully scanned the entire area, noticing alley entrances, nearby windows, parking areas and street lighting. The closest overhead light was out on the corner of Main Street, which was a half a block away. That would've made the alley very dark at 2:45 a.m. The only vehicle entries were at each end of the block, other than the small parking area behind Bernie's Liquor.

The dumpster sat close to the building, a foot away, maybe less. The shadow between it and the brick wall would've been pitch black. Lunderman assumed that's where the attacker would've been standing when Sandy Coleman was leaving the tavern. She lived in an apartment above Charlene's Book Nook, on Main. That meant her walk home would've taken her right by the alley.

He walked to the dumpster. Two boxes of rotting lettuce fumed the air. The pavement was covered with broken beer bottles, paper, and trash of every sort. Walking around behind he saw the police photographer snapping off pictures of the dead woman. She was lying face up and arms at her sides. Her mouth and eyes were both open slightly. The lower half of her body had been covered with a sheet.

The torso had been split from the pelvic bone up to the sternum. The upper and lower intestines had not spilled out during the struggle. They had been removed, after death, and carefully set out. They sat in a neat pile beside the body. The heart also had been taken out. It lay on the other side of her. The entire surrounding area was dark, congealing red.

A big white van pulled up. The big blue and red logo on the side read Channel 12 News. Lunderman watched as the cameraman and the reporter climbed out.

"Shit. Fucking bloodhounds."

The officers at the perimeter kept them out of the crime scene. The woman with the microphone recognized him.

"Sergeant Lunderman! Can I ask you a couple of questions? It'll just take a minute."

He recognized her too. It was Lana Jennings. He couldn't stand her. She was notorious for reporting unconfirmed facts and making law enforcement look like idiots on the air. Lunderman knew because she'd done it to him once. After that, he swore that pigs would fly, hell would freeze over and they would have an honest president before he'd speak to that bitch again.

"Sergeant Lunderman! Please!"
Randal tapped Lunderman on the shoulder, "Hey Sarge, it looks like you're wanted for an interview."
He turned, "That slut can go to hell."
Tom smiled, "I'll take care of it."

The light on the front of the news camera came on and the lens focused on Tom. Jennings quickly looked herself over in a pocket-sized mirror. Satisfied with her appearance she raised the microphone up and spoke.
"On me in three…two…one…"
The cameraman pointed at her and she continued, "Another brutal murder has devastated the once quiet town of Canyon City. As we told you on lasts night's broadcast, a young woman, only 17 years old, was found mutilated and stabbed to death near Red Canyon road, just eight miles north of the city limit. Her body was discovered yesterday morning, having been slain just a few hours earlier. And now, in an alley behind the five hundred block of Main Street, another horrendous murder has taken place. Standing here with us is a local detective. Sir what is your name?"
"I'm detective Randal."
"What can you tell us about these crimes? Are they connected? Is this a serial killer we're dealing with?"
"We have not yet established a connection between the two crimes. Once we've had a chance to analyze the evidence we're now collecting, we will know if it's the same attacker."
"We've had two murders in two days. Shouldn't we assume the crimes were committed by the same person?"
"No, not at all. In homicide cases, it's dangerous to assume anything."
Jennings gave the officer a sarcastic grin, "I'd say what's *dangerous* is being anywhere near Canyon City at night. Wouldn't you agree Detective?"
Randal glared at the reporter, "There is no reason for a panic situation. The police and Sheriff's departments will both be out in full force tonight. We are however declaring a county-wide curfew of nine O'clock for all residents, as a precaution."
She turned back toward the camera, "With a ruthless killer still at large, Canyon City and its residents remain paralyzed in fear. I

think it's safe to say that these crimes *are* connected. It's just a matter of time before the murderer strikes again. We can only hope that the FBI will step in. It's this reporter's opinion that the small town of Canyon City doesn't have the experience or the resources, to handle this type of investigation."

The camera light went out and she lowered the microphone. Randal was steaming, "That was completely irresponsible! The people here are already nervous without you fanning the flames!"

"What you call fanning the flames I call drama; and drama equals *ratings*, Detective. It's that simple," she smiled confidently.

"Lunderman was right. You *are* a bitch."

"Yeah? He's a prick. What's your point?"

"We're doing the interview again, and this time leave your opinion out of it."

She walked to the van, "We're finished here. Thanks for your time, Detective." Lunderman put a hand on Tom's shoulder, "You'll take care of it, huh?"

The van pulled away from the curb. Jennings sent them a stiff-palmed, Miss America wave through the window as the vehicle made the corner at Macon Avenue. The sergeant looked back at the dumpster.

"Who was on graveyard surveillance last night?"

"Officer Robbins was on till six O'clock this morning."

"His report?"

"Holland was home all night. She went to bed at nine."

"Where was he parked?"

"On the street, in front."

"Who was in the back?"

"John, you know our staff problems right now. We didn't have anyone available…" "Bullshit, Tom. Don't feed me that crap. I want two on night shift tonight. You got me?"

"Yeah John, I got you."

Lunderman pounded a stiff finger into Tom's chest, "I don't give a fuck if it has to be *you*. Just make it happen."

"John, I…"

"The bitch is getting away with *murder*. Or she least has something to do with it. This shit is happening at night. I want the second officer on at six. No later."

"Are the Feds getting in on this?"
"Yeah. I spoke with Agent Richardson a half-hour ago. They'll be here Friday morning." "Friday?"
"Yeah, I guess they've got staff problems too," he patted Randal on the back, "Let's catch the fucker before they get here, huh?"
"That only gives us today and tomorrow."
"Yep. So let's get busy."

The two investigators walked back to the dead woman. The sheet had been pulled back over her face. Even in the daylight the shadow behind the dumpster held the thick feeling of midnight.

6:3

Sally sat leaning against the counter with her head propped up in her hand. She stared down into the book she was reading, completely absorbed in it. Finished on page, she quickly flipped to the next. She was all alone in the store. The frigid weather kept most would-be shoppers at home. The local radio station could be heard faintly in the background. They were talking about school closings, icy streets, and naturally, murder.

Sally looked up from her novel. The large front window was totally fogged over. Through the moisture she saw headlights. The Nissan pulled into a space and the yellow blur of the lights was turned off. A dark silhouette exited the car and approached the door. The tinkle of the overhead bell. The powerful blast of bitter air. Inside, under florescent glow, the figure became a man. It was Jack. Sally smiled as she stood up to greet him.
"Hi Jack. Did my grandma get a hold of you?"
He swiped the wet snow off of his head.
"No, she didn't"
"Damn, she said she would."
He looked up at her, "She said *a lot* of things. But more importantly, she's left a lot of things *unsaid.* That's why I'm here."
Her smile faded while she waited for him to continue. He pulled the velvet box out of the pocket of the thick winter coat.
"I know that you won't help me until you believe me, so *here*," he held it out to her, "Do it now but don't take very long. *Please.*"

He creaked the lid open and Sally saw the necklace inside the dark velvet.

She lifted it out and held it up in front of her, “This is it, huh?”

“Yeah, like I said, as soon as you believe me you have to come back. I’m in trouble and I haven’t got long.”

“Trouble?”

“Please put it on. There’s no time.”

“Alright Jack, alright.”

She hung it around her neck and sat back onto the stool. Jack watched as the soul expelling sensation came over her. He quickly went around the counter and caught her just in time, before she fell off the stool. He gently laid her down on the floor. She watched from above as he lifted her head and removed the necklace. He looked up and around the room.

“Hurry Sally. I’m in real trouble.”

She heard him. His words seemed faint, distant, but she understood him just the same.

In a shocked amazement she floated up through the ceiling. The snow passed through her astral body unaffected as she gazed up into the overcast sky. She could feel the gusting wind pass into her and out the other side. It was freezing, yet not uncomfortable at all. It has an almost calming vibration to it. Many energies not unlike her own, buzzed around above her. It was a multi-colored light show of dancing vapor. Each one whizzed around and back, as though they were buzzards circling a carcass. Sally guessed that there were a least thirty of them, some flew very high, while others were just above her head. She gazed around the town, over the buildings. There were no other astral bodies in sight, just the ones circling above the bookstore. It was like they were drawn there by something unseen.

Are they attracted to my light?

They formed a great spiral in the sky.

Sally remembered Jack saying that he was in trouble. He’d wanted her to hurry. Perhaps the lights above them were a kind of spiritual flare, calling for help or…maybe they indicated something else. Maybe they were the things Jack was afraid of. She got an awful feeling that something bad was about to happen. She descended back down into the shop. Her body still rested comfortably on the green carpet. Jack was at the window with nervous, alert eyes. She sank down into the flesh and found herself staring up at the ceiling fan. It spun gently, circulating the air. She sat up.

"Jack?"

He turned and quickly went to her. With a hand on the stool she pulled herself up.

"It's all true. God Jack, you were right."

He set the rope and the duct tape on the counter.

"I know, but now there are things we have to do, *quickly*."

A metal-framed chair was sitting in the center of the room. The small table in the front of the store had been set aside by the bookshelves. The closed sign was hanging in the window. Jack had used his time wisely while she'd been gone.

"I need you to lock the door and then tie me up…"

He sat down with his arms straight down at his sides, "…to this chair."

"What the hell? Jack, what's going on?"

"Please just trust me. I'm *begging* you. I'll explain while you do it."

She could see that he was afraid, terrified, and desperate. Something was happening above them. A rumble, a vibration of some kind was starting. It was like a distant thunder that wouldn't end. A biting wave of static electricity came with it. The overhead lights flickered momentarily. Sally thought the energies above them must have been causing it. She didn't know what was happening but whatever it was, it was getting close.

She walked around the glass showcase and starting unwinding the rope. She tied the end of it securely to the back of the chair and then wound it tightly around his chest three times. Then she tied each of his wrists to the chair legs. Finally, she bound his ankles. Jack pulled against his bonds, testing it. It seemed secure. In fact, the only free movement he had was his head and neck. She picked up the duct tape from the smeared glass.

She turned, "What do you want me to do with this?"

"That's for my mouth, if you need it."

He told her about the previous night's events. She listened intently as he spoke. She told him about the circling entities above them. Jack thought that the energies must have been spinning with a purpose. They were a living beacon showing Jack's position. They were telling the powerful evil that was already on its way where it needed to go. Jack was starting to realize that there would be no hiding from it. He only hoped that it would be limited by his own physical strength. He couldn't stop it from coming. All he could do was try to contain it.

6:4

Night after night the rituals continued. With each screaming, struggling victim that was dragged down into the reeking shadows, another lifeless body was heaved out the next morning.

A hundred yards behind the farmhouse was a small clearing in the woods. That was the gravesite for more than fifty. Most of them had been sacrificed prior to the complete rituals, when the circle was not yet complete. They were the lucky ones. Their souls had escaped into the cosmos. They were all far from the pain of that evil place.

But the more recent ones *were* there. They would always be part of him now. There would be no escape. The consciousness of each one had been snuffed out, like a candle flame in between his fingertips. They had entered the dark pitch of nothingness, and ceased to exist. It was like that point in deep sleep when one dream ends and another has yet to begin. That moment of pure black silence. No thought, no movement, nothing. He'd sent them to that place and locked them in. All of their feelings and perceptions had dissipated like a fading vapor.

The eight spirits he had devoured so far had given him more spiritual might than any human had ever felt. The pure concentrated energy pushed against the mundane flesh. It was changing him. The ethereal pressure inside was causing his hair to fall out in large clumps. His teeth had begun to rot at an accelerated pace and his breath was horrible. He sweated all of the time and his skin had become pale and clammy. The physical strength of his body grew with his spiritual strength. He was thicker and taller. He imagined that he had grown at least three inches in height.

He scooped up the lifeless body out of the wheelbarrow easily. Standing at the edge of the large pit, he dropped it in. The mass grave was rotten with death. The putrid stench would soon reach the highway if he didn't cover it over.

He picked up a shovel and got to work. A glaze of slick sweat covered his back, dripping onto the dry ground. Flies buzzed all around the pit, quickly zipping out of the way of shoveled dirt. Half a foot of soil was packed down on top of them with his black leather boots. One more layer of bodies would be all he could get into the clearing without anyone being able to see.

He would need a new place to hide his efforts within a week. No one ever came out there anyway. They had no reason to. No trespassing signs hung on the fence out at the highway. It had been years since anyone aside from him or Linda drove up the driveway.

It appeared as though he would get away with all of it, that no one would ever know. But within two weeks time everything would change.

His carelessness would be his downfall. He *would* get caught. He would be convicted for 62 murders, kidnapping, rape, and other assorted crimes. All because of a very foolish mistake. A victim's credit card used at the wrong place, wrong time. A cashier that recognized the name on the card but didn't recognize Killien.

A report of a stolen VISA card turned into the lead law enforcement needed to solve the crime of the decade. The mass slaughter of a growing list of victims ended suddenly with the capture of one Howard James Killien. The media called him a killer, a murderer, a monster. The Gazette Telegraph headline read:

THE BEAST CAPTURED

The beast.

They didn't know how right they were.

6:5

The nylon rope was cutting off the circulation in Jack's hands. She had tied it tight. *Very* tight. The ends of his fingers had already begun to fell prickly. He could not risk her loosening them. Luckily they had bound him in time, before it came.

Jack was sure that it was almost there. If even one arm was loose when it arrived who knows what would happen.

If my hands go numb, so be it.

The rumble outside was louder now. The whole town heard it. People stepped out onto their porches and balconies to see what it was. Naturally they saw nothing. Mortal eyes could not see the spiritual thunder above the small shop. The winding lights would not illuminate the streets of Canyon City in a kaleidoscope of blinding colors. The deep hum and the constant charge of static electricity were the only noticeable differences in the material world.

The power across town blipped on and off randomly. Most thought the heavy snow was to blame. Gas stations started closing shop due to the blizzard like conditions. The Super Wal-Mart at the end of town lost power for five minutes, leaving their customers to maneuver their way through pitch black isles. The Paradox book store lost electricity for three hours.

The blackout began just as Jack turned his arm clockwise, finding a position that allowed more blood flow into his left hand. Sally looked up at the darkened florescent tubes when the lights went out. She found an oil lantern on a shelf. She pulled a silver Zippo lighter out of her jean pocket and lit the wick. She adjusted the flame. The dim yellow light illuminated the room.

"What do we do now Jack?"

"Just wait. That's all we can do. It's coming, I know it."

She continued to look up, as if to see past the ceiling into the sky. The humming was loud now. Right above them.

"Goddammit, what is that?"

His eyes went upward too.

"I don't know. Some kind of a signal I think, calling him."

"But who…*what* would call him?"

His vision found the glass enclosure. The place that Linda had disappeared behind to get the necklace. He remembered her eyes on him as he walked slowly through the store, scanning the bookshelves.

Linda.

"I told you a story yesterday."
Sally was sitting on the floor now, leaning against the wall.
"Yeah?"
"Now I want you to tell *me* a story."
"What?"
He stretched backwards against the thick rope across his chest.
"Tell me about your grandma."
Sally seemed surprised at the question.
"You want to know about my grandma?"
"Yeah. I want to know everything there is to know about Linda."
Sally couldn't imagine how that would help them at all.
"Jack, I don't think that--"
"Come on. She's that one that sold me the necklace. She knows about its power. I don't know how or why yet, but she's in on this. She knew it would happen."
Sally jumped to the defensive. She was angry and yet at the same time afraid that what he was saying might be true.
"Don't say that. You don't know her. She's a victim in this, same as you."

It was true that Jack didn't know her grandmother. They had only spoken once in the shop. It was possible that she'd been as in the dark as he was. But the blaring question that shot to the front of his mind, what he wanted to ask her so badly but decided to hold back was this.
How well did Sally know her grandmother?

6:6

The thunder in the sky rumbled almost deafeningly now. Jack knew that it was time. The evil had arrived. He watched Sally with a fearful gaze. She was covering her ears with her hands tightly, trying to block the sound. The use of his hands was a benefit he wished he had but his suffocating wrists in the yellow rope were a precaution they both were about to be very thankful for.

The bright red astral power was filling the room. It settled in slowly, bubbling all the way. Violent little tufts of vapor popped as it faded from red to yellow to shadowy black and back again.

Jack could feel it start to push against him. He quickly eyed out Sally.
His voice was straining, "No matter what I say, no matter what I do…" He paused to gasp for air, "…*do not* untie me."
He wheezed another breath into his lungs and then went limp. His head dropped down to his chest. The tension in his shoulders fell away.
"Jack!"
He remained still, slumped over in the metal chair. Sally feared he was dead.
"Jesus, Jack. What's happening?"
She stood up shaking, afraid to approach him.
"Please. I don't know what to do."
He didn't move. She looked at him closely, trying to see if he was breathing.
She took a nervous step forward.
"Jack?"
Another step.
She bent down low to see his face. Shadow. It was too dark to see.
Another step.
The rumble above them had subsided now. Everything was totally silent.
No howling wind outside.
No breathing.
Only the creak of the hardwood floor under her foot.
Another step.
She was close now.
Right over him.
"Jack?"

The lights flickered on and then off again. The lamp sitting on the glass counter made a snap as the light bulb exploded into hundreds of tiny pieces. When the shower of glass rained on the floor it made a tinkling splash sound. Sally jumped turning her head, almost falling over. She watched as the lampshade fell down around the fixture. Her heart thumped so strong inside her chest she felt it in her throat.
A moment of light, and then nothing.

Once again the only illumination in the shop was the kerosene lamp she'd lit earlier.

Jesus Christ.

She tried to catch her breath and calm down.

"Please Jack, don't be dead. Please…"

She turned back toward him. A pale face glared back at her. She screamed and fell backwards onto the hard floor. The face that had until recently been Jack's was grayish in color. Except for the dark eyes. Thick rings of almost black flesh hung under the sockets. The drying lips were cracked and bleeding. Blood also stood in its mouth, flowing from the darkening gums. The face looked like Jack, and it didn't. It wheezed at her, smiling.

Sally scrambled backwards on the hard wood. When it spoke, she knew that it wasn't him. The voice crackled and hissed.

"Who the fuck are you, bitch?"

Oh shit, oh shit, oh fuck.

When the back of her head smacked the wall she realized she had backed away from it as far as she could go. It pulled hard at the ropes. They held tight against him, squeaking. What Jack had hoped for was true. Its astral might meant nothing here. It was limited by the body's own strength. Its defiance raged in a growling scream.

"Let me loose you whore!"

Sally stayed where she was, crying. She didn't want to look at it but she had to. It was disgusting, horrific, amazing. Her words finally came.

They shook off her tongue, "Who are you?"

It looked up from the ropes.

"The new and improved Jack, and you are?"

"S-Sally."

"The pleasure is mine, I'm sure. Now loosen the ropes, bitch!"

She clasped her hands together in an attempt to make them quit shaking.

"We're gonna stop you, you know."

Its laugh was thick and deep. A thin line of bloody drool hung down from its chin. "Even your God cannot stop me!"

She remembered the scripture in the forbidden prophecy. She'd read much more of the story than Jack had heard. Linda had only

told him part of it. It had all seemed so ridiculous yesterday. But now, looking into the blood-shot eyes of a killer who'd stolen Jack's body, the unbelievable had become conceivable.
The fairy tale had become real.

6:7

As Sally looked into Jack's eyes, everything she thought she knew crumbled around her. The evil that she had never believed existed was there, inside his dark gaze. In all that he thought, all that he did, in everything that he was, lived the only pure evil Sally had ever seen. It *was* real.

But it did not originate from some all-powerful demonic force, tempting the world with its hate. Evil was inside in all of us, just as she always thought. It was loneliness. The solitary, lack of love. Anger, hate, guilt, sadness, and fear did not need more than one person to thrive. Those things easily fed on themselves, inside a single soul.

Love however, depended on others to exist. It required one to give and at least one to receive. It couldn't live inside pure loneliness. Sure, one could love themselves but even that would diminish underneath the pain of one who was completely alone. It was absence of love that created a need to control, despise and hurt others.

That coupled with the power the dark entity had found, was the source of the evil that blazed in his eyes. It had been created, fed and had flourished right there on earth. It not only lived inside him, it had completely consumed him.

Sally figured that love was the only cure for such a condition, but for him there was no going back. It was far too late for that. The only true sin man had ever committed was allowing that spirit and others like him to be unloved.

Yes, the world had taken upon itself the business of creating monsters. While society was busy pointing fingers, not willing to accept its own blame, children continued to grow up uncared for and unloved. They began to despise the world that seemed to hate them. In the vast sea of population on the planet, they were the ones that were utterly alone. Lashing out at the ones around them was the only thing that seemed to give them any purpose at all. So beget rape, abuse, murder, and every other hate crime a resentful mind could imagine.

The criminals created victims, which in turn, became criminals themselves. The circle spun round and round. Loneliness was a contagious disease, spreading from one to another. As Sally watched the evil spirit smiling, with eyes ablaze, she knew just how deadly a solitary man could be.

Jack's energy floated above Sally looking down. Her and the thing that had stolen his body had been silently staring at each other for ten minutes. It was grinning, studying her.

She didn't know what to do and couldn't think of anything to say. So she just sat quietly, waiting it out. She prayed that Jack would come back soon. She hoped he could return at all. It spoke again.

"All right sweets, here's the deal. If you cut me loose I won't *rape* you before I kill you. Have we got a bargain?"

Sally crossed her arms, "Fuck you."

His smile got bigger.

"I'm not the bad guy you know. You may think I am, but I'm not."

Her words were sarcastic, "Oh yeah? Then who is?"

He ignored her question, "Do you want to know what Hell is like? Do you?"

"No."

He ignored her answer, "Hell is where people like you and I go when we die."

"I'm *nothing* like you!"

"Oh but you are. In Jehovah's eyes we are all damned, except a choice few. Abraham, Noah, Jesus. The list is so short that I could name them off in just a few minutes. And the rest of us? Well, we are destined for fire."

"Liar!"

"Just think about it a moment. How much time have you spent serving God? *None*, I'd expect. How much time have you spent in prayer, seeking his will? Same answer, I would guess."

He paused to soak in her reaction. She stared down at the floor. Her hair was hanging down over her eyes.

He started again, "Your God calls to him those that are close to him, that is all. Hell waits patiently for most of us."
Sally's eyes were angry, "What's your point?"
His stare seemed to burn into her skin. She could almost feel its heat penetrating her soul. As he looked through her, into the heart of her being, Sally's hands started shaking again. Sweat ran down her face, stinging her eyes. She knew that no matter how evil they perceived him to be, no matter what his intentions were, there was some truth in what he was saying. He'd been there. He'd experienced it. It was real.
"When you are drifting through the core of damnation…
…when your soul is on fire and the fear and pain are boiling in the center of you…
…when you would do anything, and *I do mean anything,* to make it stop…
…you'll wish that I had consumed you, made you part of me. At that point, in the very *pinnacle* of torment, non-existence would be a *blessing*. If I had eaten you up, your consciousness would be gone and I would take the pain for you. So you see, I am *not* your enemy…I'm your *savior*."

6:8

Jack watched from above as Sally and the entity spoke to each other. She could not see him hovering over them, but Jack knew that *it* could. It hadn't yet acknowledged him, but it knew he was there nonetheless. Everything it had said and everything it was going to say was for Jack's benefit as well as Sally's. Its eyes, *Jack's eyes*, stayed with the girl. "Men and women are very different creatures, you know. Not just on a material or societal level either. On a spiritual level."
Sally stayed silent.
It continued, "The female spirit, much to the dismay of the male idea, is the stronger of the two. The determination is sharper, the concentration denser, and the threshold for pain is thicker."
"The threshold for pain?"

"Yes, my sweet. Agony is not limited to the flesh. Astral pain is much more complete torment than one could ever experience in this place. Hell depends on it."

Sally didn't know what to say. It was almost as if the son of a bitch was paying her a compliment. She watched him closely. His face had become relaxed, nonchalant. "Gender goes far beyond the sexual organs. They are different sides of energy, completely opposite signatures."

She sat up against the wall and folded her arms in front of her.

He held a casual smile, "They even taste different, male and female. Of course, I prefer women. More gristle mind you, but the flavor is superb."

Sally's frown was cold and disbelieving. He was amused.

"I do not mean that I have eaten the actual flesh. That would be crude, *disgusting* really, and would serve no purpose. What I'm talking about is the essence, the life force. The soul. That's where the power lies, inside."

He had always been one to talk with his hands, motioning here or there as he spoke. He found it extremely irritating that he was not able to gesture with those previous words. He felt it would have had so much more impact if he'd laid his fingers on his chest. But alas, his arms were still down at his sides, wrapped in nylon rope.

He pulled hard against it, making sure it was still tight, proving to himself that he hadn't missed anything. The knots she had tied held strong around him. He would have broken Jack's arm to get out of his restraints if it had been possible. He wanted so much to pounce on top of that girl in front of him. To beat her, to rape her, to kill her. But she remained safe, for the time being.

There would come a time where she would not be so protected. He was positive of that. And when that moment came, there would be no mercy. She would scream until there was no blood left in her body. Her soul would scream until there was no consciousness left in it. He would eat her up with more enthusiasm than he'd ever had for anyone. She had defied him. Sitting there across that room, acting as though she were worthy of even being in his presence, she was mocking him.

Yes. The bitch had to die. And he knew just how he would do it.

Slowly.
Very slowly.

6:9

If they were going to fight this thing they needed to know more about it. They had to find out who, or what they were up against. Sally pushed herself up from the wood floor. She kept a safe distance between herself and the thing with the blood-shot eyes. He carefully followed her every movement. She walked to the stool behind the counter and sat down.

"Tell me who you are."

"Haven't we gone over this?"

"You never gave me your name."

"You still think you've got a chance, do you?" He smiled, "A chance to beat me?"

She looked down at the purple velvet box on the glass case. A greasy handprint had been smeared onto the shiny surface. It looked like frost.

"We *are* going to beat you."

His bloody grin was pouring with ferocity and self-righteousness. The high powered confidence dripped onto the floor in long red streaks.

"Knowing my identity will not help you."

"Humor me."

The jagged red lines in the whites of his eyes were like lightning. The anger of the storm was in his vision. There was nothing that would stop it now. He would tell her his name. The words coming out of him sounded like a punch line to a bad joke. It amused him to say it.

"In life, I was known as Howard James Killien."

6:10

Killien stood at the bathroom mirror with his mouth wide open. His shiny blackening gums dripped with dark blood. With his index finger he pushed against the loose tooth at the front of his mouth. He'd already lost three teeth and it looked like he was about to lose another.

On a nearby radio, Janis Joplin could be heard wailing out the chorus of *Me and Bobby McGee*. Singing along with the tune happily, he wiggled the tooth back and forth. He felt around the counter for the pliers. With them in hand, he curled up his lip and viced down on the tooth, watching his reflection carefully. It didn't take much force to pull it out. The root and a long strand of glistening nerve went with it. Dark brown fluid dripped into the otherwise bright white sink.

The astral pressure inside his whole body pushed at his flesh. He could feel it vibrating just underneath his skin. Killien ran his hand over his balding skull. The diameter of his cranium had grown to at least three inches bigger. His forehead protruded out in a kind of monstrous visage, making his eye sockets look dark and sunken. The flesh tone was bleached almost totally white in spots, while other patches still held some color. His fingers had thickened and the wide gold bands on them were tight. With all of the souls he'd now consumed he had become the most spiritually powerful man alive. Killien was, in fact, the largest human spirit who had *ever* lived.

With a continual consumption of souls he would soon reach the might of the Elioud, the third class of angelic giants who'd once walked the earth. He figured another twenty should do it.

He grinned down at the bloody tooth in his hand. Dropping it into the trashcan, he knew that the feast would not stop at the Elioud. He was shooting for full angelic power. He needed to reach that goal before the true shift could begin. Once there, he could take any mundane mass he wished into himself.

He could eat the whole world. He would do what God's adversaries could not. They were powerless over creation because they were never a true part of it. Their power had once mingled with it, but the energy had been separate. Killien was, as all humans were, part of God. He always had been. Only a true piece of creation could manipulate creation, if it held enough might.

The spiritual strain inside of him made his muscles and bones ache. He continually had a pounding headache and his elongating spine stabbed at him with the pain of growth. He was a half a foot taller than a few weeks ago, before the first Black Communion ritual.

His eyes met their reflection in the mirror. Killien still could hardly believe that the horrible face he was seeing was his own. He appeared as a kind of Nosferatu, minus the pointy ears and fangs. He leaned up close to the looking glass, examining the pale tones of his face.

"Blah," he said in his best Transylvanian accent.

Another tooth fell onto his tongue. He spit it into the sink and laughed. He pulled his shirt open. The thickened torso was powder white, except for a small area over his stomach. The blackened sternum and ribs underneath showed through the skin easily. He dropped the shirt to the floor behind him. His shimmering black spine sat on top of the torn flesh. It was bulging and twisted.

Another tune came over the airwaves.

The song was *Spirit in the sky*. Killien sang along happily.

When I die and they lay me to rest. Gonna go to the place that's best.

When I lay me down to die. Goin' up to the spirit in the sky.

Goin' up to the spirit in the sky. That's where I'm gonna go when I die.

When I die and they lay me to rest. Gonna go to the place that's the best.

BOOK SEVEN:
WAGES OF SIN

7:1

When God returned to the battlefield he saw that the killing was over. His people had held and the Philistines had withdrawn. He looked down at the dead giant's body angrily.

King Saul dropped to his knees, thanking his creator for giving young David the power to kill the demon. God, not wanting to hinder the human's faith, let him believe that it was he who'd visited David in the forest. He changed Goliath's carcass into ethereal vapor and took it back into himself. He knew then that something was wrong. A small part was missing.

The blood.

Lucifer was planning something. Of that he was sure. But the mystery of the stolen fluid would remain hidden to God until many years later. By the time he realized his enemy's intentions it would be too late.

The Philistines had conspired with the devil and God could not let that go unpunished. He waited three days to allow them time to reach Gath, the city of the Philistines. Karradel the scribe was with them. He went to the great temple of Dagon and descended down into the lower chamber. He meant to hide away the dark scripture and talisman where only he could find them.

Just as the afternoon sun sank under the horizon, God's punishment began. Huge blasts of lightning exploded against that ground and buildings. The clay walls crumbled into dust. The people ran, screaming. Fiery chunks of rock fell from the sky. They nearby fields caught fire and the city was surrounded by flame. Karradel knew that there would be no escape. He remained in the lower chamber of the temple, hiding from God.

When a stone crushed the house of idols it shot a thick stream of sparks into the air. The chamber where Karradel was had not been totally destroyed. He was still alive below the rubble, trapped. He cowered in the back corner of the chamber grasping the talisman.

The center of the rock from the sky was flowing red-hot liquid. A blast of heat filled the small room with twelve hundred degrees of fury in seconds. Karradel's skin burst into flames. The vial and the book fell from his hands into the clay dust and burning wood. The devil's magic protected them from the temple's underground oven.

Outside, the last of the living shrieked in pain at the searing heat. God's boiling rage washed over the city in minutes. As always, it had been swift and devastating.

So would be Lucifer's punishment. God knew just what to do. He headed for the outer realm, wasting no more time or energy on the Philistine city. It was left to burn.

7:2

Killien.

A shaking chill went down Sally's spine. She knew that name. He was the one that had murdered all of those innocent people. He had kept her grandmother trapped in that house and drove the sanity out of her. He was the reason for Linda's ruined life. Sally had grown up without her grandmother because of him. He had been put to death in the electric chair twenty years earlier, and now, somehow, he'd come back. It was almost unbelievable. No one else would've accepted it, but she now knew that anything was possible.

She believed him. It was him. It made sense to her. Out of everything she'd heard in the last few hours, it was the only thing that made any sense. But, what did he want? What did he mean to do? Maybe he wanted to finish off the survivors of his cult. Sally remembered reading the newspaper clippings in the attic. She had read that there were two survivors. Linda and another girl. She couldn't remember her name. Sally wondered if she was still alive. And if so, was she still in the state hospital? She would have to find out. The two who remained from the cult were the only ones who might have the answers to the questions that were burning her mind. She knew that the talisman the prophecy spoke of was real. She knew that its power was real. Her own grandmother had sold it to Jack. That is how Killien had gotten the opportunity to return. Then it struck her.

Oh my God.

Linda was in on Killien's plan. She was helping him, she had to be. Sally realized that she didn't know her grandmother at all. Everything she'd told her the past few months was all bullshit. She was a murderer too, the same as him. She was not a victim. She'd *never been* a victim. Her grandma had been a killer twenty years ago, and was now trying to start it all over again.

Oh my God, Linda.

She knew what she was doing when she gave the necklace to Jack. She knew that Killien would come back. She had to know. Linda knew the magic was real. Killien really had devoured souls like the prophecy described. And Linda had been his lover and his accomplice, all along.

7:3

Killien was sitting at the kitchen table eating a ham sandwich. His discolored gray fingers were like thick stone wrapped around the bread and meat. His teeth had all fallen out now and his gums were turning black. His facial features were mostly the same except the pale hue of his sick skin. The last of his hair had fallen out days ago.

Tonight's ritual would make twenty-four souls that he had consumed. His next victim sat up against the wall across the room from him. He smiled at her as he gummed his food. She was tied up at the wrists and ankles with twine. A wide piece of duct tape covered her mouth.

A slight breeze gently moved through the trees outside. Killien watched out the window as a small cloud of dust wafted up from the dirt road. It danced in the air and then settled down onto the leaves on the other side of the gravel, dusting the freshly shined black boots behind the evergreen. The man was dressed all in black, including the military style helmet. The weapon he held was fully automatic. He gripped it tightly against the dark Kevlar vest. When Killien saw him he was motioning for two other agents to move up into position.

There would be no ritual tonight. The frightened girl sitting on the linoleum would live to see another day. He got up slowly from the kitchen table and tried to look calm as he retreated into the basement. At the top of the stairs he closed the door and barricaded it with a long two by eight-inch board. He rushed down into the shadows. Linda was sitting in the library reading. He stopped at the door.

"They've found us. You know what to do."

She opened the top drawer of the desk. Inside lay a nine-millimeter handgun. She handed it to him. Killien checked the clip. It was full.

Linda rushed to the empty cell next to the ritual chamber. She stepped inside and locked the iron bars behind her. With the doors secured he pointed the pistol between the bars and pulled the trigger. The shot echoed deafeningly throughout the darkness. Linda writhed in pain. The bullet had entered her lower leg and snapped the bone.

He could hear them in the kitchen upstairs. He worked quickly going to each cell and sending a bullet inside. When he got to Elizabeth's cell she was standing at the entrance. She looked him in the eyes. The nightmare was over for her. She was almost free. A lifetime of anguish and torment ended with a burning hot chunk of lead inside her brain. Blood spattered onto the scratchy green blanket lying on the floor. The thick wool absorbed the fluid quickly. It sucked in the pain of her broken childhood. It was soaked through with unbelievable experience. Those parts of her would stay behind, inside it now. She no longer needed them. Elizabeth's spirit soared up into the sky.

Killien turned and glared into the cell across the hallway. Lisa sat waiting. She was the last. Her ears were ringing from the six previous shots. The battering ram broke through the wood at the top of the stairs. A deep voice called out from above.

"Federal agents! Put down your weapon!"

In the ten seconds that followed, there would have been plenty of time to shoot Lisa and then himself. But he wanted her left alive. It would look much more convincing to the police if Linda wasn't the only one.

His work had to continue. It was his destiny. The dark scripture and the necklace were safely hidden away. They would not find them. Only Linda and Killien knew where they were. She was the key to his return.

He gave the trembling girl a smile. He chose to spend the last few moments he had bidding her farewell.

"Goodbye my sweet Lisa. It's been great fun."

The FBI was at the bottom of the steps. Killien held the pistol in his mouth. The end of the barrel was hot against his tongue.

A sharp blast tore through his shoulder, sending him reeling to the floor. The pistol disappeared into the shadow of Lisa's cell. There were three men with rifles over him before he even realized he'd been shot. He was face down on the concrete with a hard boot in the middle of his back.

Others scattered. "Who's got the weapon?" a voice called out. "Secure the area. Get these cells open."

The handcuffs made a *click-click-click* sound around the bleeding man's wrists. The agent looked over from his prisoner. Lisa was pointing the nine-millimeter down at Killien.

"Put the weapon down ma'am. We're here to help you."

She kept staring at the monster that had raped and beaten her, the evil man that had forced them to be murderers.

"Please, ma'am. It's over."

She lowered the gun and sobbed. Turning it she grasped the barrel and passed it through the bars to the man in the FBI jacket. She sat down and rocked back and forth on her knees until the ambulance came.

She became violent when it was suggested that her and Linda ride together to the hospital. To avoid problems, another ambulance was dispatched.

Killien was taken to the emergency room in an armored van. The rest were transported in body bags.

7:4

Killien knew that what he'd admitted to Sally would hit her like a train. He knew that she would put the pieces together. He had known that moment he saw her who she was. He'd only been toying with her earlier, forcing her to introduce herself. It had entertained him, seeing if she would lie to him or tell the truth. But that had become boring, and anyway, this was so much better.

To watch her eyes as she realized that her own grandmother was part of it. To watch Sally's world crumble down around her. He smiled watching her faith in goodness pour out of her eyes in salty wet streams.

She saw him glaring at her with that toothy smile, "Fuck you, *bastard*!"

A howl of laughter escaped him. It was deep and harsh. It filled the whole room. His stare didn't leave her until she retreated behind the counter, out of his view. She tried hard to cry quietly, in the shadows, so not to provide any more amusement for the demon that had taken over Jack. The rasping laughter continued just the same. She wanted to find to duct tape and cover his mouth. Anything to make him stop. But she was too afraid to approach him. She couldn't let him see her. She would never let him see her again. If he saw her weakness, she would be forced to see his power. If they were going to have any chance at all of stopping him she was going to have to be very careful.

She hoped he didn't know too much already. But of course, he did. He knew her and Jack and Linda. He knew everything he needed to know to win the game. He'd had twenty years to ponder it from every angle. He was positive he would soon be the God of men. Looking back into the darkness behind him with a straining neck, he knew exactly who he wanted to consume first.

7:5

Killien's work for tonight was complete. He could feel it. The body he occupied was no longer giving him any resistance at all. His astral signature was totally changed now. It matched Jack's perfectly. His right to the flesh now equaled its previous owner. The ritual could now commence. But he knew that there was no time left that night. He knew that even if the body would not expel him, something else was coming for his soul.

He'd been gone too long from his place in the cosmos. It was calling him. He could sense it coming for him. He would have to endure Hell's punishment one more time.

But when its grasp let him go as it always did, his time would come. Tomorrow night he would say a final farewell to the spiraling pain and once again be alive to finish his transcendence.

He grinned up at the spirit floating above, "Thank you Jack, for everything. I've got quite a surprise for you tomorrow. You're gonna love it."

He managed a crackling laugh before Hell's grip surrounded him. Jack had a pretty good idea of what Killien meant by a *surprise*. In one blinding ethereal flash, he was ripped away. Jack followed up through the ceiling and watching him disappear into the sky.

Killien was gone for now. But Jack knew he would be back. They only had one more day to stop him. They only had about twenty hours before the game was over. Jack and Sally both knew that they were losing. Killien now held all of the cards and it would take a miracle for Jack to not only save himself, but the whole world.

7:6

Jack settled down into his body. It was sore all over and the taste of blood was in his mouth. He had rope burns over his reddening arms and a pounding headache.

He looked up, "Sally?"

She was still in the shadows behind the counter.

"Jack?"

"Yeah. He's gone."

She stood up shaking, "How do I know it's really you?"

"I swear, it's me. Did you hear what he said? We don't have much time. *Please*."

She slowly made her way around the room to have a look. Even in the dim light of the lantern she could see that the dark circles under his eyes were gone and his face had more color. He was spitting the blood out of his mouth.

She started to untie him, "Jesus, Jack if it's not really you, I swear I'll kick your ass." "Don't worry. It wouldn't take much to kick my ass right now."

It was getting close to 3:00 A.M. and his body was exhausted.

"God, you were right. My grandmother *is* part of it. She has to be," Sally started to cry, "What do we do now?"

With the last knot loose he sat up, stretching.
"We need to find some answers. We need to know who Howard Killien is."
Sally had an ashamed look on her face.
"I know who he is."
Sally spent the next hour telling Jack everything she knew about Killien, the cult and Linda.

The lights came back on at 4:00 A.M. She went into the back room to make some coffee. They were going to need it. There would be no sleep for either of them that night.

7:7

Sally quickly shuffled through the papers she had pulled out of the box. Jack anxiously waited, looking over her shoulder. She set a clipping aside on the counter. In tall bold letters it said,

THE BEAST CAPTURED.

It was a faded front page from the Gazette Telegraph. Another shorter article was from the Rocky Mountain News. It read in much smaller type,

SURVIVORS OF MURDEROUS CULT HOSPITALISED.

Sally scanned down the paragraphs searching for names. She saw Howard James Killien, numerous investigators and then, almost at the end of the article, Linda Holland and Lisa Stockard. They had both been taken to the Colorado State Hospital in Pueblo.

7:8

"What if we went and talked to Lisa Stockard?"

Sally was still scanning down the article in the newspaper. Jack was leaning over her shoulder.
"You mean go to the state hospital?"
"Yeah. They have a psychiatric ward there. That's where Linda was until a few months ago. Maybe Lisa's still there too."
"There's no telling where Lisa ended up. She could be in some other state, as far as we know, if she's even still alive."

She looked up, “We have to try. She’s the only one who might have some answers for us.”
Jack agreed. There was too much at stake not to try, but even if they found her, would they be allowed to speak to her?
“Let’s say we do find her, and let’s say they let us in. What if she’s so far gone from everything that’s happened to her that she can’t tell us anything?”
Sally folded the paper and set it back in the box.
“There’s only one way to find out.”
She pushed his coat at him, over the glass showcase.
She smiled, reassuringly, “I’ll drive.”

The Colorado State Hospital was located in Pueblo, normally a thirty-minute drive from Canyon City. Due to the slick highway, it took almost an hour. Jack spent most of that hour deep inside his fear and regret. He thought about that woman in the alley, the look of her face as she felt death’s weight on her throat. She hadn’t deserved to die, not like that.

Jack had to clasp his hands together, to keep from shaking. It felt as though the shadow in the alley, his own shadow, was over him now. It stood above him, grinning and waiting. It was ever darkening, casting its anger over Jack. He was sure that if he didn’t find a way out from under its pitch-blackness soon, he never would. His whole world would become the pain, the fear…the blood.

His breath was short and stuttering as he clamped his fingers together tighter. His back muscles seized into a vibrating cramp. Jack’s soul, soaked through with helplessness, made him feel like he was going to explode into a million pieces. He started to slowly lean forward and back, in a kind of rocking motion, in the bucket seat. It was the only thing that seemed to calm the anxious tension.

Out of the corner of her eye, Sally saw him moving back and forth, staring blankly out the window. His torso looked like it was floating gently in a swimming pool. She couldn’t think of anything to say, so she said nothing.

7:9

Jack cleared his throat to get the attention of the woman behind the counter. She had been busy typing on the computer keyboard. She turned and smiled, "Can I help you?"

Sally spoke up, "Yes. We would like to speak with Lisa Stockard, if that is possible." She tried to sound polite and respectable. They nervously waited for a response. They both expected to be asked many questions about their business with Lisa. They also expected to be denied. But they had no other options. She knew more about the cult that anyone, aside from Linda.

The receptionist said, "One moment please," and picked up the telephone.

After a short pause the person at the other end answered.

The woman looked up at Jack and Sally as she spoke, "Yes. Lisa Stockard has some more visitors."

Her vision shifted down to the desk, "Yes, all right."

She hung up. Looking at Jack she smiled again.

"You can have a seat over there if you like. Someone will be right with you."

"Thank you."

Jack tried not to sound surprised.

More visitors? Someone has been here talking to her?

A nurse soon pushed through the stainless steel double doors and approached them. "Hello. I'm Nurse Stephens. I'll take you down. Follow me please?"

Sally was dumbfounded. This was far too easy. They obviously thought that they were someone they weren't.

The nurse led them through the doors leading into a long hallway. She continued halfway up, stopping at the elevator. She pushed the down arrow and waited. The light above the doors indicated that it was currently on the fifth floor. She turned to Sally, "Your people were just here yesterday. I'd hate to upset Lisa. I suggest that you be as brief as possible."

Sally began to speak, "Actually we…"

Jack interrupted, "Don't worry ma'am. It shouldn't take long at all."

When the woman turned back toward the elevator Sally gave Jack a confused look. His silence seemed to say back to her, *you'd better let me do the talking. I don't want to screw this up.*

A ding announced the arrival of the transport they would take down to sub-level two. All three stepped inside and rode in silence as they descended into the hospital basement.

They stopped with a slight jerk, and then stepped out into a large room. A big screen television was playing a re-run of Gilligan's Island. Five women looked up from their card game at a table on the far side of the room. A Ping-Pong table sat empty. Sally stared at the little white ball next to the red paddles on the floor. It had a dent on one side. The flat spot in the plastic held a dark shadow. Somewhere inside that shadow, she could see what looked like a face. She quickly looked away.

Her vision found a young girl leaning against a wall. This gauze bandages covered both of her wrists. Sally imagined deep scars underneath where the sullen looking girl had attempted to drain the blood from her body. She pressed her eyes closed tightly for a moment and then she felt Jack's hand on her back. It felt warm, kind.

Her nervousness faded away and they walked quickly to catch up to the woman who had already made it to the nurse's station. She was talking to a man at the desk.

"You okay?" Jack whispered, leaning close to Sally's ear.

"Yeah," she whispered back, "let's just get this over with quickly."

The nurse pointed to a woman sitting by herself in a thick cushioned chair in the corner. She hugged her bent legs up close to her chest. Her body bobbed slowly, back and forth. "That's her." She gave them a disapproving glare, "Just like I told'm yesterday. Introduce yourselves politely and speak to her in a calm tone. If she gets agitated, she won't talk to you."

7:10

"Hi Lisa."

The woman was still rocking in place.

"I'm Sally Benton and this is Jack Sawyer. Can we talk to you?"

"It sounds like you're *already* talkin' to me."

They sat down on a couch across from her.
Lisa looked them over carefully, "You ain't the *police*. Cops dress nicer than you."
Jack looked down at his wrinkled coat, "No Lisa. We're not."
Sally sent her an unsure smile, "We'd like to speak with you, if you don't mind."
Lisa sat staring at her blankly.
Sally continued, "Do you remember Linda Holland?"
"I don't know nobody by that name."
"Are you sure? She was a victim of the Howard Killien cult twenty years ago."
Lisa's face twisted into a scar of hate, "That crazy *bitch* weren't no *victim.* She could better be described as a, uh, *accomplice*."
"So you remember her?"
Lisa looked up angrily, *"I remember everything."*
"I understand that this is probably painful for you but…"
She stabbed at Sally with an intense glare. Her eyes were surrounded by dark purple skin.
"But you're not here to spare my feelings, so why don't you just get to what you want to ask me."
Sally was unnerved by her straight forwardness. Lisa didn't seem insane. She just seemed pissed off.
Sally cleared her throat and asked, "Was there just one type of ritual performed or, were there more?"
"We did all kinds of shit."
"Well, other than the, uh…" She didn't want to say the word in fear of upsetting Lisa, but she didn't know how else to say it, "…*sacrifice* ritual, could you tell us about the others?"

Her back and forth rocking stopped. She looked at Sally and smiled. Her remaining teeth were dark yellow.
"You want to know about banishing and possession, *don't* you?"

Sally tried not to appear caught off guard. But the fact remained that the woman sitting there with them knew *exactly* what they were after. While Jack and Sally were uncomfortably surprised, she had become overly pleased with herself.
"The devils are at it again, huh?" Then she added sarcastically, "Is what's in *my* head gonna save the world?"

Jack spoke up for the first time, "Let's just sat that any information you can provide would be very important to us."
Lisa gave them a disgusted glare. She took a deep breath and put her feet down on the floor. She leaned in close to them.
"All right. My cell was the closest to their little…*meeting* room. I heard them talking *all the time*. And, I've got a *photographic memory*, so I remember all of it."
She wiped her nose and continued, "One time they brought this man down there. I don't know what he looked like. I only seen him once. They did the banishing ritual on him. They used the bird and called out some such crap from that book. *We cast thee out from thy temple*, or some shit like that."
She paused to see if they doubted her self-proclaimed photographic memory.
"It was a *fucking* long time ago. Gimmie a *break*."
Sally tried to sound empathetic, "It's alright. Go on."
"Okay. He was cast out of his body. You know, his *soul*. And then Killien hopped right in. He possessed him for an hour or so, until the body spat him out."
Jack was confused, "What do you mean?"
"Look, anyone can take over a body with no spirit for *a while*. But it will eventually knock yer ass out, cause it doesn't belong there."
"So he couldn't control him for good?"
"Well, not at *first*. You see, the body needs energy it recognizes, otherwise it rejects it, just like an organ transplant. If it doesn't like you, you're outa there."
"But after awhile the body starts to recognize the spirit? It starts to accept it?"
"Yes. But not because the *body* changes. Because the *spirit* changes."
Sally's puzzled look was obvious. "I don't get it."
"Each mortal body has only one astral signature it will mesh with. As a soul spends time in that body, it will begin to take on that signature, and the more time it can remain in the body. And after awhile, it don't take long neither, that spirit will have as much right to the person as the original does."

Jack understood what was happening now. Killien had been trying to steal his body.

"But he couldn't go all the way. The more his energy matched that man's body, the less it matched his own." Lisa laughed to herself, "The sonofabitch's own body started kicking *him* out. It served that asshole right."
"What other rituals do you know about?"
"There were the binding spells."
"*Spells*? There were more than one?"
"Yeah. One of them bound a body and a spirit together, after the body *accepted* it of course. After that the soul was locked in, it couldn't leave. As long as there was life in the body, the energy was fused together with it."
"That's what Killien is trying to do. He wants to steal my body, for *good*," a chill went down Jack's spine.
Lisa looked at him, "If he's trying to take you, he wouldn't be performing *that* spell."
"Why not?"
"The whole point of all of it for that sick fucker was to gain power. He was becoming a god. And how did he do *that,* you may ask. Well the sacrificial ritual was more than just that. It was the Black Communion. That's where he absorbed the dying person's soul. *Death* for the *dead*."
"My *God*."
"Yeah. And you need to *travel* to do that."
Sally looked at Jack, "He'd want to continue his work."
Lisa's voice became a whisper, "It's the *other* binding spell he'd be looking to do on you."
"Tell us."
"The other one lays claim to a mortal body. It makes the universe recognize it as *his*. That way he would still be free to travel, perform rituals, and *everything*."
"But what would that do to me?"
"If he took your place on earth, well, you'd have to take *his* place. You'd switch with him."
"What's his place?"
"If there's any justice at all, I suppose his place would be in Hell."
Jesus.

Jack remembered the swirling torment, the pain he saw at the outer realm. *That* was Hell. The souls there were screaming in the pain. And Jack had seen *him*. He was sure it was Killien. He was the only one that had the power to leave. He was glowing bright, very strong.

My god, I could end up in that place. I can't let that happen. But how do I stop it?

"How do we beat him? Please tell us."

"If he has as much connection with your flesh as you do, God help us all."

"There *has* to be a way."

"You couldn't do it by yourself. You'd need help."

"From who? *God*?"

"Let's just say I've been present while Killien consumed more than twenty souls. He's almost as powerful as an angel."

"As powerful as an *angel*?"

"No. *Almost.* He's not a god yet."

"So we would need the help of an angel?"

"Don't be fooled. There are *two kinds* of angels. While one might help you, the other might trick you."

"How do we know the difference?"

"God casts away those who don't follow him. If you can find God, you can find his angels."

Jack remembered the extraordinary feeling he'd gotten from the exploding cloud.

"*Heaven.* That's where God is. I've been there."

"He and the place are the same. If you've seen heaven, you've seen God."

I touched God?

The wonderful sensation of bliss that he'd felt had been from God himself. Jack could barely comprehend it.

Lisa didn't want to them to leave just yet, "And the *book*, you'll need the book if you want to use the spells against him."

"But how?"

"I don't know. I don't know *everything*."

A nurse walked up and put a hand on her shoulder, "It's time for lunch Lisa, alright?"

She stood up.

"Just know that it's a war. It's been going on since the beginning. You can be the turning point or you can be a casualty. Either way, you're not just fighting for yourself. You're fighting for all of us."

7:11

Sally stood in the frigid air next to the Nissan. She shivered waiting for Jack to unlock the door. They got in and he started the engine. Cool air blasted at them from the vents. He turned down the fan.

"We need that book. Do you think you can get it?"

"I don't know Jack. What if I got caught?" What if she…"

Sally could hardly believe that she was afraid of her own grandmother.

"Think of what's at stake. We have to get it."

"I know, I…wait. The house next door to hers is empty. It's been up for rent for a month now. If I could get in there I could wait till she's not home, or *something*."

"I'll drop you off at your car. Please, do whatever it takes. Just get the book."

"And then what Jack? What do we do, even if we get it?"

"I don't know."

The winter storm that had subsided that morning was beginning again. The temperature was down to fifteen degrees. By nightfall if would be below zero. It had started again. Jack hoped that he would have an opportunity to see the sun again. With each passing minute, it seemed further and further away.

7:12

Linda rested her cheek on the receiver. After three rings the woman at the other end picked up. Linda's voice was friendly and cheerful.

"Hello, Betty? Yes, this is Linda. You're still coming, aren't you?"

A pause.

Linda held the plastic charcoal lighter in her left hand. She clicked the trigger and a flame shot out the end. She held it up staring into the orange fire as it twitched.

She spoke again, "Yes, of course *gin* rummy…Well, I don't know how to play regular rummy either."
Another pause.
"Yes…Oh and Betty, go through the alley and come in the back door, would you? The front's jammed completely shut. Must be all the moisture we're having…Alright, fifteen minutes. See you then."

7:13

Jack watched as Sally sped away in the Volkswagen. He could not go with her. He had his own task to accomplish. He thought about what Lisa had said. Could everything that was happening now really mean the end of the world? It seemed ridiculous.
The death of God? God can't die, can he?
He didn't even believe in God before all of this started happening. And now, he was rushing to find him. He had to if he was going to save himself and everything, from Killien.

He clicked open the deadbolt with the key Sally had given him. He entered the bookstore. The metal chair was still sitting in the middle of the room. The yellow nylon rope lay in a winding pile on the floor. He pulled the purple velvet box out of his deep coat pocket. With the lid open he took a few seconds to watch the ever-flowing liquid in the glass vial. The blood that had once pumped through the veins of the Nephilim looked black and cold.

7:14

"Goddamn storm," Linda said under her breath, looking out the window.

She hated snow. She hated being cold. She hated driving on slick streets. But she would have to. This was it, the day they'd waited twenty years for. If it were going to happen, she'd have to leave the house. Her lover was ready to come back to her. He'd spent enough time in the other world. His place was there, with her. Their work needed to continue. It was fate that had chosen them for their grand task. Killien would be a God. She would be the beneficiary of his power. He wouldn't kill her. She meant too much to him. She was sure that he would create a new world for them, away from all of the pain of this one. Humanity would no longer exist. They'd be the last two, living in their own heaven.

If she had known Killien's *real* plan or what Lucifer would do if he were loosed, she would have stopped then and there. If she had felt like she was in any danger at all, she would have stopped. But her lover had promised her eternal life, and she believed him. And even Killien himself didn't know what trickery the devil had planned.

A good strategy always has many pawns. They were all proof of that. Jack was the only one who realized just how expendable he really was.

A knock sounded at the back door. Linda got up from the kitchen table, smiling through the window at her neighbor. Opening the door she said enthusiastically, "Hi Betty. Come on in."

The woman wiped her feet on the mat and entered. She lowered her snow-covered scarf as she spoke.

"It sure is coming down out there."

"It sure is. Say, follow me to the bedroom. I want to show you something."

"Alright," she said, walking slowly.

Betty stepped into the room and Linda shut the door behind her, reaching for the nightstand. When she turned around she was holding a large silver knife with a wide blade.

"Have you ever done any acting Betty?"

Staring uneasily at the blade she responded, "No. I can't say that I have."

"None at all?"

"Not even in grade school. I've always been too shy for that type of thing."

Linda's eyes lit up, "Well you won't have to worry about being shy today."

"I'm sorry?"

Linda lunged forward and sliced the woman across the chest. Blood poured as Betty fell to the floor. Gripping her wound, she weakly attempted to crawl away.

Linda was over her with the dripping knife, "You see, it doesn't matter *if* they catch me. It only matters *when.* That's why I need you to put on a good performance today."

The woman on the floor gagged. Her lungs heaved at the air around her.

"Oh, I didn't tell you? You'll be playing me today," She stepped up, "I know what you're thinking Betty. What's your motivation? Right?"

She took a handful of gray hair and pulled the head up. The blade was at Betty's neck. "Here's your motivation, Bitch."

The cold steel sliced through the jugular, emptying her bloodstream onto the carpet. Linda calmly sat down on the bed, watching her neighbor's body twitch.

7:15

Jack soared higher into the void. It had been a long time since he's seen other astral beings of any kind. It appeared that they were all behind him now. He flew as fast as he could into the pitch-black nothingness. He was sure that was the direction he'd gone before, when he saw Heaven. Only at the time he didn't know it had been God himself. But now, it was different. There was nothing out there. It had all moved. He kept going, hoping that he would find something, anything that could help him. He couldn't stop thinking that if he didn't find God, he was damned inside a course of events that could not be stopped.

A tiny light appeared far in the distance. It was like a faint star. He couldn't decide at first if it was real or his imagination. He thought perhaps that he needed to find it so desperately that his mind was playing tricks on him. But as he got closer her saw that it was really there. It got brighter as he approached. He kept going full speed. It was getting bigger.

The mundane world was so far behind him now he didn't know if he'd ever find his way back. He couldn't be concerned with that now though. He'd have to worry about that when his task was complete. If that ever-brightening star he saw was God, he couldn't figure out why he would've moved so far out. Sure, God could move about as he pleased but Jack wondered if there was some reason he'd traveled so far. Did what was happening now have something to do with it? Was he, the creator of the world, afraid? Or maybe just strategically positioning himself for a battle? Maybe the final war between God and Lucifer, the great Armageddon, would take place here, at the edge of the universe.

Jack was close enough now to see the exploding rainbow of energy. Blinding lightning curved around the perpetual blast in huge arcs. Dots of astral energy swam around it randomly like tadpoles in an aquarium. They were God's own angels and were drawn to his power, like moths to a light bulb.

He raced straight toward it, watching it grow bigger as he neared. Finally he was close enough to feel its warmth, its vibration. It felt different than before. The peace and comfort he'd experienced, the bliss of ultimate calm had been replaced with frustration and confusion. There was a fear that lived inside that cloud. Not for itself, but for the whole mundane existence. Jack did not displace the field of sadness for mankind. It passed through him and he could feel every part of his being become saturated with it. He was dripping with God's regret.

And yet, somewhere deep inside all of it was a will, a desire that could not be overlooked. It was a fire that burned with determination and strength. It was telling Jack that it hadn't given up. It felt almost as if God himself was telling him not to lie down and die just yet.

The cloud took up his entire frontal vision now. He was close. A large glowing astral mass was flying quickly up behind him. He turned, throwing himself into its path. He had to get its attention.

It did not stop or even slow down. It plowed into him full force, sending him backward into the cloud. When the momentum finally let loose he was at least ten feet inside the mist. Its power surrounded him, snapping at his glowing body. Then a pressure started building at his back. The heat pulsed in ever quickening bursts. And then, as if being shot from a cannon, Jack was pushed out of the cloud. His astral form sucked into a small tight sphere as he flew. He tried to stop himself. He couldn't. The etheric ball started to increase in speed.

God no.

Jack strained against it. He pushed with all of his might.

Please, I need to get back.
It was no use. He would just have to ride it out. Faster and faster he flew. The stars and planets went by so fast that they had become just a slight variance in his vision. A faint streak and then blackness. Something was ahead of him.
A speck.
A blue light…Earth.
He entered the atmosphere like a comet.
Clouds.
Ocean.
Land.

He crashed into his body with the force of a train. He hit so hard the mortal flesh shook under the impact. Part of his energy overshot the mark and took a few seconds to gather itself and re-enter. Jack opened his eyes. He had a pounding headache directly behind them.
"Shit."

Two hours he'd traveled to get there. God had sent him back in less than two minutes. All of it was for nothing. He hadn't gotten the help he needed. They wouldn't even stop to recognize him. He hadn't accomplished anything. He didn't have time to go back now. He had wasted too much already. Without angelic assistance he'd damned the whole world and everything in it to nothingness.

If a book were to remain telling the history of the world, the universe and all existence, Jack imagined that there would be an entire chapter dedicated to him. The man who's mortal desires and selfishness had, in effect, killed God and ended everything.

But he knew that there would be no books, no lineage of the human race, for there would be none left to read it. The only ones who'd know his sins, or that he had ever existed at all, would be the ones that had tricked him.

Jack thought that the devil must be very pleased with the plans he'd laid. They were in full fruition and there was nothing he, or anyone, could do to stop it.

7:16

Officer Robbins sat in his car eating a ham and cheese

sandwich and sipping coffee that was still too hot to drink. The unmarked ford's engine was running and the heater was on full blast. It would've been too cold to sit there otherwise. It was parked halfway down the block but still close enough to see the front of Linda's house.

He'd been there for just over an hour and he hadn't seen anyone enter or leave. Linda carefully peeked through the closed blinds in the front room. She was looking right at him. She knew she was being watched. It was obvious. The ford was the only car on the block with billowing white exhaust pouring out the tail pipe.

"Jesus. They think I'm a damn fool."

She went into the dining room mumbling curses under her breath.

Opening a drawer on the china cabinet she muttered, "Goddamn, fucking Canyon City hicks."

She lifted the nine-millimeter handgun out of its resting place.

"They think they're smarter than me," she said with a cold smile.

Linda quickly screwed on the silencer, extending the guns length another four inches. That would make it more difficult to hide, but her heavy winter coat would provide enough coverage. It hung down past her knees. She could have hidden a shotgun under it, if she'd needed to.

Standing in front of the full-length mirror in the bedroom, she pulled the thick brown coat up over her shoulders. She checked the safety on the side of the pistol before tucking it against her stomach and wrapping the coat around it snuggly. The large black buttons would be left undone. She couldn't have those getting in the way at the wrong moment. Pulling the belt forward, she tied it tightly around her waist and the nine-millimeter barrel. A brightly colored scarf was wrapped over the back of her head, across her mouth and over her nose. She pulled the brown hood on so it hung down, hiding as much of her forehead as possible.

Only her eyes and hands were showing. The rest of her was perfectly disguised and due to the extreme weather, would look no different from anyone else who'd dare venture out on a day such as that one.

A cold blast of snow and wind chilled her when she stepped out onto the back porch. She didn't bother locking the door, she never locked the *back* door. It was Canyon City for Christ's sake. There wasn't any crime there to speak of.

Feeling inside her coat pocket she found the broken seam and felt her way through until she found the cold steel of the pistol. She held onto it tightly as she slowly made her way down the slick steps. She couldn't have a gun falling out the bottom of her coat. She smiled to herself, *My oh my, what would the neighbors think?* She laughed under the scarf as her feet crunched across the frozen white grass in her back yard.

Sally watched closely as her grandmother started down the alley on foot. She stayed far back from the window, in the shadow of the room until Linda was out of sight. This was her opportunity. She went out the back door and across the yards, entering where her grandmother had just left. She was scared to death that she would come back and catch her looking through her things. She didn't know where Linda had gone or how long she would be so she had to find it quickly.

Her job was an easy one. The forbidden prophecy was there, on the bookshelf, sitting between a dictionary and a hardbound copy of *Paradise Lost*. Sally glanced at the back door before sliding it out. She flipped through it quickly, scanning the pages. It seemed to be all there, but she'd only seen it once before. She couldn't be sure.

Hurriedly she went back to the door and creaked it open slowly. Her eyes scanned the yard and alley. There was nobody in sight. Sally almost slipped descending the icy steps but caught the iron railing with her right hand just in time. She looked around nervously once more before heading back to her car that had been parked two blocks away.

Linda walked down to the end of the alley and made a left. She crossed Elm Street and stepped up onto the sidewalk. Halfway up the block she could see the white exhaust drifting up from the back of Officer Robbins' car.

He noticed her coming up the sidewalk slowly, in his rear view mirror. She was being blasted by the icy wind. He only glanced at her momentarily, and then went back to watching her house. As he sipped his coffee he had no clue that the home he was now looking at was empty and the suspect he was staking out was now coming up behind him, clenching her long coat tightly together, trying to stay warm.

It took her a couple of minutes to fight her way through the howling wind and the barrage of whipping snow. When she had gotten up along side of his car he looked over at the old woman. Linda stepped over into the grass beside the concrete. Her left foot found a slick patch of packed snow and she let out a helpless wail as she fell onto the ground. The policeman watched her fall.

"*Shit.*"

He jumped out of his car to help her to her feet.

"Jeez ma'am, are you alright?"

"*Oh my…oh…I don't know.*"

"Let me help you."

He took her arm and pulled her up to her feet, "Are you hurt?"

"Maybe, if I could just sit for a moment…" she said in a weak, pathetic voice.

"Sure. Here, sit in my car."

He led her slowly to the passenger door and opened it for her. Linda reached out with her left are to support herself and she lowered her body down into the ford. Her right hand never left the deep pocket of her coat. With the door shut, Robbins walked around and got in the driver's side. She looked out the windshield as he closed the door. There was no one else on the street. It was just them and the storm.

Turning he said, "Would you like me to call someone for you…"

The barrel of the silencer was pressed hard against his right cheek. His eyes became wide as hers narrowed.

"What the fuck?" he cried frantically, pulling away.

The nine-millimeter made a loud *pop* sound inside the car. Blood splattered out the back of his skull and onto the snow-covered glass. His body twitched only once and then became still.

"It was so nice of you to help me officer," she teased, reaching over and turning off the ignition.

She grinned as she stared over at his dripping face. Sliding over, she gently laid him down onto the seat. Linda tucked away the pistol, checked herself in the rear view mirror and opened her door. She casually peered around as she closed it from the outside.

Looking down through the windshield she was satisfied that it looked like an empty vehicle. Anyway, without the defroster on it would soon be covered with a thick blanket of snow, just like all of the other parked cars.

She crossed the street grinning under her scarf. She carefully made her way up the frozen steps and entered her house through the front door. She had no need to hide any longer. Her little *problem* had been solved. She could now leave without anyone following her.

She began to gather up her things. It was time to go. He'd be coming soon, and she wasn't going to keep him waiting.

7:17

Sally was flipping quickly through the pages trying to find where she had left off at her grandmother's house. When Jack sat up she jumped back from the counter.

"Shit!"

"It's all right. It's me"

"Goddamn it Jack, you scared the hell out of me."

He got to his knees and then pushed himself up, off the dark carpet.

"I didn't accomplish a thing. They wouldn't listen to me."

Sally's eyes didn't leave the book. She scanned down each paragraph searching for the answer Lisa had hinted at that morning.

"Wait. I may have found something. Listen to this."

She began to read from the second section of the forbidden prophecy. It explained the nature of the spiritual energy.

"The *living* spirit is the same in all living things, save one difference. The soul of man has consciousness. Other life does not."

Jack watched her finger following the words across the page.

"What does it mean?"

Sally looked up, "I guess its means that say, a dog's energy, doesn't have an individual will. It has astral matter inside it, but that's not what controls it."

"So what controls the dog? What makes it bark or eat or...*whatever?"*

"It's all run on instinct, I guess. Its brain."
"So animals don't have a consciousness? They don't think?"
"No, not on a spiritual level anyway. Just a physical one."
Jack thought of a cartoon movie he saw once, "Okay, so all dogs *don't* go to Heaven. So what?"
Sally continued reading, "The soul of a man can exist inside a shell not of human form." Sally sat back and thought for a moment, trying to see the significance of the last line. Jack spoke up, "*Jesus*. I get it now. The *binding* ritual."
"Huh, what about it?"
"Don't you see?" We could lock the son of a bitch inside. Trap him."
"What? Inside a *dog*?"
"No, not a dog. It would have to be big enough to contain him. A horse maybe, or a cow."
The entire conversation was beginning to sound like some kind of science fiction daydream he might've had when he was a kid.
His eyes met Sally's, "It sounds crazy, doesn't it?"
She smiled at the desperate, almost embarrassed expression on his face, "No crazier than anything else I've heard in the last couple of days."

Jack remembered the relentless yapping of his neighbor's dog. He would've loved to lock Killien inside of it. He hated that animal. But Killien's energy inside of him had pushed so hard against his flesh it had made his gums bleed and muscles ache. He was afraid that if he locked him inside a dog it would soon be the size of a grizzly bear. That wouldn't work at all. They needed something bigger. Much bigger.

There are horses in fields all over Penrose, but what am I gonna do? Go steal one?

And even if they were successful in binding him with an animal, wouldn't he then be in control of that animal? Would energy with a will of its own take over the body, overpowering the instinct?

If so, escape for his soul would be no more difficult than starving himself to death. It would be an agonizing, painful way to die but as Jack thought of Killien passing through the center of

Hell, he assumed the powerful entity could endure just about anything.

Binding the energy would only be a temporary solution. But it was possible that, if the animal could be kept alive long enough, Killien's energy signature would no longer match his. It would then match the flesh in which it was bound. It would have to start over with someone else.

Naturally Killien would know that would happen. He would most likely kill the body immediately. Jack thought about the next day's headline.

Suicidal Horse Jumps in Front of Bus

or

Depressed Stallion Plunges from Royal Gorge Bridge.

Jack was sure Killien would find a way even if he were trapped inside a stall.

Horse Breaks Neck in Bizarre Alfalfa Accident.

There had to be another way.

But how? How do you cage something that Hell can't even contain?

The answer had to be somewhere within the lines of the book. It was the only hope they had. As Sally kept reading Jack said a quiet prayer to a God he hadn't spoken to since he was a child. It went just as he remembered it used to. There was no answer. God did not reply.

The silence was deafening.

7:18

Linda angrily looked over each book, one by one, that had been removed from the bookshelf before dropping them onto the dining room floor. She knew exactly where she'd left the scripture. A woman in her position would not forget a thing like that. It was too important.

"Goddamn it," she muttered to herself, "What the hell?"

Her hand clamped into fists. She kicked at the pile of papers and books at her feet. *Someone has been here.*

She was almost sure that she knew who had taken it.

"You little bitch, I'll kill you."

Linda walked to the window, peering into the side yard. The empty house next door was dark inside. She could see no movement. She rushed to the front room and carefully spied through the blinds, taking care not to touch them.

The officer's unmarked sedan sat quietly, collecting snow. Her granddaughter was no where in sight.

Damn it.

Linda didn't need the scripture. Every line of the ritual, every phrase, was inside her head. She knew it all by heart. All the magic that would be needed would flow off of her tongue effortlessly. The text wouldn't be required until after tonight's task.

Linda knew that her granddaughter would be there. Sally was going to try and stop them.

Walking into the kitchen, the old woman checked the clip. One more would top it off. She reached into her pocket and pulled out a bullet. It felt smooth between her fingers, as she looked it over closely. It was a high velocity hollow tip. At close range, it would practically rip Sally's head off.

7:19

Linda set the green oven door aside, onto the linoleum. With the top rack removed, the stove had room for her friend's upper torso. She looked down at Betty's blank stare. Her skin was pale, bluish-white. A wide gash hung open across her neck, exposing the fat and muscle.

"Jesus Betty. You need to lose some weight," she grunted, dragging her neighbor across the slick floor.

Linda rolled her over and lifted her up, into the oven. She glanced inside making sure the pilot light was out before setting Betty's head and shoulders on the bottom rack. The body was up on its knees and bent down, facing the oven floor. Linda backed away slowly, taking in the image.

She grinned, "God Betty, you look just like me."

The long plastic charcoal lighter was in her hand. She clicked the button and a small flame popped out the end. She held it up in front of her face, gazing into the twitching fire. Her index finger relaxed and the flame disappeared with a *click*.

"Lights every time," she said, approaching the oven.

7:20

Linda stepped out the front door, onto the slick surface of the porch. She turned and locked the dead bolt. Her car had been warming up for fifteen minutes. As she looked out at the windshield she saw that the defroster had melted most of the snow and ice. She carefully made her way down the steps and out to the hatchback.

Officer Nichols pulled up in the alley. Looking at the clock on the dash, it read 5:52. He tried Robbins on the radio, "Twelve, this is seven, over."

There was no response. He tried again. Nothing.

He called to the station, "Control, this is seven. I'm on location. I'm not getting an answer from twelve, over."

A woman's voice cracked over the CB, "Maybe there's something wrong with his radio. I'll send a patrol by."

"Ten-four, control. Seven out."

Linda drove her care carefully down the street and to the highway. The patrol car passed her going the other direction. When he arrived he saw Robbins' unmarked vehicle, covered in snow. He didn't bother to find a parking spot. He stopped in the middle of the street. Opening the door he saw Robbins lying over in the bench seat. "Hey man, you sleepin' on the job or what?" He bent down to see into the car.

"Shit!"

He ran back to the patrol car with his hand over the pistol at his side. He ducked into the vehicle and grabbed the microphone. "Officer down! Officer down! I need backup and an ambulance now!"

Nichols almost spilled his coffee when he heard the transmission over the radio. He stepped out of his car, drew his weapon, and headed for the back of the house. He could see a light on in the kitchen and the dining room.

He kicked the door in and said, "Fuck surveillance. I got probable cause."

When it broke open the window smashed into a thousand shimmering pieces, raining down on the floor.

"Police! Come out with your *fucking* hands on top of your head!"

He stepped into the kitchen. The smell of gas was thick in the air. The oven and the stovetop had been on full blast for almost twenty minutes, after the pilot flames had been blown out. The whole room was stagnant with fumes.

Looking down he saw a woman on her knees with her head and shoulders inside the oven. The fold down door had been removed. It was setting on the floor next to her. *Jesus. She's trying to kill herself.*

He rushed over, grabbed hold of her around the waist and pulled.

The entire kitchen and dining rooms roared in a magnificent explosion. The heart of the blast was directly in front of the policeman. He was dead instantly.

The woman in the oven, Mrs. Betty Anderson, had been deceased for hours. Unlike Officer Nichols, it had not been the fire that had ruined her afternoon.

Her day had gone to the dogs at three O'clock.

7:21

The highway was all but deserted. The snow had been coming down so thick that visibility was almost nil. Many motorists had given up their travel, pulling over onto the shoulder, hoping the storm would subside. The heavy blanket of white across the road had camouflaged its surface. It was difficult to tell where the pavement ended and the ditch began. The few cars left on the stretch of highway between Canyon City and Penrose were not going more than ten miles per hour. That made the twelve-mile distance, for those who did not find themselves in to ditch, take over an hour. Linda had left town twenty minutes before. Her car had just warmed up enough to begin to sooth her aching hands.

She hated driving in that kind of weather but she had no choice. It was happening tonight. Everything she'd worked for the last twenty-five years had all come down to now. She knew, no matter how much she hated the storm, it did seem appropriate for their task. The beginning of the end of this ill-conceived world would start with a storm to end all storms.

The blizzard had sent most to their homes, desperately hiding from its anger. And those caught in its wake would cower fearfully under it, and some would even die. But not Linda. She wasn't afraid of its power. She fancied herself a part of it and smiled at its glory. She knew full well where she was going and would *walk* to her destination if she had to. The snow and ice wouldn't stop her. It was *protecting* her.

It was almost as if the world itself knew what needed to be done to bring it all to an end. Linda imagined that it grew tired of its own existence and was as anxious for it to be over as she was.

The earth and heavens were crying out for a new beginning and she was about to answer their call.

7:22

The ever-thickening layer of snow on the tall elm sparkled in the glow of the street lamp. The tree's arms hung low under its weight. A long branch high up at the top creaked under its extra sixty pounds of punishment.

A loud crack announced to the surrounding parking lot that it could take no more. As it fell down through the other branches shimmering white clouds exploded at each impact. The last collision sent it spinning into the lines, ripping them down to the ground. The branch came to rest on the icy pavement, but not before denting the hood of the squad car. Inside, Officer Montoya spoke into a receiver that had just gone dead.

"Hello?"

He looked up at the switchboard.

"Shit."

Pulling the curtain back, he peered out into the storm. The cold air slowly seeped in around the metal frame. He squinted through the raging white flakes, cupping his hands around his eyes against the icy glass. The phone wires hung from the far pole and led down into the grass by his car. A single branch lay on the nearby pavement collecting snow. He quickly went back to the board.

He plugged in numerous cords, checking each one, “Damn it.”
He picked up the CB microphone.
“Patrol five, this is control. Do you copy?”
“10-4, control. Go ahead.”
“Yeah. A tree branch just took out the phone lines. There are no office lines. 911 is out too. We’ve got nothing, over.”
“That’s a 10-4. I copy that.”
“Stop at a phone and call the Sheriff and the phone company.”
“You got it. I’m on my way.”
“Thanks five. Over and out.”

7:23

Jack listened nervously to Sally’s narration of the forbidden prophecy. It was almost 8:00 p.m. They were running out of time. Killien would come by midnight at the latest. The metal chair and nylon rope was ready in the center of the room. He looked down at his wrists. The rope burns he’d received the previous night were sore.

Sally glanced up every few sentences to make sure he was all right. She wanted to be positive it was Jack she was reading to, not Killien.

“The male and female spirits are different sides of power. The soul of a man cannot bind together with the body of a woman. A woman’s soul shall not bind with a man’s body. The power will always remain opposite.”

“Jack leaned in close looking at the upside down words across the counter from him.

“So men and women aren’t just physically different. We’re spiritually different too.” Sally kept going, “At birth, the child assumes the visage of the parent of the same gender. Only after seven years have past will the spirit develop to individual.”

Her eyes left the page, “What the fuck does that mean?”

Jack understood, “It means until a child reaches seven years old its astral signature is identical to its same sex parent.”

“Huh?”

“For instance, my son Christopher is six years old. Until he reaches seven he’ll have the same exact astral signature as…” Jack realized that the words that were coming out of him meant something terrible. *"...me."*

Fearful horror washed over Jack's face. The tears flowed. "Oh God, *no*."

7:24

Linda turned off the headlights and put the car into park. The heater fan was on high and she held her aging fingers in front of the hot air.

Across the street a porch light faintly glowed behind the white blast of sparkling flakes. The wind was gusting up to forty miles per hour and the temperature was at ten below.

She watched the dark sky above the house. She was waiting for it.

The signal.

They would come soon. It wouldn't be long now. The last twenty-five years of her life would mean something, finally.

An anxious smile curled the corners of her lips into the shadows of her cheeks. Her eyes were glazed over with anticipation of what he had promised her.

A single tear escaped the corner of her eye. It ran down past her nose and into her mouth. She could taste it.

A slight variation in the night sky. Then another. Then rumble started in low, almost unobservable. But it was getting louder. The twisting entities in the pitch black were nothing to the untrained eye. To Killien they would be a beacon in the storm, calling him. To Linda, they were a starting gun.

It was happening. He was coming. It was time for her to begin. Her smile was big now; she was shaking with excitement.

Praise the new God. Hallelujah.

7:25

The trial came quickly after his capture. With the families of the victims demanding justice, prosecutors did not want any time wasted. Killien sat calmly in the courtroom with his shoulder bandaged and right arm in a sling. A confident smile occupied his lips most days as lawyers pointed cold fingers at him, calling him a murderer, a Satanist and a psychopath. He did not flinch once, even when they leaned closely over him, shaking fists of outrage. He only grinned.

He knew they were right, of course. He was a murderer. He was proud of that. It made him feel powerful to know that no one else in that room could have done the things he'd done.

Now, he hated the word Satanist. He couldn't stand it in the least. It conjured thoughts of people chanting out weak spells and sacrificing chickens. He in no way wanted to be associated with that kind of behavior. It also implied that he worshiped Satan. That was so far from the truth that it was almost laughable. Sure, he had been using the tools Lucifer had provided for him, but not once had he ever prayed to him or thanked him for such opportunity. Killien imagined that the devil would soon be thanking him.

And how about psychopath? Well, he loved the word psychopath even more than murderer. It was the kind of word that said, *I'll not only kill you, but I'll do it in a creative and unusual way*. Oh yes, that pleased him very much.

As the prosecution gave their closing statement to the jury, as the young lawyer went on about atrocities and crimes against humanity, Killien smiled quietly.

As the man in the designer suit, black tie and freshly shined shoes reminded them of the overwhelming physical evidence, Killien paid no attention to what was being said. He was busy with more amusing thoughts. He was not concerned about the jury's decision or what punishment he could look forward to. Those things were obvious. He was guilty. Any fool could see that. His punishment would be capital. There was no doubt in his mind.

He did not fear death. It would only be an inconvenience to him, at best. He'd be back, and when he did return he wanted to remember the faces that had convicted him. The lawyers, members of the jury, the judge. He'd return for all of them. He had already decided their fates.

Death waits patiently for everyone. The people in the courtroom that day were willing to help Mr. Killien along to his.

And he, in turn, was willing to help them find theirs, in the most creative and unusual way possible.

He began to laugh. It started as a low chuckle under his breath, but soon turned into a gaping howl. The lawyer stopped speaking. Every eye in the room glared at him in shocking surprise and horror.

The judge banged the gavel thunderously, yelling, "I demand quiet in this court of law or I'll find you in contempt!"

The laughing ceased immediately. The calm was like a dark, black vacuum in space. He looked into the judge's eyes as if seeing right through them and out the other side. Killien whispered into the center of the silence, scratching it like sandpaper.

"Contempt...*indeed*."

And he laid hold on the dragon,
that old serpent, which is the devil,
and Satan, and bound him a thousand years.

Revelation: Chapter 20 Verse 2

BOOK EIGHT:
DAMNATION

8:1

God went blazing up and out of the mundane world. He soared to the outer realm. The great spiral of Hell was waiting. Lucifer was inside the place he had created, with many of the fallen ones. It was their refuge, their home. God called out to him.

You have betrayed me for the last time, evil one! Become now what you have made and feel it's torment!

A huge blast of ethereal mass expelled from God's anger. The fallen angels fled in fear. Lucifer alone was in God's grip. He struggled, unable to move. A thick layer of concentrated vapor surrounded Hell and its master, fusing itself together and locking Lucifer inside. He raged in the spiraling prison. Its walls imploded against him, creating a devastating, torturous pain like none had ever felt.

With the devil trapped he called out, *Here shall you remain for all time. Your lies and deceit will stay with you. All that oppose me shall join you here in Hell's fire.*

God appointed a group of his angels to guard the borders of the prison for the damned. They were to be sure that nothing escaped.

So it was done. God looked upon the terrible thing he had created and felt his new weakness. It had taken much of his energy to contain his enemy. His mass was now so much smaller that he would have to be very careful in choosing how and when he would use his magic. God knew that if Lucifer ever were to escape from Hell, his enemy would hold more power than he.

The creator of man had in essence, trapped himself. No longer did he have the power to interfere in the mundane world. He would only watch from a distance.

The searing heat and pressure held Lucifer tight in its grip. The pain was so great that the devil lost the ability of free thought. His consciousness had become the torment. The center of his power had become tornado's core. Any that entered would feel his punishment. The reality of damnation had been born.

Lucifer's only hope was the plans he'd already laid.

8:2

Sergeant Lunderman walked up behind the fire truck. He looked over what remained of the back of the house. The boards were charred and crumbling. The windows were gone. Numerous firemen and police were scattered around the smoldering structure. The back wall was completely gone and he could see straight through, into the blackened kitchen. Lunderman stopped the fire chief.

"You've got two bodies inside, correct?"

"Yes sir. In the kitchen."

"Is one of them a sixty-two year-old woman?"

The chief glanced over at the burnt building and then back at the investigator.

"At this point, it's kinda hard to tell."

The bodies had been burned beyond recognition. It was going to take some time to sort things out.

"Can you at least tell me what started the fire?"

"Yeah," he said, pointing at a melted piece of plastic in the yard.

"What's that?"

"That is a charcoal lighter. You know, they're used to light a barbecue."

"Right."

"The whole back of the house was full of natural gas. So when they clicked the lighter…"

"Boom."

"Yup. You got it. We also found some melted nylon string and duct tape on the floor, along with pots and pans, you know, usual stuff."

Lunderman walked up and peered into the kitchen. The bodies hadn't been removed. They were still there. They themselves looked like charcoal.

A fucking grill lighter? What the hell?

Two of his officers and the prime suspect were dead. The case appeared to be solved. He couldn't help thinking that something wasn't right about it though. He couldn't put his finger on it but he was positive. Something about the way it had happened was very, very wrong.

8:3

Stacey went into the bathroom with an armload of toys. She dropped them into the water at Chris's feet. The rubber duck made a squeak sound when it hit the side of the tub.

The six-year-old said, "Thanks mommy!" as he grabbed for the green plastic sailboat. "You're welcome, babe," she responded, trying to smile.

Jack hadn't called for a while and the fear for her husband was making her crazy. She had spent most of the day pacing the living room floor. The last time she spoke to him had been three O'clock. Looking over at the digital clock with the large red numbers, she saw that it was 7:30.

Chris made explosion sounds as his boat with the imaginary cannon tried to sink the yellow duck. After a successful hit, he pulled it under the sudsy water with his small fingers. Air bubbles popped at the surface as he squished it against the ocean floor. He, being the captain of the ship, laughed heartily.

Stacey went down the hallway to try to calm her nervous energy. Walking through the front room she felt something cold and wet under her bare foot.

Did Chris spill something earlier?

She knelt down and pressed her hand on the carpet. It was icy cold. Looking over to the tile area in front of the door she saw small pools of water and melting snow. As she lifted her hand up from the wet footprint she knew they were not alone in the house.

Jack.

Pushing herself up she squinted into the dark kitchen.

"Honey, are you here?" she whispered.

Silence.

She turned her head slowly as she scanned the room. Her eyes had not made it back to the hallway when the baseball bat struck her across the chest. She screamed, falling backwards onto the hard surface. Linda said nothing, raising the weapon up for a second blow. Stacey grasped her chest, fighting to breathe. She did not see the next swing of the bat. Nor did she expect the third.

Her cheek found a cold pool of water on the white tile. Blood ran into her hair and across her cheek. Her body became still.

Back in the bathroom, the green plastic boat was sinking. It had a large bite taken from it by the purple dinosaur.
It never even saw it coming.

8:4

Christopher looked up at the old woman standing in the doorway. He did not recognize her. She smiled at him intensely.
"Hi there," she said in her friendliest voice.
"Hi," he responded in his most unsure voice.
"Your mother had to step out for a moment, so I'll be putting you to bed. Is that okay?" "Where'd mommy go?"
"Oh, she'll be right back. Don't you worry about that. Now let's get you dressed."

Gently dropping the baseball bat that she'd been holding behind the wall onto the floor, she entered. She dried him off and them helped him into his Blues Clues pajamas.

Walking down the hallway, he did not notice his mother lying at the front door. With his light clicked on he crawled into bed. She closed the door behind them. She went around the tall chest of drawers and shoved against it. It slid about a foot, scraping the wood floor. Chris knew that wasn't right.
Tears welled up in his eyes, "Whatcha doin'?"
She gave it another shove. It was halfway blocking the door now. Looking over, she gave him a big smile, "Why, I'm blocking out the monsters, of course." He held his teddy bear tightly against his chest, "I don't believe in monsters."

The last push sent the chest of drawers scraping directly in front of the door. She placed her hands on her hips and laughed in a whispery hiss.
"You don't believe in *monsters*?"
She approached the bed, "Well…you *should*."

8:5

Jack hung up the phone. He had let it ring more than twenty times. Sally was putting on her coat.

His son was in as much danger from Killien as he was. He knew that the evil spirit had two ways to win. If he couldn't have Jack's body, he would take Christopher's. That had been his plan all along.

"No answer. *Damn* it."

"God, Jack. What are we gonna do when we get there?"

"I don't know, I don't *know*."

She tried to sound reassuring, "We'll think of something. We are gonna beat him Jack. We *will*."

He felt inside his coat pockets making sure he had the necklace and the cell phone. Sally was holding the book in front of her. He picked up the pile of rope off the floor.

"You'll have to drive."

"I'm not a very good driver in this kind of weather, I…"

"*Please*. You have to. Just be careful."

She looked out at the road under the street lamp. Packed snow and ice covered the entire surface. The pounding wind pushed the falling snow into large circles. The storm had become a blizzard. Sally rarely had driven when the roads were icy. She even hated going out in the rain.

Jack opened the door and pushed out into the dark. Sally pulled the front of her coat together and followed him out. She looked up into the dark sky filled with angry whipping dots.

Oh my God. I can't do this.

But she would have to. Jack would not be there to drive. His body would sit next to her in the passenger seat, but the rest of him would be flying.

8:6

The cold tile was wet underneath her cheek. The back of her head was sticky with blood matted hair. Her chest was tight and swollen and her neck was exploding with sharp pain.

Her eyes opened slowly. She tried to make them focus on the

surrounding room but they would not. Everything was a bright blur. It wasn't until she pushed herself up from the floor that the swirling dizziness took hold of her. She tried to remember what had happened. All that came back to her was pain. And then she heard him. Her son. Screaming.

Christopher.

She stumbled and fell against the couch. Her head felt so heavy. Her eyelids were weak. Fickle thoughts danced in and out of her mind like flies. She tried to grab hold of one of them, any one, but they only faded away.

Another scream.

Stacey got to her feet again. She slumped into the recliner and picked up the phone. The hazy numbers glowed green and melted into one another. With 911 successfully pressed she held the receiver up to her aching skull. A steady beep-beep-beep was all she heard in the speaker.

Crying.

She stood up and attempted to steady herself.

A woman's voice.

The bedroom.

With the phone still in hand she went to the door.

"Chris?" she said in a weak, groggy voice.

The female words behind the wall did not stop. Stacey pushed her voice louder.

It made her ribs ache, "Chris?"

That time a response.

"Mommy! Help!"

She turned the knob and shoved. It only opened a few inches before it met the chest of drawers and stopped.

Oh God.

She stumbled backwards against the opposite wall. She had found a thought she could hold onto, her son. She had to get to him, had to help him.

She flung herself forward with as much force her weakened body could gather. She screamed when she hit the door. Her ribs and back ripped with agony.

The tall wooden chest fell into the room and the door snapped loudly as the hinges broke away from the frame. It stopped falling when it once again met the chest. Stacey was now lying on top of the flat, angled surface and sharp splinters. One of them drove deep into her hand as she rolled off and fell onto the hard floor of Christopher's room. "Mommy!"

Her son was on the bed crying. Linda was standing between them. The pistol was in her hand.

"You are supposed to be dead, bitch."

Christopher kicked at Linda. The heel of his foot met the back of her arm. The gun flew into the shadows. When it hit the floor a loud crack filled the room. All three of them screamed at the gunshot. The bullet entered the muscle below her right knee.

Outside in the blizzard, the wind muffled and contained the pain. Everything within remained well hidden behind the blasting wall of the storm.

8:7

The large mass of dark yellow energy was nearing the outer layer of Hell. As he passed through the glowing membrane, the pain subsided. The torment had lost its grip on him once more and he was loose to re-enter the mundane realm. He quickly sped past the angels approaching him. He started toward Earth. As he got farther and farther away from the ethereal prison that had punished him for twenty long years, his soul smiled. He looked back only once, for a moment.

The next time I see you, I will be the stronger.

Turning, he continued at full speed. His new body was waiting for him. His transcendence was waiting.

8:8

Her knee buckled underneath her when the bullet ripped through the muscle. Linda shrieked as she fell onto the hard floor. She was lying on her side, looking at an upside-down pair of bare feet. Stacey had also dropped to the floor, facing the other direction.

Christopher was frantically crying leaning over the edge of the bed. The pistol was somewhere in the shadows. Linda let out a wailing, "Aaaahhh!" as the pain caused her whole body to seize in a twisting knot. Blood poured from the open wound.

Stacey gathered her strength and kicked hard, smashing the old woman in the face. She rolled backwards into the bed as Stacey scrambled to get to her feet. The slick pool of dark red on the floor made her slide in her off balanced dizziness. Her legs swiped out from under her and once again she hit the hardwood screaming.

Both women (in excruciating pain, and determined to stand before the other) fought to pull themselves up. Christopher jumped backward crying when Linda grasped the bed frame. They each struggled to an upright position, standing unsteadily on their feet.

Covered with sticky blood, Stacey swung at the blurry figure in front of her. With the fist easily dodged, Linda took her own offensive. Limping forward on her good leg, she shoved. Stacey slid into the wall. She almost fell, but caught herself on the closet frame. She immediately threw a backhand, connecting with Linda's jaw. The old woman slid into the corner of the bedpost and tripped, with blood flying, down into the shadowy opposite side of the bed.

With Linda in the darkness yelling, "You bitch cunt!" Stacey grabbed her son's hand and led him out of the room, stepping carefully over the chest of drawers and broken door.

"You fucking whore!" Linda screamed, watching them leave the room.

The mother and son ran down the hall to the back bedroom. She felt along the wall with her hand in the darkness. Once inside, she closed the door and shoved the large oak dresser with all of her remaining might. It was too heavy and wouldn't budge against the thick carpet. Stacey ripped out the bottom drawer so her fingers would have something to grab. She began to lift. It was made of thick wood, full of clothes and excruciatingly heavy. She strained at the weight, crying.

Through the door they heard Linda fall into the hallway.

"Goddamn it!" she shrieked in the shadows.

She had a bed sheet tied tightly around her leg to deter the blood loss. Painfully, she got herself off the floor and starting limping, carefully hopping on the good leg. She grunted at each jolt to the floor. The pistol was once again in her hand, sticky with sweat and blood.

Seven bullets remained waiting inside the clip and one in the chamber. She raised it up at arm's length and pulled the trigger. It cracked through the center of the door and splintered the other side.

Stacey screamed and heaved. The huge oak dresser went up on end and then toppled over onto its top, blocking the door. The attached mirror and frame smashed under the impact. Linda popped off two more shots at the bedroom.

Stacey yelled, "Stay down Chris!"

He was lying flat on the brown carpet, his tears and snot streaming down into the fibers. A bullet cracked through the door and into the opposite wall. Another shattered the pane in the west window. Stacey dropped to the floor and crawled over to her son.

The winter air chilled the room in seconds. Linda was just outside the door. Her lungs gasped for air. They could hear her wheezing. She felt lightheaded from the pain in her leg. The blood flow had stopped. The tourniquet was tight.

Banging on the door with her fists she yelled, "You cannot stop it! He comes *now!*"

Killien was soaring downward into the streetlights over the house. He entered the hallway through the ceiling.

Linda screaming.

Blood.

She'd been shot.

Furious, he sped down into the room.

A woman and a boy on the floor.

Christopher was crying. The dark spirit smiled, approaching the child. The cloud bubbled and popped, swimming.

Killien's time had come. His energy's signature matched Jack's exactly. His son would be no different. They boy was small. It would be a tight fit to say the least. The pressure would be tremendous, but the six-year-old's body was about to accept the killer's power just the same.

8:9

Sergeant Lunderman was sitting at his desk when his partner walked in. He was holding a picture of Linda Holland, studying her face. Tom set a folder down on the desk.

"Jesus, John. The bitch is dead. Let's move on."

"I don't think so, Tom."

"She was gonna off herself by huffin' some gas. Officer Nickols walked in on her. She torched the place. What's so hard to believe?"

Lunderman looked up, "Why use a grill lighter? Why?"

"Lotsa people have'em. I've got one of those things in *my* kitchen."

The Sergeant flipped open the folder.

"What's this?"

"Missing person's report. It just came in."

"Betty Anderson? How old is she?"

"Uh, I don't know. In her sixties, I think."

Lunderman bent down and unlaced his shoe. He unwound the string out of each eye on the boot. He held the lace up for Tom to see.

Tom watched the Sergeant confused, "What's goin' through that brain of yours?"

"The fire chief said he found a melted grill lighter, duct tape, and nylon string, like a shoelace or something."

"Yeah?" he said watching one end of the lace get tied to the handle on the desk drawer. The other end was then fed through the trigger hole on the lighter.

"Tom, tell me the difference between this lighter and a regular one."

"A regular lighter has to be lit with your thumb. That lighter's got a button."

Lunderman tied the loose end to the same desk handle, "Right." He pulled the lighter away from the desk. The string depressed the trigger and the flame popped out.

Lunderman smiled, "You can't do that with a Bic lighter."

"What are you saying? She set us up?"

"Wait a minute," Lunderman said with wide eyes looking at the report.
"What now?"
"Betty Anderson isn't missing. I know exactly where *she* is," he said looking down at the black and white picture of he'd just received of the burnt bodies, "It's Linda Holland we need to be looking for."
Lunderman slid the folder across the desk, "Look at Betty Anderson's address."
"218 Elm. That's *Holland's* block. Shit!"
He stood up, "Shit is right. Let's get to work. Start with an APB on the bitch's car."

8:10

Sally drove the Volkswagen nervously down Royal Gorge Blvd. The light sprinkling of lazy snowflakes that had begun earlier in the day had grown into an unforgiving barrage of icy pellets. The wind roared through the trees, carrying its frozen message to the reddening faces of those who dared step outside. Packed snow and ice covered the road from one side to the other.

They were coming up on Ninth Street. On the corner a dark colored sedan sat quietly up against a telephone pole. The passenger door had been crushed and the window broken into tiny chunks of cracked glass that lay on the seat and floorboard. Blood from the driver's face and arm was smeared and frozen to the steering wheel. With the window gone the storm was now free to enter the car and swirl about the man inside.

Three people had pulled off to the side of the road to see if they could help. A woman was running over to the Loaf –n- Jug station to call 911. She slipped and almost fell twice as she hurried across the darkening parking lot.

A tall man opened the driver's side door. It popped and creaked. He kneeled down to peer inside. The occupant was laid over onto the bucket seat on the other side. His face was resting in a pile of shimmering little pieces of what was, until very recently, part of the windshield.

He wheezed loudly. The warm fluid was gurgling in his

throat with each breath. His chest had collided with the wheel and bounced into the dash. One of his ribs had been broken and jammed into his left lung.

The cold slickness of a leather glove was felt on his numbing hand. The stranger was leaning over him. He told him that an ambulance was on its way. He told him that everything was going to be all right.

Half-conscious now, he heard the voice as if it was in a long tunnel. It felt distant and distorted. He could not answer the tall man. He was suffocating. Blood was filling his lungs quickly. His eyes were wide now. His body shuddered violently as it struggled for air. He knew the ambulance would not make it in time. The accident played over in his mind in slow motion as he gasped.

The necklace was around Jack's neck and lying on his chest. The buzzing filled his ears as he became disconnected with the flesh. His spirit vibrated up and through the roof. A distant siren could be heard behind the howl of the wind. It was six blocks away.

The stranger could do nothing as he watched the man drown in his own blood. Jack saw flashing lights approaching. Sally slowed her car down as they passed by the totaled vehicle.

They big white van with siren blaring pulled into the parking lot. Five people now stood around the crashed car and pole. The canopy light of the gas station blinked alive and little sparkles of glass and snow lit up the pavement.

Jack did not wonder if anyone had gotten hurt in the crash. He could see what all of the others could not. A smoky puff and them a brilliant blue-yellow haze rose up out of the buckled metal of the sedan. It hovered above the car in the florescent light. Jack saw it float up into the darkness above the roof of the gas station. It paused momentarily to look back down at the accident and the people below. That moment passed quickly and it turned back to the night sky. It dashed away, into the storm and it was out of sight in just a few seconds.

Jack looked down at the sheriff deputies' car as it stopped along the curb. The EMT was over the body. He would try to revive the man for almost ten minutes before giving up. He didn't know that the soul had already soared up into the storm. Only Jack knew that.

What lay inside the blue car was just an empty shell of tissue and bone. The former owner was well beyond the blizzard snow. The mundane world had been washed away. He was entering the astral plane.

He was not coming back.

8:11

"You open this door, you fucking bitch!" Linda screamed, heaving her body at the closed door. Stacey said a silent prayer in the shadows.

Please God, help us.

She watched to see if the woman who had attacked them was going to be able to break through. It had taken every ounce of Stacey's strength to pull the dresser onto its top. She hoped the barricade would hold.

Christopher felt the rock solid pressure behind him. It started at his neck working its way down his spine and across his shoulder blades. With his spirit pushed forward, standing halfway out of his small body, he turned to see the source of the pressure. His physical and astral eyes saw the dark room behind him and the churning, crimson power at the same time. With a final shove, the boy fell into the air in the middle of the room, floating above his mother. He tried to cry out but the control over his mortal body fell away too quickly. His panic was heard only in the spirit world.

Killien took over the flesh before it could fall to the floor. The huge mass condensed itself into the six-year-old, straining into a black, almost solid energy. The muscle and skin vibrated against the entity it now contained. Blood flowed from the mouth and eyes as sweat poured. He looked out over the bedroom with Chris's vision. The joints in his elbows and knees ached at every movement. The vertebrae in the spine felt like rusty blades, carving their way through the tissue in his back. Violent strands of astral electricity danced powerfully around the flesh in jagged flashes.

Stacey, lying on her stomach watching the barricaded

door, was completely unaware of what was in the room with them. Her son hovered above, crying. He yelled, desperately trying to tell her that she had been wrong. There were such things as monsters. There was one right behind her.

Christopher's spirit looked down at the small body that now moved without him in it. His astral self screamed for her help. She couldn't hear him. There was no communication between the two dimensions they occupied.

The six-year-old fingers shuffled through the pencils in the cup on top of the desk. He found a nice, freshly sharpened one and pulled it out. Then Chris's eyes searched the floor. A black boot with a thick heel lay on its side under the bed. He knelt down and slid it out, looking at Stacey. She was still watching the door. He smiled at her with bleeding gums and clenched teeth.

Holding the sharp point above the center of her back he said, "Hello, mommy."

With the heel of the boot, he hammered it in. The pencil drove deep into the muscle. Stacey shrieked, rolling over. The floor met the yellow painted wood and snapped it in two. The weight of her body pushed the remaining length of it inside.

She gasped in horror looking up at the grin Christopher's face was sending her. His dark eyes looked sunken in the sockets, surrounded by pale skin. Bloody drool hung in sticky strands down from his mouth.

She knew it was not her son she was seeing. It was the thing that had taken her husband. It had stolen Jack's body, and now somehow it had stolen Christopher's. The monster had infested her baby and there was no doubt in her mind.

It meant to kill her.

8:12

It only took a few minutes for astral Jack to reach Penrose. He raced to his house frantically, hoping that he would beat Killien there.

Oh God, let my family be all right.

When he arrived, he realized his hopes had been for nothing. The nightmare had already begun. His wife lay writhing on the bedroom floor, hurt and bleeding. Linda pounded furiously on the barricaded door and his son Christopher hovered above all of it, crying.

Oh God, no.

Stacey desperately pulled at the carpet trying to crawl away. With every move her body made her impaled back blasted her with agony. Killien found a pocketknife in the drawer of the desk. His small fingers pulled it open. Turning back, he walked to her. The back of her shirt was soaked with a large dark stain.

He raised the blade up above her neck. Jack's soul screamed.

Stacey, turn around! Please!

"My sweet mother, your time is up."

Stacey turned and saw the flash of the blade coming. She rolled over to dodge it. The wrenching pain in her back made her scream. The sharp graphite and wood went deeper. She shoved at her son's body and it went reeling to the other side of the room against the wall. Killien knew that even in her weakened state, she was still larger and much stronger than the body he had possessed. It was time to go perform the ritual.

He stood up on the trunk in front of the window and pulled it open. With the screen kicked out he bent down and jumped out. He landed shivering in the freezing snow. Killien pushed the six-year-old to his feet and ran around the house to the front porch.

Jack followed, ineffectually blasting at his son's body. The concentrated power inside was like an iron wall. It sent Jack ricocheting across the yard. Christopher's face smiled up at him.

"I knew you'd come, Jack. You're just in time. The fat lady is about to sing."

Killien opened the front door and entered.

8:13

Sally lit a cigarette and took a deep drag. She'd been driving for forty minutes and she was only halfway there.

The blinding snow made the sky look like space. She imagined the scene in *Star Wars* when they hit light speed. The millennium falcon's windshield filled with bright streaks as it buzzed away in a flash. She only wished she could go that fast now.

The needle on the speedometer was sitting on twenty. Even that was too fast to be safe. It was hard to tell where the highway ended and the ditch began.

A pair of headlights was coming up behind her. A spinning yellow gumball flashed above them. It was a snowplow. She watched as it got bigger in her rear view mirror.

"You're goin' a bit fast, doncha think?" she said out loud.

It was clearing the right lane, the one she was in. The blade on the front of the truck created a huge wave of slushy snow, fifteen feet in the air. It came up fast, changing lanes. When it blasted past the Volkswagen the wave of muddy slush covered Sally's windshield.

"Fucker!" She yelled, quickly reaching for the wiper lever.

Her foot pressed onto the brake pedal and the car began to slide.

"Shit!"

Her cigarette fell into her lap. It glowed bright orange between her legs. She turned the wheel to try to control the slide and reached down. The end of her finger touched the burning tobacco.

"*Aaah!*" The tires went over a big patch of ice and the Volkswagen swung sideways.

"Noooo!"

Pumping the brakes did little good as the car continued sliding around in an uncontrollable circle. When it finally came to a stop the car was turned completely backwards and the driver's side tires were in deep snow. Sally gently pushed the accelerator. The tires had nothing to grab hold of. They spun in place.

The plow truck driver hadn't paid any attention. He kept driving. Jack's body was spiritless in the passenger's seat. There were no other vehicles in sight. Sally sat facing the wrong direction.

She was all alone.

8:14

Oh God, what have I done?

Jack's own selfishness had begun all of it. His wife lay bleeding and his son possessed and it was all his fault. If he only had his mortal body he might've been able to stop it, stop Linda from performing the ritual. But Sally hadn't arrived yet. She was still somewhere out in the storm. Even if he was in the flesh, Killien had power over him too. One thing was certain. Killien had thought the plan out well. But there was one element he'd had no control over.

Linda.

Jack followed down the hall to where they were. She lay unconscious on the floor. Christopher's body was screaming at her.

"Get up you stupid bitch!"

Jack couldn't stand the words come out of his son's mouth. He saw the tourniquet and the blood. She had been shot. She wasn't dead though. In shock maybe, or just passed out, but not dead. He could see her breathing.

Killien couldn't perform the ritual on himself. The only person who could was an old woman with a bullet in her leg and possibly dying. He was steaming.

"Wake up or I'll kill you! *Whore!"* With a hard slap across her cheek he yelled, *"Fuck!"*

The small face with the dark eyes turned around to confront Jack. "She'll wake up. You'll see," he smiled, "But even if she doesn't, I'll have you to play with…" the voice became a raspy howl, *"…for the rest of your miserable life!"*

Killien's energy jumped out of Chris and the boy's body slumped lifelessly to the carpet. The power was like a huge shadow of electricity with long ribbons of anger whipping behind it. The center glowed blood red, snapping its static charge.

It lunged forward, tearing at the weaker spirit. It felt like jagged claws in Jack's ethereal nerves. He cried out in pain for none to hear. None but Killien, who was pleased and dug even deeper. Jack could only shudder at the paralyzing voltage stabbing his astral spine. He struggled to break free but the vapor was everywhere. The amperage of hate was not just a physical pain, but it was also brimming with an emotional Armageddon. Twenty years of pure, unhindered Hell was pouring out of Killien. Jack was its destination.

8:15

Freezing sleet grated at her pink, numbing face. She tried to hold her head down, away from its harsh beating. Sally's canvass sneakers were soaked through, and her toes felt like icy rocks. Her jeans were wet too, up to her knees. She stood in a drift of snow that was more than a foot high. She grunted, leaning into the back of the Volkswagen. Her feet, with very little traction, slid backwards against the weight of the car. The gearshift sat in the middle, neutral position with the engine running.

She shoved and then let off and then shoved again, trying to create a rocking motion that might provide some momentum. It wouldn't move. The tires were deep in the snowy mud. She pushed again, trying to dig her shoes in. Sally slipped backwards once more.

The curved metal of the hood on the Volkswagen looked like a big smile to Sally. It was like the car itself was mocking her.

You can't move me, little girl.

"Fuck you!" she screamed at the car.

She backed up to it, lifting the bumper as she pushed at the ground like a leg press. Nothing.

The ones that depended on her were still seven miles away and it didn't look like she was going to get any closer.

"Damn it!" she yelled, kicking the tire.

The cell phone.

She almost slipped running around the car. Getting inside she felt the warmth of the heater. Jack was still silent, as if sleeping. Digging through his pockets she found the phone. She clicked it on. A green light illuminated the screen. It read,

OUT OF RANGE – NO SIGNAL.

"Fuck!"

She grabbed his shirt and tugged.

"Please, Jack. Come back. I need you…*please*."

8:16

Christopher floated above his mother, sobbing. The shaft of wood in her back thundered with sharp pressure. Her head was still spinning from what was probably a concussion. Her ribs ached. They were badly bruised. It hurt to move. It hurt to breathe. It hurt to cry, but she cried anyway.

Just outside the door, they heard a scratching of fingernails scraping wood. The old woman's fingernails. Linda was waking up, enduring her own agony. The wound in her leg made her whole body pound, all the way up to her neck. She was groggy and confused.

"What happened? I…"

Slowly, she sat up. The cool steel of the pistol was next to her leg. With it in hand, she pulled herself up, gripping the doorknob with the other. She rested her body's weight on the right leg, leaving the other to hang loosely on the carpet. The boy was lying a few feet down from her. She leaned against the wall and limped to him. She felt more lightheaded with each step. Thinking she might pass out again, she paused. Her vision was narrow, in a black tunnel. Christopher was at the end of that tunnel, just below her.

With tightly closed eyes she tried to will away her pain. She'd waited so long for this and she wasn't going to blow it. She couldn't. Her lover was counting on her.

Outside, above the frozen grass, Jack was suffocating. He could do nothing to break from Killien's punishment. They spun around in a drifting spiral of electric pain. Then they saw her. The shadow in the window. Linda was awake. The iron grip let loose of Jack in an instant. A face inside the powerful mist smiled.

"This has been fun Jack, but I gotta go now," he said before turning back toward the house.

Jack's energy flashed bright yellow, boiling, *Nooo!*

He started to follow but a force was holding him back. Focusing his attention behind him, he saw it. An enormous brilliant blue entity had appeared. Its bright haze was powerful. It spoke to him. It was the language he'd heard the entity use during

his first travel. It was the tongue of angels.
Go back. Sally needs your help. Hurry.
He turned to the house.
But, my family. I need to...
It stopped him.
No Jack. You can do nothing here. Go now.
Jack pleaded with the spirit, *Please help us.*
We cannot interfere. You are God's vessel. Only you can stop it.

Then Jack remembered a verse in the forbidden prophecy. It had spoken of energy signatures and living things. He looked down into the yard. The frigid wind and snow blasted at the frozen grass and little tree. The thin branches and trunk bent away from the blizzard's push. A soft white haze glowed from inside it.

He knew what he had to do. But in order to do it he needed his body and the book.
He also needed Sally.

8:17

Jack flew hard and fast over the eastbound highway.
Where is she?
He had to find her quickly. The ritual was beginning, and he didn't know how long it would take. Fearing he was too late already, he tried to go faster.

Sally sat crying behind the wheel of the little car. She blamed herself for sliding off the road. She wondered what could be happening at the house. Had her grandmother hurt anyone? She wondered how she could have been so stupid to believe her. Looking back on it now she saw how Linda had fooled her. She had been so utterly nice. Sickeningly nice, in fact.
She's the textbook fucking example of nice.
Her picture could've sat right there, beside the definition. Of course no one would've ever expected her big grin would have anything at all to do with the knife she held behind her back.
Oh no, not at all.
Sally flipped through the book she had stolen from Linda's house. The answer had to be there somewhere. She just wasn't looking hard enough.

Or perhaps, (she thought in a flash of cliché wisdom) *maybe I'm looking too hard.*

Either way, she did not have the solution and her frustration made her turn the pages with an impatient slap.

The blowing snow dusting up from the roadside hid all but the faintest red blur, from the taillights. Jack saw that the Volkswagen had spun around on the ice backwards. He couldn't see the shine of the headlights until he was just above the car. They were almost completely covered with shimmering white. His body took a gasping gulp of warm air when he settled into it.

Sally jerked in surprise, "Jack! God, I'm so sorry. The car's stuck."

Opening his eyes, he looked over.

"We've got to hurry."

He opened his door and went around to the front of the Volkswagen to push. Sally put the car in reverse and gave it some gas. The tires spun in place as Jack bent down. With his shoulder and arm tight on the hood, she revved it. He fell forward as the car began to move. Up in the middle of the highway she turned the wheel and backed slowly to turn around. Once it was facing the right direction he got back in. She saw his red face and sad eyes.

"What's happening? What do we do?"

"Just drive. Get there as fast as you can. I'll tell you everything."

She got it up to thirty miles per hour, hoping they wouldn't hit a bad patch of ice and slide again. She listened to what her grandmother had done to Stacey and she heard about Christopher. Jack took the book from her lap.

"I've got a plan. I don't know if it will work, but we have to try."

She listened to what she had to do. When they got there she would have to act fast. Jack finished what he needed to say and left his body once again. He had to get back to the house.

Sally was all alone again. She drove on through the blizzard as the fear welled up inside her. As much as she now hated her grandma, as important as tonight's outcome was to the whole world, she didn't know if she was capable of hurting Linda. If it came down to a standoff, Sally feared that she would lose.

8:18

Linda, light headed and weak, struggled to remember the words. The boy lay on the bed in front of her. With one hand over his forehead and the other over his heart, it began. She spoke in the spiritual tongue of the sons of God.

"Flay hooth de moki sartinase! Com hotha too beesh!"

The body shook in a violent spasm.

"Fron too ny *lunda* beesh!"

The wind rumbled against the walls. A window in the kitchen shattered.

"Luciphim de *Naldophim*!"

Stacey could hear the words faintly behind the ringing in her ears. With her strength gone, she couldn't move. She could only listen.

"Neephylym no meeka, *Yahovaphim!*"

Jack swooped down through the roof. He looked around for Chris' spirit. He was still in the room with his mother.

Christopher.

Daddy.

He embraced his son. They cried, their energy mixing at the edges. Linda called out a final incantation, "Xiaba de namtho can day!"

A thick bolt of astral lightning cut down from the sky, into the room and entered the body and spirit. It surrounded them with a clap of light and thunder. The charge threw Linda backward into the wall with her muscles seizing into a painful knot.

And then it was gone. The small eyes lined with blood opened, staring up at the dark texture of the ceiling. The straining pressure inside was still there, but the flesh was his. The body would soon grow into the size needed for its large occupant. All that was required was a little time and Killien knew that it was no longer against him.

He was the proud owner of a new body. With universal law, *God's law*, now broken he lay there lingering for a moment. He was in no hurry. He had all the time in the world.

The six-year-old laugh was twisted with the thick rasp of years of experience. Linda sat up, welcoming him to the realm of the living.

Christopher, clutching his father, frantic and confused, had been disconnected from everything he'd ever known. His place had been stolen.
He had nowhere to go.

8:19

Killien climbed over the broken door and entered the hallway. The house was getting cold. The blizzard's air was pouring in the broken kitchen window. Snow was gathering on the sink and floor.

The rumbling hum of the entities above the house was gone. They were no longer needed. He had sent them away. He stood facing the back bedroom, calling out to Jack. "Come and see my new home Jack! Come and see what you helped me to do!"
Jack's spirit passed through the door. He stared down the corridor. A murderer stood at the other end, grinning.
"Come and see my friend. See what you have done for me."
Bastard!
The powerful one could hear him, even from inside the flesh. It could always hear him. "Don't look so disappointed. This was meant to be."
Get out!
Killien crossed his arms, standing with confidence.
"Oh no, Jack. I'm not going anywhere. I like it here."
Go to Hell!
"I guarantee you, *Hell is coming*. It will be here very soon, but…" a big toothy smile took over what used to be Christopher's face, "*…it's not coming for me*."

8:20

Sally's car slid around the corner as she turned off the highway onto Fremont Drive. She let off the accelerator and it straightened out. She hoped she could find his house. She knew where Pike Avenue was but in this weather she doubted she could see the house number.

When the Volkswagen got to Fourth Street, it turned right.

The lights from the houses were vague yellow blurs behind the thick fog. Hers was the only car on the road. She drove carefully down the middle of the street keeping a watchful eye on what she assumed was the edge of the pavement.

Taking a Kleenex from her pocket, she wiped the collecting moisture from the side window. The stop sign at Pike Avenue was almost completely covered over with snow. Only one spot of red showed through. Turning left, she squinted trying to see the number on the first mailbox. It definitely started with a three, that much was apparent. But then again, *all* of the addresses on that block began with a three. The second number was covered over in white and the third looked like an eight, though it was impossible to be sure. The next mailbox was on the opposite side of the road. She slowed down to read it.

Is that a seven?

No. Not a seven.

A one?

She hit the brake. The tires skimmed the ice for another few feet and stopped. Sally threw her door open and ran around the back of the car. Her sneaker caught a slick spot and she slid down onto the hard surface.

"Ouch! Fuck!"

With her hip aching she pulled herself up. Her gloved hand swiped the snow off of the tall thick address on the mailbox.

Jack and Stacey Sawyer, 331 Pike Avenue.

"This is it!"

Leaving the car in the middle of the road, she started across the yard. The frozen grass crunched under her feet. Holding tight to the railing she went up to the stairs of the porch. It was slick. Her heart was thumping. She was afraid of what she would find inside.

What if it's too late?

Her mind shot to an image of her grandmother lying dead on the floor. Sally's hands shook with cold and fear. Each breath she took was panting, short. She reached out for the doorknob. The body in her head was no longer her grandmother's. Linda was now standing over the corpse. The slump in the darkness had become Jack's wife.

Oh, God.

The face was bloody, eyes open with a blank stare. She closed her eyes and tried to shake off the picture in her mind.

Keep it together, Sally. Keep it fucking together.

With the knob turned, she slowly creaked open the door.

8:21

Linda was watching out the kitchen window. She saw the Volkswagen with its engine running out in the street. With baseball bat in hand she limped over to the front door.

Holding it as if she were up to bat, she waited. Slowly the brass knob turned. The blast of freezing wind entered with the dark figure.

Sally turned, pushing out the storm. The door clacked shut. It was dark in the living room. Sally felt for a light switch. Her heart was pounding, shaking her whole body.

Movement.

A shadow.

Sally's voice was weak, "Who's there?"

Silence.

Oh shit, oh...

The bat swung hard into Sally's stomach. She fell forward, screaming.

On her hands and knees.

The pain.

She rolled onto her back to block the next swing.

Linda's face, smiling, "I'll kill you bitch!"

Sally raised her foot and kicked. Her wet sneaker connected with a bloody leg. Her grandmother howled in distress as she fell. She hit the floor and the tourniquet loosened. The blood flowed.

Killien's six-year-old laughter echoed behind them. It no longer mattered what happened to Linda. The ritual was complete. The body was his.

Astral Christopher felt a tingling sensation. It started in the center of his energy, pulling upward. Jack could feel it too.

The anguish.

The punishment that had ripped Killien away.

It was coming.

Jesus, no.
The powerful grip was nearly there.
God, don't let this happen.

Jack held tight to his son, trying to protect him. The searing stream of hate blasted into the room. It paused for a moment, staring at Killien inside the boy's body. With the ritual complete it could no longer recognize him as its target.

Nonetheless, it was about to take *someone* back with it to pay for a murderer's sins. That was its reason for being. The blackest part of Hell's core was waiting. It was bound to its purpose.
Its new purpose was Christopher.

8:22

The powerful grip surrounded Jack and Christopher with a fiery swirl. The anguish snapped at them as they struggled. A wall of rock solid mist formed between father and son. They were ripped apart. Jack screamed, end over end. The young spirit, now trapped inside a liquid ball of searing heat, strained against its captor.
Daddy!
Jack's energy fizzled and swam in violent flashes. He desperately pounded the dense surface.
No!
The shifting red sphere did not waver. The walls did not give way.
Don't take my son.
It was invincible.
Please, take me. Oh God, please.

It sat motionless in front of Jack, looking at him without feeling, without caring. It hovered there, blankly staring at him. Its attention then focused inward at Christopher, tasting its new soul. Then, in a bright flash of one instant, it whisked him away.

Jack's ethereal yell reached out to the unforgiving sky that had just swallowed his helpless son. He shot up through the roof ineffectually following Hell's stream. It led up into the darkest blackness he had ever seen. Jack's soul was frantically crying, soaring into the void. The terrible path led into the very heart of damnation.

The words Killien had spoken rang in his mind, settling into the most desperate cracks in his being.
When you are drifting though the core of damnation...
He flew as fast as he could but he couldn't keep up. He was losing them.
...when your soul is on fire and the fear and pain are boiling in the center of you...
He caught one last distant glimpse of his son's face through the wall of the sphere.
...when you would do anything, and I do mean anything, to make it stop...
Christopher writhed in pain, screaming for his daddy to save him.
...You'll wish I had consumed you, made you part of me...

Jack's energy exploded with fear and horror. It was his fault. He alone held the responsibility for all of it. It was he who had wanted to know the secrets of the universe. Only now was he finding out the cost of those secrets.
His own son was about to pay the price for him.
At that point, in the very pinnacle of torment, non-existence would be a blessing.
All Jack could do was watch them disappear.

And the seventh angel poured out his vial
into the air; and there came a great voice
out of Heaven, from the throne,
saying, it is done.

Revelation: Chapter 16 Verse 17

BOOK NINE:
REVELATION

9:1

God was energy, as was every angel in the universe dimensions. The astral substance was the only thing that existed in any universe. Mundane matter was only one form of that energy. All that any mortal had ever known, the earth, the sky, the planets and stars, were at one time part of an entity they knew as God. To form creation, he took from the only power source he had, himself. He had separated his own power to create a new world. In doing so he had made himself weaker.

And on the Seventh day, God rested.

Also, with every miracle he performed on Earth or otherwise, he became less than what he once was. He had become so much weaker in fact, that he and Lucifer were almost equal in strength. Lucifer, made up of similar astral energy, was also a God. For a deity was only an angel with the power of creation and manipulation. The lower angels could not be classified as anything more than demi-gods, due to a lack of concentrated astral might. They controlled some manipulation magic, but it was limited to each individual's energy structure. They did very in strength. Every angel was not created equal.

Lucifer (being second only to God) found that, as time went by, the differences between them had become less and less. The once Master and servant were now peers.

When God fused Lucifer with Hell's spiral he used up the last energy he could afford to separate. He had, in effect, trapped himself. He could no longer interfere in human activities; he could only watch from a distance if he wanted to remain the dominant power in the astral universe.

Just as God's adversary had been bound to Hell, so had the devil's talisman been bound with the earth. He had used very powerful magic in melding the necklace and the scripture to the mundane realm. God could no more destroy them than Lucifer could escape from his torment.

The threat of the dark Messiah would exist as long as the world was in existence. The devil's magic had intertwined with the mundane universe, and all of humanity. It lived in the small spaces between us all, waiting.

9:2

Sally scrambled to her feet. Linda was still lying on the floor, trying to tighten the tourniquet. Sally pounced on top of her.

A shriek.

An arm pinned under a hard knee.

“Biitch!”

Kicking.

She pushed her open hand forcefully into Linda’s face. The back of her head made a *crack* sound against the floor. A hand emerged from the shadows beside her. When it entered the dim light Sally could see that her grandmother was gripping the pistol. She gasped.

Leaning over, she grabbed Linda’s wrist shoving the hand and the gun down. With her right arm loose, the old woman punched her across the jaw. Sally could taste the blood as she fell over. When she spun around the cold metal was pushed against her forehead, scraping her skin. She froze.

Linda forced a painful smile, “I’ve got you now, you little cunt.”

Killien’s eyes were lit up with amusement.

He walked closer, “You ladies sure know how to throw a party.”

She spoke to him without looking his direction.

Her eyes stayed on the girl, “Would you like me to kill her, my love?”

Sally tried to swallow, but couldn’t.

He clasped his small hands together in front of him with anticipation, “No. I’ve got *special plans* for her.”

She felt sick. Her heart pounded like a machine gun. Sweat and tears ran freely down her face. Sally had once again found herself in the same room with a killer. Only this time, there was no nylon rope holding him back.

He was free to do as he pleased.

9:3

The brilliant blue entity stopped Jack. It held him powerfully from chasing his son.

Let go of me! I have to go. I have to...

Its haze was blinding, blocking the path.

Christopher!

The giant entity held him in place. It spoke to him.

You must confront the dark one.

Jack sobbed, *No...No.*

In the distance he saw a crack of lightning break through the sky. It flashed bright white. It got bigger with the second crash. With the third it did not fade away. It remained. Something was pushing its way into the mundane world. The white jagged line in the blackness sat crackling in the distance with Jack staring into it. It began to open.

A huge explosion poured through the lightning, ripping the crack wider over the horizon. The multi-colored fire blasted around in circles, feeding back into itself. Its low rumble vibrated Jack's astral matter and bit at his ethereal skin.

Inside the house, Killien could feel it too. He threw open the front door and stepped into the cold. He called out to the creator of the world he'd hated his whole life.

"So, you have come to witness my re-birth." he paused to laugh, "How appropriate that God has shown up for the beginning of his own end!"

The explosion answered with thunder that shook the entire universe. For a few seconds every being in existence felt the searing charge of God's anger. Jack's energy sucked up into a ball in the wake of the electric pain. Killien, master of the Black Communion and the eater of souls, dropped to his knees in agony. The thunder subsided slowly and he got back up to his feet, slowly.

"You are powerless! You can do nothing! Lucifer's magic has seen to that! I have beaten you!"

The cloud of light became silent. It stayed where it was, watching from a distance. Jack flew toward it.

Do something, please! Help us!

The bright blue spirit was with Jack. The angel of God spoke again.
He cannot fight this battle. You are his sword and shield. Only you can defeat the dark one.
Jack was furious. He couldn't believe that God wasn't going to help them.
Are you just going to sit there and do nothing? What kind of God are you?
He stopped his approach.
I hate you!
God remained silent. He could only watch.

Jack's son was gone. His wife lay bleeding, possibly dying. Sally could do nothing. Jack had become saturated with guilt and fear. He was exhausted.
Weak.
Powerless.
He hated himself for what he had done.
Jack's battle would have to start from within.

9:4

The terrible storm raged on. There was at least a foot of snow on the ground and in some places twice that much, where it had drifted up into the glistening hills of white.

The windows in the front room were completely covered over with frost. Very little light found Sally's silhouette in the corner. She was shivering. The temperature in the house had dropped down to forty degrees with the howl freely entering both the kitchen and bedroom windows. The heater had been running for more than a half-hour, but couldn't keep up with the violation of outside air.

Linda kept a careful eye on Sally and only glanced out to the yard once, where Killien was standing. She'd heard him yelling a few minutes earlier. She couldn't hear what he'd said but she had heard the voice just the same. She held tight to the pistol keeping it aimed in her captive's direction.
A sound.

The doorknob.

Powerful wind filled the room as the door opened. Killien walked in. The six-year-old had to push hard against the storm's blast to close the door. He turned calmly, peering into the dark shadowed corner.

"Alright Sally, let's play," he hissed with a grin.

Her frantic breathing stopped to say, *"Fuck you!"*

Her defiance pleased him. He knew that shortly her pain would please him even more. He wished that he had a circle of seven to perform the ritual. He would have loved to eat her up, devour her. But he did not. He'd have to settle for a slow death.

He headed to the kitchen in search of cutlery. The girl that had tied him up and defied him in the bookshop watched as he shuffled through the silverware drawer. She was still standing up to him, mocking his glory with her *fuck you* attitude. That could not go unpunished. Numerous knives clanged on the linoleum before he was satisfied.

"Ah…" he whispered, pulling out a nice sharp one.

The blade was perfect, razor thin and smooth. He smiled, turning toward her. It was time for the part he loved the most. The slick shine on his hands, the feeling of power and control.

Yes, she had angered him.

And for that, he was going to show Sally her intestines.

9:5

God, please help me.

Jack's energy sucked into a tight yellow ball. It snapped with anger and guilt swam through in violent surges. His astral body glowed with florescent, popping fear.

I can't let this happen. I can hardly believe that it is happening. If anyone would've suggested that this was even possible a week ago, I would've laughed in their face. But now that it's happening to me and the people I love, I can do nothing but believe. It's all my fault.

As Christopher's soul was dragged closer to hell, Jack wondered if he could bargain for his son. Maybe they would take him instead. *Maybe…*

He knew it wouldn't work. Hell wouldn't listen to him. It didn't care about its captives. It only knew that it had a quota to uphold.
Oh God, Chris.
If only I hadn't gone there, met her. I know that she has been using me from the beginning. She set me up and I went along happily, smiling all the way. I'm such a fool. Nothing I've learned is worth this. I'd gladly give up the secrets I've been shown to take back the things that have happened. There has to be a way to stop it.
I know now that God won't help us.
It's up to me.

Killien had cheated his way out and Chris was left to take his place. It was just as Lisa said it would be.
You'd switch with him.
It seemed that there was nothing he could do now.
Please, hold on Christopher...Please.

9:6

Jack swooped down into the Volkswagen. He lowered into his body. The mundane eyes opened wide as he gasped. It was cold. His frantic breathing created big puffs in front of his face. The book was on the seat beside him. Grabbing it, he opened the door.

The hard frozen grass crunched under his feet as he ran across the yard. When he got to the porch he heard it.
It was Sally.
She was screaming.

9:7

The silver blade was right in front of her. It danced gently back and forth in a kind of swish that might conduct an orchestra. Sally was the only instrument being played and her vocal chords were becoming raw. She jumped backwards and hit the wall hard.
"Bastard!"
He glanced back at Linda.
"Bring me a chair from the kitchen and find me something to tie her up with."

He would have to restrain her. She was a strong, young woman with a lot of adrenaline on her side and he…well he was only six years old.

Linda lowered the pistol and walked toward to kitchen. She did not see the shadow outside the window. She didn't see him, watching her. The front door flew open with the weight of Jack's body behind it. It struck her in the shoulder, knocking her down. She hit the floor and the gun went off. It made a small hole in the white textured ceiling.

Killien turned away from Sally. He let out a growl of anger. The small body slumped to the carpet when he jumped out. The popping dark energy sizzled behind him in whipping snakes. The center of the stirring cloud was blood red.

Sally got to her feet and pounced on top of Linda. The old woman wailed, straining her arm's length for the gun. Sally picked it up. She pushed it into the back of Linda's head.

"Don't move grandma…" she could barely believe the words coming out of her own mouth, "…or I'll kill you."

Linda turned and lunged at her granddaughter, growling with rage. Sally jumped back screaming. She squeezed the trigger. The pistol kicked backwards in her hand. When Sally caught her balance, she looked up with a jerk.

Linda was on her back with a dark red stain covering her stomach. Sally lowered the gun and slowly stepped forward. Linda was still. The room was dark but she was pretty sure her grandma wasn't breathing. Sally cried. Her whole body was an uncontrollable, shaking spasm.

Killien blasted at Jack, sending his spirit backwards, out of his body. Killien settled in once again taking over. He looked at Sally with mortal eyes. Jack watched his body approach.

God, no.

He looked down at his son's body lying on the floor. It had to same astral signature as he did. If Killien could do it, so could he. He flew down into it and his ethereal mass compressed into the flesh. The pressure of his large spirit in the small body felt strange. It made the skin tingle. He felt like he couldn't breathe for a moment.

He opened Chris' eyes, "Look out Sally!" he yelled, as he got to his feet.
She looked up.
"It's me Sally," Killien said, trying to sound like Jack.
"Don't listen to him. *I'm* Jack," Jack said with his son's mouth.
She stood up and backed away from them.
"Jesus."

She didn't know which one was which. There was no way to tell.
He knew just what to say to make her believe him.
"I know now what has to be done," he said.
"Don't listen Sally, he's lying" the other said.
He looked at her calmly, "There's only one way to beat him," he paused, "Kill both of us."
"No! It's a trick!"
"You know it's true, Sally. I've already lost Christopher. He's gone. Don't let that asshole win."
"No!"
"Do it now. You can't save me, but you can save the world from him."

Sally's eyes were wide. The gun was shaking in her hand. She was so afraid she could barely hold onto it. She looked at him. Her swollen eyes were brimming with cold tears. "I can't do it Jack. I'm sorry, but…I can't."
"Sally, no!"
"I understand. I started this mess. It should be me who ends it," he said reaching out his hand.
The six-year-old cried, "Stop!"

Jack's skin felt cold as she set the pistol into it. Killien accepted the weapon with a smile.
"The plan! Stick to the plan we talked about in the car!"
She turned, "Huh?"
She didn't realize the truth until the hard fist struck her jaw.
"I knew you couldn't do it, you stupid bitch."
Blood filled her mouth, "Bastard!"
He laughed.
"It appears that I'm back in business, wouldn't you say, Jack?"
She pulled herself up.

"God, I'm sorry. I'm so sorry."
"You are powerless against me. You might as well give up."

Of course, it was true. Jack had tried to fight him before. It was like hitting a brick wall. His eyes got wide.

The wall.

He looked up.

The ceiling.

He found the hole made by the bullet only a few minutes before. He got an idea. Jack knew that he was much smaller and weaker than Killien was. That was obvious, but the bullet that had punched through the ceiling was small too. It hadn't been its size that caused the damage, it had been its *velocity.*

He looked at Sally, "I'll be right back."

He soared up through the roof. The small body slumped down on the floor.

Sally cried, "Jack! Don't leave me!"

Above the house he hovered, peering into the storm. God was much closer than before. The exploding cloud hung in the sky, waiting. He headed straight for it. Jack remembered that first time he ever saw it and how it had pushed him away. And the second time, how it had sent him reeling back to earth like a comet. The first had been like a warning saying that he didn't belong there. The next was more like a punishment, with more force. What would the third be like? Jack was about to find out. With any luck he'd shoot straight at his body, just as before.

God, I hope this works.

The huge cloud of exploding light was about to become the most powerful gun in the universe, and Jack was going to be the bullet.

9:8

Jack raced toward the exploding cloud at full speed. The huge blasts of rippling color became brighter as he neared. He hit the outer energy and a biting charge filled his astral body. The pain clamped down and around him. The static was so intense he lost consciousness as his energy imploded into a small glowing sphere.

When his momentum came to an end, he was farther inside the

cloud that he'd ever been. Astral lightning danced and snapped around him in growing flashes. It vibrated faster and faster. The white-hot bolts broke apart, creating tiny hair-like streaks. The jagged light was gaining in vibration and speed.

Then, it released.

The shot sounded a thunder that shook the sky. The astral energy blasted out of the cloud like a cannon ball. The blur was an ethereal comet ripping down to Earth. God's aim had been true. Jack was headed straight for his mortal body, for Killien. The impact would announce the beginning of the final battle.

God and Lucifer.

Divine and evil.

Jack and Killien.

The dark messiah had attacked all of creation with a rage that had threatened to consume it. But the rage was no longer his alone. The creator had just entered the fray. Armageddon was on, and God had just opened fire.

9:9

Killien stepped up and hit Sally across the jaw with the butt of the pistol. She fell into the shadows screaming.

He walked slowly, "It looks like you've taken care of Grandma real good, don't it Sal?" He kneeled down to Linda, picked up her wrist and dropped it to the floor. It landed with a *thud.*

"I don't think she's goin' anywhere, do you?"

Sally crawled into a dark corner. Killien smiled into her shadow. "How did it feel, Sal, to take a life? Wasn't it glorious?" he stood up, "Shooting someone isn't as personal as I like to get…but, whatever it takes to get the job done, right?"

Sally didn't say a word. Her panic would barely let her breathe. She pushed into the empty corner and stood up, scraping against the wall. She wanted to run but Killien was standing in the center of the room. There was nowhere to go. She had seen the spirit world that Jack had shown her. Death wasn't the end. Being dead didn't scare her as much as the way Killien intended to get her there. It was the pain that horrified Sally. She stepped up shaking, out of her black corner. If she was going to die, she wanted him to have a clear shot.

She managed a few wobbling words, "If you're gonna kill me, then do it."

He was surprised, "Brave little Sally. My oh my."

Do it you bastard.

He lowered the pistol, "It's not so easy Sal. Not by a long shot."

He squatted and reached down, picking up the knife. Standing he whispered, "Where would you like it Sal? Your choice."

Outside crackling blast of thunder filled the sky. The surrounding area sizzled with static. They felt it in the house, the electric charge. Killien paused, cocking his head.

Jack blasted down from the sky, through the roof and into Killien. The two energies splashed together in a blinding astral collision. Searing pain thundered through the impact. It was a lifetime of agony in one, horrifying moment. The invisible explosion pounded the room with deafening static. The grinding sound was like bees buzzing over a loud speaker.

The static charge sent Sally flying backwards.

She hit the hard floor yelling, "Jack!" as she covered her ears.

Jack's mortal body was thrown to the floor limply. The powers had separated into sloshing yellow-black pools. When the momentum subsided they were lazily drifting liquid, defying both gravity and time. The spiritual shrapnel floated in slow motion and to each, seemed to last forever. The color began to soften, finally, as the separated pools started to find each other.

When the last glowing piece joined with Jack he took on a human like shape once again. He looked down at Sally on the floor. He saw Killien's energy still trying to gather itself. He dropped down into his body quickly. There wasn't much time. His body jerked alive as he took control once again. He sat up with muscles aching. He could taste the blood in his mouth. The pressure behind his eyes was tremendous. It was the worst headache he'd ever experienced, but he couldn't concern himself with that now.

Sally was behind him on the floor. She was dazed. Her skin was still tingling.

"Sally!"

She slowly got to her feet.

"Jack?"

"The ritual! Do it now!"

The book was lying on the floor. He scooped it up and opened the front door. Wind and snow blasted in, swirling around and through the huge entity trying to collect itself. It glowed brighter red with each hazy cloud that re-joined with it. Sally followed Jack outside. He dug deep in his pocket for the necklace. The purple velvet box fell into the snow when he pulled out the talisman. He stopped at the little tree in the middle of the front yard. Turning, he gave the necklace and book to Sally.

"Do it now, *quickly*. Just like we talked about in the car."

She kneeled on the freezing snow. Her body shivered as she flipped through the chapters. Pulling a silver Zippo lighter from her pocket, she clicked the flame alive. The pages illuminated with a dim, yellow glow. She bent down over the lighter to try to protect the flickering light from the storm's howl. Jack ran around Sally and the tree, stopping about ten feet further in the yard. He turned and yelled to her.

"Say the last line when you see the impact!"

She squinted at him.

Impact? What impact?

He saw the confusion in her face, "Don't worry, You'll know."

"Oh God, Jack. I don't know, I…"

"I trust you Sally. Just do it."

He looked behind him into the swirling sky, "I'll be right back."

Right back? Right…Oh shit!

She knew what had happened moments before, the last time he said that. She flipped to the back of the book. Running her finger down the page, she found it.

Killien's energy screamed and snapped with fiery rage. He blasted out into the yard. He looked down at her. He knew what she was doing.

I should have killed you when I had the chance.

She couldn't see or hear him. She began the ritual, raising the stone bird up to the tree, calling out the first magical words.

"See flothica dos can day!"

The blood in the vial glowed red-hot and swam in violent circles. The etheric energy expanded out in a great yellow light and washed over the tree. The edge of the energy went up Sally's arms and over her face. She could feel it pushing at her soul, as well as the astral matter in the tree. Her spirit was just outside of her flesh, vibrating. It was far enough out that she could see the astral realm, and the physical one with her mortal eyes, at the same time. She could see him. Killien's huge cloud was staring at her, boiling.

Fuck!

She tried to sound out the next line. Her words wobbled in icy cold terror. "Wha…Whatha…"

Keep it together, Sally. She thought to herself, *You can be scared later.*

Killien approached her.

He has no power over you. Do what you're here to do.

He hovered down close to her shivering body. She shrieked, jumping backward and fell into a snowdrift when he screamed in her face. The rasping howl echoed over the yard and across the street. He looked over and saw Jack's body lying in the snow. His face whipped around toward her, seething, *Be right back, sweets.*

She saw him go to the body.

Oh, shit!

She had to hurry. Pulling herself up onto her knees, Sally continued the ritual where she had left off. With the next line spoken, the white glow inside the three pushed up and out, into the air above. Her eyes scanned over the last words in the ritual. Killien stood up in Jack's body, smiling at her. She could see the dense red energy popping at the edges.

He walked to her with powerful, dark purpose, "Alright you little whore, you've been a thorn in my side long enough. Time to die." His fists were clenched.

Her scream, *"Nooo!"*

He stomped over to the kneeling woman and kicked her in the chest. The bottom of the hard-soled boot felt like a brick striking Sally's sternum. With the air knocked out of her all she could manage was laying on her side, heaving to fill her lungs. The bitter, icy snow soaked into her clothes as she struggled.

He stood over her, watching her push up onto her knees. Grabbing a handful of Sally's hair, he pulled her up. The panic in her face pleased him as his hands wrapped around her neck. With wide eyes she scratched and kicked at him. It felt like a vise around her throat. Her vision was blurring. She dug her fingernails into his forearms, pulling against the thick grip. Jack's fingers only got tighter around her throat.

Can't breathe...

The world tunneled in around her until all she could see was his face. Blood stood in his eyelids, running down over the clammy, pale cheeks. His cracked lips were smiling at her, exposing the darkened gums and red stained teeth. Thick veins sat pumping, just underneath the skin on his face. Sally stared into Killien's bleeding eyes. A snapping energy illuminated the devil's face. The glow made the pale skin bright red, while the pouring blood was flowing black as oil.

Sally's strength fell away from her. Her arms dropped limply to her sides. Her suffocation was nearly finished. She could only stare blankly at death as it squeezed her life away. The end of the black tunnel was fading. Only a small light remained.

It was not the crimson blur of Killien's spirit. This light was blue. It was getting bigger. A ripping vibration came with it.

He could feel it too. He turned his head to look.

Over his shoulder, in the sky.

A comet.

A rocket.

Jack.

Killien only caught the slightest glimpse of the approaching light before the ethereal bullet struck. The ball of astral lightning ripped through Killien like a shotgun blast, ripping him into glowing shrapnel. Sally fell off her knees backwards into the shimmering snow. She gasped for air.

"Jack..."

She couldn't see him. He was gone.

Got to finish it.

She crawled to the book and wiped the snow off the page. Breathing heavily to catch her breath, she forced out the final words. The nearby floating strips of energy glowed brightly. They cycled closer and closer, burning white hot. A crackling streak of lightning exploded into the tree. The remaining nearby pieces of ethereal mass sucked into the center of it.

The light faded and the dark shadow of night once again dominated the yard. Sally felt her spirit settling back in as her astral vision disappeared. She went to Jack's body. It was motionless.

"Please Jack, come back."

Her tears ran unnoticed down her numb cheeks, "Please."

She went back over to the necklace.

I've got to find him.

She pulled it up out of the drift.

A voice behind her.

"Sally?"

His eyes were open. He rolled over spitting blood out of his mouth.

"Jack!"

The power locked inside the little tree raged against its new prison. It was now blind to the mundane world. The terrible pressure inside the thin branches vibrated. Killien was screaming in pain.

9:10

The brilliant blue angel that had spoken to Jack swooped down and surrounded him. Its power formed a bright sphere around his astral body, pulling him upward. His whole being felt calm, as if being submerged in warm water. It carried him into the sky increasing in speed as it went.

The grip of Hell's stream was approaching the tornado at the outer realm. The torment spun in huge spirals. Christopher watched in horror as they got near. A fizzling sound crackled all around the powerful layer surrounding him. It grew louder and louder and then…

…nothing.

The sphere that contained him melted away as quickly as it had appeared. Christopher was free. He watched the ethereal stream dissipate into nothingness, fading into the black sky.

Another stream formed inside Hell's core and shot past him, toward earth. It had a new purpose. The little tree's astral mass drifted lazily above the yard. It would soon find itself in the core of the devil's tornado.

Jack watched the blur of passing stars through the filmy energy.. He knew where the angel was taking him. The distance that would've taken him over an hour lasted only a few minutes within the entity's powerful speed.

The great spiral of punishment came into view. The tornado's eternal glow lit up an otherwise black void. The sphere melted away as Jack was released. He was still miles from Hell's storm. Jack looked over the distance, searching. A small, bright spirit was approaching. Jack knew right away that it was his son. Relief washed through him and he began to cry. They embraced, their energies mixing at the edges.

They looked out into the night sky, toward Earth. The mundane world looked so small from where they were, so insignificant compared to the endless astral universe. But, as they gazed at the tiny speck in the distance, they knew better. It meant everything. It was home, at least for a while.

As Jack sped off hand in hand with his son back to the place they loved, he realized that there was so much more to learn. He also realized he would have forever to learn it.

9:11

When they got back, the street was scattered with Sheriff's cars and ambulances. He gave his son a final spiritual hug and they descended down into their bodies. Jack was lying on a stretcher next to Stacey's. His eyes popped open and he sat up.
The EMT shouted, "He's awake!" to the other.

Jack hopped down and went to Stacey. The driver was telling him to lie back down. He paid no attention. His wife was lying on her side with a white sheet pulled over her shoulders. She was looking at him. He took her hand.

Her voice was weak, "Jack? Is Chris okay?"
"Yeah baby, he's fine."
"Did we do it, Jack?"
"Yeah, we did. Be still now. Don't worry about anything."
Officer Lunderman spoke up from behind him, "Jack? Jack Sawyer?"
"Yes."
"Can you tell me what happened here, sir?"
"Yes. The old woman. She attacked my family."
He looked up at the house. Linda was still inside. The officer watched the ambulance staff attending to Sally.
"What about the girl, the granddaughter?"
Jack and Sally's eyes met. He sent her a kind smile.
"She saved us. We wouldn't have survived without her."
"We're going to need a full statement from you--"
"No problem."
He walked away, Lunderman followed.
Jack kneeled down in front of Sally, "You okay?"
She grinned at him, "Yeah Jack, I'm alright. Chris?"
"I think he's gonna be okay."
He looked over her red, frostbitten face with the cracked lips and smeared mascara. Her dark hair was a mess and her shirt was torn at the neck. He took her hand and their eyes met.
He gave her a serious smile, "Thank you. Thank you for saving my son."
She grinned, "We did it together, partner."
"Friend."
She turned her hand over and gave his fingers a squeeze, "Yeah…you bet."

Jack looked up into the sky. It had stopped snowing. The sun was beginning to show below the distant horizon. The white haze would clear away by noon. The clouds would break apart and move on, leaving only blue sky. They would appreciate that sun that day. It would not be taken for granted.

But as the old timers often say,
If you don't like the weather, just wait a few minutes. It's bound to change.

After all, you never know when another storm is just around the corner.

9:12

A cool breeze pushed through the branches of the little tree they had planted in the spring. Its thin arms swayed in the wind. From the street, it looked like any other elm sapling, sitting quietly in the melting yard.

A closer look would find that the brown skin was turning dark and a black, sappy ooze drooled down its rotting spine. The physical integrity of the tree was diminishing as the dark power inside the small prison raged. The swirling energy bubbled and spat. The astral pressure was more than the sapling could take. Its molecules screamed silently against the tremendous push. The thin branches dripped with desperation.

It was almost as if the tree itself was aware.

Aware that it had already begun to die.

0:2

And so we find ourselves back where we began, inside the questions. We have always had them and as long as we are on the earth, we always will. They will continue to thrive, sitting ever so uncomfortably between our hopes and fears.

As life's path winds in a different direction for each soul bound to the earth, we can find comfort. Comfort in the knowledge that we all are on a similar path of growth and learning. The answers lie in the journey and even as a soul nears death, the path for them is far from over. As long as a spirit remains open, inquisitive and questioning, its growth will continue. All knowledge comes from, and lives and breathes inside the questions.

We can realize that they not only drive and sustain us, they give us meaning. Just so long as we remember this:

If the answers were laid out in front of us like some great map of truth, the questions would simply disappear…

www.ingramcontent.com/pod-product-compliance
Lightning Source LLC
Chambersburg PA
CBHW020613310726
48979CB00008B/1461/J
* 9 7 8 0 6 1 5 1 8 1 3 8 7 *